D0812936

Tom Clancy's
Net Force Explorers:
High Wire

Created by Tom Clancy and Steve Pieczenik

Copyright © 2001 NetCo Partners

The right of the authors to be identified as the Author of
the Work has been asserted by them in accordance with the
Copyright, Designs and Patents Act 1988.

First published in 2001
by HEADLINE BOOK PUBLISHING

A HEADLINE FEATURE paperback

10 9 8 7 6 5 4 3 2 1

All rights reserved. No part of this publication may be
reproduced, stored in a retrieval system, or transmitted,
in any form or by any means without the prior written
permission of the publisher, nor be otherwise circulated
in any form of binding or cover other than that in which
it is published and without a similar condition being
imposed on the subsequent purchaser.

All characters in this publication are fictitious
and any resemblance to real persons, living or dead,
is purely coincidental.

ISBN 0 7472 6195 4

Typeset by
Letterpart Limited, Reigate, Surrey

Printed and bound in Great Britain by
Mackays of Chatham plc, Chatham, Kent

HEADLINE BOOK PUBLISHING
A division of Hodder Headline
338 Euston Road
London NW1 3BH

www.headline.co.uk
www.hodderheadline.com

Acknowledgements

We'd like to thank the following people, without whom this book would not have been possible: Mel Odom, for help in rounding out the manuscript; Martin H. Greenberg, Larry Segriff, Denise Little, and John Helfers at Tekno Books; Mitchell Rubenstein and Laurie Silvers at Hollywood.com; Tom Colgan of Penguin Putnam Inc.; Robert Youdelman, Esquire; and Tom Mallon, Esquire. As always, we would like to thank Robert Gottlieb without whom this book would not have been conceived. We much appreciated the help.

Chapter One

'Get out of the way!'

Andy Moore jumped, put his hands out to break his fall, and came up in a tumbling roll that threw the sawdust lining the huge steel-barred cage in all directions. The thick sawdust made it hard to get traction for a moment but he dug his feet in and lunged forward again. He threw himself into a slide like he was stealing second base, arms outstretched before him. He caught the edges of the steel platform supporting the large steel hoop above and pulled himself under it.

Almost immediately, the steel hoop above him ignited in a pyrotechnic blaze of violet sparks that spread into yellow and orange flames. The sudden heat fell just short of hot enough to sear Andy, six feet below.

Out of the frying pan and into the fire, Andy thought. *Now that's the story of my life.* Lying on his back, he glanced back at the great predator pursuing him.

The lion, only one of the dozen great cats inside the cage, measured ten feet long from snout to tail and stood over three feet tall at the shoulder. Its long, barrel-chested body was at least five hundred pounds of rippling muscle. The wedge-shaped head seemed to dwarf even that huge body, but most of that effect came from the long black mane that contrasted with the tawny fur covering the rest of the animal.

Andy gazed deep into the lion's emerald green eyes. He saw only his twin reflections and the hunger raging through the animal.

And maybe there was a little irritation in the eyes as well. Andy knew he had that effect on his share of people.

The big cat paused at the edge of the platform and snarled angrily at the leaping flames above. The sound rumbled through the cage. The lion gnashed its teeth in an explosion of flashing ivory.

Hot saliva dripped from the huge jaws and slathered across Andy's cheek. *Gross*, he thought.

'You are not safe! Keep moving! Napoleon is not stupid, young Andrew!' Heritzel Crupariu stood outside the large cage, gripping the steel bars. He was a tall, broad-shouldered man dressed in an electric blue silk shirt and olive jodhpurs. A white ascot wrapped his neck. He wore his dark hair slicked back and a handlebar mustache.

'It's Andy,' Andy corrected automatically.

Drawn by the sound of his voice, the lion glanced down at him, slitting its eyes.

Fear shot through Andy then like an electric current. Still, he couldn't keep the smile from his face. Even though he had a shock of unruly blond hair and blue eyes, no one would have mistaken the boy's smile as anything close to angelic. At sixteen, he was athletic and wiry, used to thinking fast and moving faster. Danger was something he thrived on – as long as his mom wasn't around.

Andy returned the great predator's gaze full measure. When he noticed the shifting muscle mass in the lion's legs, the young Net Force Explorer hooked a foot under one of the supporting legs on the other side of the platform.

'Young Andrew,' Crupariu pleaded. 'Andy, please. Napoleon, he is not playing the cat and mouse game with you. You will only antagonize him.'

'I know what I'm doing,' Andy replied. *At least, I hope I do.* The way he generally worked, he tended to find out if he really knew what he was doing pretty quickly.

Napoleon swatted one immense paw at Andy's head.

Three of the girls in the stands around the cage screamed

shrilly. They were dressed in pink and white outfits sporting tons of sequins that left their arms and legs bare. Before Andy had crawled into the cage they'd been working with the horses.

The paw sported huge hooked claws designed especially for rending flesh. An adult male lion, Andy remembered, could easily eat over sixty pounds of raw meat in a single sitting. Of course, once Napoleon finished with him, there might be enough left over for a few late-night snacks, but not enough to go around to the other cats in the cage. The lion's paw crashed down toward Andy's head.

A warning tremble shuddered through Andy. He quelled the reflex and took control. Getting booted out of the sim at this moment would be ego damaging and embarrassing rather than dangerous. But he wasn't going to let it happen, even if it wouldn't really hurt him.

Andy flexed his leg, kept his foot hooked on the support leg, and pulled, sliding himself through the sawdust and to the other side of the platform. His smile was still firmly in place as he rolled to his feet and sprinted.

He spared a glance at the five young girls who had been working with the horses. The girls were all petite, and they looked like they were maybe his age, but he didn't know for sure. It was hard to tell, given the present situation. He paused a moment to treat them to a sweeping bow, one arm outstretched.

The girls clapped in immediate response, then squealed in fresh terror.

Turning, Andy saw that Napoleon hadn't remained stymied long. The big lion bounded toward him, muscles bunching and releasing beneath the tawny coat. Andy shifted to the side, dodging the animal by inches.

'Where's the whip?' Andy shouted to Crupariu.

The man pointed inside the cage at his feet. There, coiled like a black leather snake, a bullwhip lay in the sawdust. But, draped seemingly casually on the raised platforms along the way, four female lions were regarding Andy with growing interest. For the moment, the hunt belonged to Napoleon. But it appeared as though that might change at any minute.

Glancing over his shoulder, Andy saw the lion spin faster than anything that big should have been able to. Despite his love of excitement and danger, things weren't looking too good right now.

Around the cage the seven other big cats – four black panthers, two Bengal tigers, and a snow leopard – stayed on their perches and kept their distance from the lions. Napoleon and his pride obviously ruled the cage. The panthers, tigers and the leopard lounged on platforms painted bright red, yellow, blue, or lime-green. Their tails flicked back and forth as they regarded the chase with what seemed to be only passing interest.

Crupariu yanked on the door to the big cage again, cursing in his native language at his inability to open it. 'You should get out of there, Andr— Andy!'

'In a minute.' Andy skidded through the sawdust and reached down for the whip. His fist curled around the haft instinctively. *Man, if only Matt or Leif or the Squirt could see me now.*

His friends were fellow Net Force Explorers, and they had a taste for adventure, too. But none of them had faced something like this.

'Andy!' Crupariu shouted. 'I do not think your mother would approve of your actions. Please, get out of the cage.'

He was right. Sandra Moore would definitely not approve.

Andy pushed away from the cage bars into open space. Hoops flamed overhead, making a trail across the narrow, elevated path. 'Hey, Napoleon,' he told the lion. 'Ever heard of Waterloo?' He shook the whip out, then cracked it expertly, running the braided leather out to its full length.

The whip's tip snaked out and sliced the air only inches from the lion's wet, black nose. The *sssnnnap!* of the whipcrack froze Napoleon in place.

Crupariu and the bareback riders in pink and white clung to the steel bars.

With obvious reluctance, Napoleon lurched back and sat. Thunderous growls that vibrated in the air rumbled from the lion's great maw.

'Okay, then,' Andy said. He wore denim shorts, a favorite pair of rundown cross-trainers, a black tee-shirt with a Space Marines logo on it as well as a picture of a 50-ton unit in blazing action, and a North Carolina Tar Heels ball cap. He wasn't exactly dressed for the lion-tamer gig.

Napoleon shifted, starting to rise.

'Nope,' Andy said, cracking the whip only inches from the animal's face.

Napoleon's muzzle jerked to the side. The female lions watched with more interest. Two of them stood up on the raised platforms where they waited.

Perspiration dampened Andy's chest and shoulders, and slipped down his arms. Either it was hotter in the cage than he'd thought or he was more nervous than he was willing to admit. Maybe it was a little of both.

He glanced at the female lions again as they continued to shift. Andy knew as long as he controlled the male lion the rest of the pride would follow. He cracked the whip again then pointed at the nearest ramp leading to the elevated path above his head. 'Up,' he ordered.

Napoleon coughed in irritation and shook his large mane.

Ssssnnnaaappp!

For a moment Andy thought the big animal was going to ignore the whip and the authority in his voice. And if that happened, he wasn't sure what he was going to do except possibly become lion kibble.

Crupariu yanked on the cage door again but the locking mechanism still wasn't releasing.

Ssssnnnaaaappp!

The big lion batted a paw forward in irritation. Then, when Andy cracked the whip only inches from its nose again, the lion turned aside and galloped up the slanted incline leading to the elevated path.

Andy grinned, and tried not to show too much relief. *I knew I could do this. Just a matter of knowing who's the boss.* 'That's right, you stubborn hunk of fang and fur. Now we're going to do things my way.'

Napoleon glared down at him, emerald fire showing in the cat's slitted eyes. The lion's tail flicked the air as the beast padded up the incline. At the top of the incline, the lion stopped.

'You know the routine,' Andy said softly, knowing the sound of his voice was part of the lion's expectations. *Okay, the lion has acted a little wonky, but there's no reason to believe this isn't going to work.*

The lion tensed on the narrow platform, and for a moment Andy thought it was considering throwing itself on him. Then, gracefully in spite of the way the narrow platform bowed under the pressure of five hundred plus pounds of sinewy muscle, the lion turned and trotted along the elevated path. It padded through the flaming hoops without pause.

Feeling pleased and a little more confident, though the thought of becoming a cat munchie hadn't totally deserted him, Andy watched as Napoleon moved along the path. The lion entered the smaller cage at the other end of the big cage and plopped down.

Crupariu remained silent but the four bareback riders turned on the applause and called out to Andy.

And the crowd goes wild. Andy grinned hugely, feeling cocky. *I could take a couple hours of attention like this.*

Crupariu's expression remained dour and unconvinced. The man folded his arms across his chest.

With maybe only a little hesitation, Andy turned his attention to the four lionesses. 'Break time's over, ladies. It's showtime.' He cracked the whip at the nearest one.

Snarling angrily, one lioness leaped up and vaulted to the nearest section of the elevated path. In quick succession the other three got up and followed, finally joining the male in his cage.

'Close them off,' Andy called out as he coiled his whip and walked up toward the snow leopard.

Crupariu pulled a lever next to the door. Metal shrilled against metal, the sound harsh enough to put Andy's teeth on edge and prickle the skin at the back of his neck.

Above, a heavy steel door slammed closed on the lion cage. In the next moment the elevated path shifted to a new cage as the door there opened.

'The main cage door,' Crupariu called out, 'still won't open.'

Andy nodded, fixing his attention on the snow leopard. The animal's beautiful white fur patterned with black diamond markings disguised the efficient killing machine that the cat really was. 'We'll take a look at it after I get the cats put up.' He flicked the whip.

Yowling and spitting, the snow leopard pushed up and leaped to the huge yellow and red striped ball suspended near the elevated path. The animal pushed and spraddled and sprawled across the spinning ball till it found the balance point, then it uncoiled and landed effortlessly on the elevated path. A moment later and the leopard was in an individual cage as well.

Another burst of applause and cheers came from the bareback riders. They cheered again when he succeeded in caging the two Bengal tigers.

But when Andy approached the remaining four black panthers he knew instinctively from their body movements that things were going to be different this time.

'Watch them,' Crupariu urged hoarsely.

I am. Andy paused as the four panthers went into action, unconsciously coiling the whip. *And they're watching me!*

With fluid grace and an economy of motion, the four black panthers jumped to other platforms, slowly surrounding Andy.

This cannot be a good thing, Andy told himself. The silence of the bareback riders lent the moment even more tension. He spoke, hoping his voice didn't crack, not believing how dry his throat had suddenly become. 'Which one is the alpha cat?'

Crupariu spoke softly. 'Kartik. The one with the scars beside his maw.'

Moving slowly, circling so he could try to keep all the cats in view, Andy spotted the scarred leopard. The animal's coat, like its three companions, was black as soot. A webbing of pink and gray scars marred the wedge-shaped head, puckering the blue gray lips as though fishhooks had ripped through them some time in the animal's past.

Andy faced the great beast, staring up the nearly ten feet that separated them. He flicked his whip toward the panther, cutting the air with a *crack!*

Immediately, Kartik dropped to a prone position on the rectangular platform, causing it to sway slightly. The panther's ears flattened and it spat fiercely.

Chills rippled the back of Andy's neck. 'Move it, Kartik,' he said in a steady voice. 'Time to get back to your cage.' Movement flickered in the corner of the young Net Force Explorer's vision. He drew his arm back and cracked his whip in the direction, only a few inches from the cat's face.

Stubbornly, the panther retreated, but the other two cats merely shifted position.

'Get out of there,' Crupariu advised.

'Not yet,' Andy replied.

'It's not going to work.'

Andy didn't argue. He'd talked himself into the cage with the big cats; he just hadn't figured on being in there alone. He cut the whip twice more, wielding it expertly, driving the other two cats back. 'C'mon, Kartik, I'm Andy Moore, and I eat Space Marines for breakfast. I'm not going to let a few overgrown housecats be any kind of problem.'

Regally, Kartik drew up on its haunches. The great cat

glared down at him with deep yellow eyes. The other cats sat up as well, looking remarkably interested in the proceedings.

Andy flicked the whip at Kartik again.

The panther's mouth opened again; only this time, something that Andy had no way of expecting happened.

'I say,' Kartik enunciated in a very posh English accent. 'You can be a most irritating chap.'

Andy stared.

'Persistent,' one of the other panthers added in a feminine voice. 'Might I suggest we consider terming it that?'

'Of course, my dear,' Kartik said patiently. 'You know I have always favored your opinions in these matters. But persistence can be such a dreadful bore.'

'Perhaps we should try to reason with the pathetic creature,' the female leopard suggested.

'Personally,' another panther said in that uppercrust accent, 'I have always felt humans to be limited in the social graces. Much too fixed on whole competitive hierarchy to properly debate philosophy.'

Kartik blinked both yellow eyes indifferently. 'We could try getting along, couldn't we? I mean, a peaceful coexistence isn't completely out of the question, hmmmmm?'

Although he'd been in a lot of weird situations in life, on the Net, and as a Net Force Explorer, Andy wasn't quite set up for this turn of events. Nobody had said anything about talking panthers. He darted a look at Crupariu over his shoulder. 'Nobody said anything about talking panthers,' he repeated, this time aloud.

Crupariu pulled on the jammed gate again. The metal clanged but it still didn't budge. 'They have never talked before.'

So they wait till I show up to demonstrate the skill? Great. Andy glared back up at the panthers. 'We have a problem here.'

Kartik's tail flicked like a restless cobra. 'I should say so.' The cat's yellow eyes focused on Andy – it felt like being lined up in a hunter's gunsights.

'There's a routine involved here,' Andy pointed out.

'*Your* routine,' the male panther snarled, then licked its chops. 'Not ours, human.'

'Perhaps,' the female panther put in, 'we could put the matter to a vote.'

A sudden image of the panthers huddling together before every performance to discuss the need to put on a show or not flashed into Andy's head. It was *not* a happy image.

'No,' he said.

Kartik's head cocked to one side. 'No?'

'Uh-uh.' Andy shook his head slowly.

The four panthers shifted above him, peering more forcibly down from the platforms.

Definitely reading the menu, Andy told himself. 'I'm being brutally honest here. How can Crupariu put on a show if you insist on running it?'

'Why, darling,' the female panther purred, 'have you thought perhaps we might have ideas of our own for the show. Instead of leaping up onto these staggered platforms all willy-nilly and zipping through those flaming hoops like we haven't a care in the world, perhaps there is some other form of entertainment we could give the audience.'

Andy was afraid to even ask what entertainment that might be. 'No.'

'I told you,' the other male panther said. 'Humans are much too limited by their own sense of self-importance.' It cleared its throat. 'I have a suggestion, if I may be so bold.'

'Yes?' Kartik responded.

'Forget about a peaceful coexistence.'

'Then what?'

The male panther shifted restlessly, gazing at Andy. 'Eat him.'

The panthers looked at each other, obviously weighing the choices.

Terrific, Andy thought. *At least they're diplomatic.*

'Young Andrew!' Crupariu bellowed. 'Get out of there!'
The man tugged fiercely on the jammed door but to no avail.

Andy stood his ground. This wasn't supposed to be
happening. Crupariu had mentioned he'd had problems
with the animals before but nobody had said anything
about this. Not only was his innate stubbornness rising to
this occasion, but his curiosity was as well. Both of those
facets of his personality had led him into dangerous waters
before.

The cats' votes came in swiftly.

'Allow me to follow my own convictions,' the female
panther said. 'I abstain from voting in such a barbaric ballot.'

'Eat him,' the second and third male said together.

Kartik gazed down remorselessly. 'He's lunch.' Even as he
got ready to pounce, the female bunched her muscles and
leaped.

Andy hurled himself out of the way, streaking for the cage
door. He grabbed a platform support, aware of the *whumph*
of panther pads plopping against the sawdust piled on the
floor. Pulling himself sharply to one side to take advantage of
the support, he felt the steel vibrate in his hand when Kartik
charged into it.

'Run!' Crupariu shouted.

The bareback riders screamed like a Greek chorus
broadcasting straight from Hades.

Andy ran, knowing he was only heartbeats ahead of the
savage jaws and relentless claws that followed him. Ahead,
Crupariu tugged fiercely on the door, managing somehow to
pull it almost an inch open. Unfortunately, that inch wasn't
going to be enough to let Andy through.

Incredible sadness filled the faces of the bareback riders.
'He didn't fix the panthers,' one of them said.

Still at full speed, Andy rammed a shoulder into the steel
bars of the door. Pain flared through his arm and he felt
certain he'd dislocated the shoulder.

'Andrew!' Crupariu grabbed Andy from behind, pulling

him tight up against the bars as if Andy might somehow fit between them.

Working on automatic pilot, wishing he could think just a little faster, knowing he was thrown slightly by the panthers' actions and talking ability, Andy turned. Then he immediately wished he hadn't.

The panthers advanced in rapid, snarling fury. There was no more talking. Pinned by Crupariu's grip and unable to move, Andy raised his arms to defend himself.

The fangs slashed through his arms and he felt the warmth of blood cover them. His bones snapped with brittle, hollow pops. Pain flooded his mind and he reached out to the blackness waiting to claim him, going into it willingly.

Chapter Two

Heart pounding, still feeling the ravaging claws and fangs sinking into his flesh, Andy opened his eyes. *Okay*, he told himself as he looked across the small, low-ceilinged room, *chill out. They're not here.*

'Hey, Andy, are you okay?'

Andy ran his hands across the rough wooden surface of the table in front of him. Thankfully, he didn't pick up any splinters. A split log seated in leather straps, hammock-style, made up the bench he sat on. The floor beneath his feet was hard-packed earth instead of wood.

'Andy?' The slender old woman tending the iron, pot-bellied cook stove in the corner started toward him. She wore loose-fitting dungarees with the cuffs rolled up halfway to her knees. The sleeves on the man's white shirt she wore were rolled to mid-forearm. Her gray hair was tied back in a bun. Her heavy boots, too big for her feet, clomped against the hard-packed earth and caused puffs of red dust and gray wood ash from the stove to rise.

'I'm fine,' Andy said, but he couldn't get the sight of the attacking panthers from his mind. He still felt their claws and fangs.

'You look a mite peaked,' Miss Dorothy said. 'Maybe you should run a diagnostics on the system.'

'The system's fine.' Andy pushed himself up from the bench. 'I just got kicked out of the circus veeyar.'

Miss Dorothy represented his personal veeyar's operating

13

system. When the Net's safeguards had automatically kicked him out of the lions' cage, they had returned him to his veeyar. Crupariu, the lions' cage, and the Cservanka Brothers Circus remained just outside Alexandra, Virginia. Andy's home, virtually and in reality, was here in the suburbs over twenty miles away. Strangely enough, his body remained at the circus.

'You keep frowning like that,' Miss Dorothy said as she added more kindling to the potbelly stove, 'and your face is going to stick.'

Andy realized Miss Dorothy was doing her job of prompting him to think out loud so the OS could interact with him in problem-solving mode. He pushed up from the table. 'I had better get back there.'

A lot of kids on the Net kept one particular veeyar for their personal work, Andy knew, but he liked creating new ones. His current one was a Pony Express station just outside Indian Territory that had regular runs to California and Texas. The veeyar was still new enough that he had a lot of fun with it.

The building was a two-room affair that afforded little privacy. Miss Dorothy lived there in the single bedroom that held just enough room for her cot and a single chest of drawers. The riders that ran the routes slept on the floor in the main room when they couldn't sleep in the saddle anymore and it was rainy or too cold to sleep outside.

The Pony Express station had started out as part of a homework assignment in history class at Bradford Academy. Andy had researched and designed the veeyar, then taken his class through the everyday routines of the Pony Express riders.

The times, and the history project, had been exciting to Andy. Even after the project had been graded, Andy had decided to keep the Pony Express station for a while as his own personal veeyar OS. Andy had a short attention span. It took a major effort to keep boredom from creeping into his everyday life. He was always looking for things that were different or offered excitement.

In this veeyar, Andy's clothing had automatically changed to black dungarees, a homespun blue shirt, calf-high boots, a red checked bandanna around his neck, and a heavy woolen poncho with Southwestern colors and designs worked into it. He topped the whole outfit off with a flat-brimmed chocolate brown hat that had seen better days.

'So why do you think you were kicked out of the Cservanka Brothers Circus holo-projector links?' Miss Dorothy mixed another batter-filled bowl. She was always cooking and cleaning inside the veeyar.

'Maybe it's a glitch in the system. They shipped their computers from Europe along with the animals and the performers. Damp, motion, and computer systems don't mix. Or maybe they picked up some kind of weird virus in one of the performances.'

'They're not from around these parts?' Miss Dorothy asked.

'No. They're from Europe. From Romania.'

Miss Dorothy nodded. 'Gypsies.'

'They're not gypsies.'

Miss Dorothy treated him with her eagle-eyed gaze. 'You said this was a circus.'

'Yeah.'

'Then they're probably gypsies. A lot of carnivals and circuses were started by roving bands of gypsies in Eastern Europe in the last thousand years.'

'I don't know if that's true,' Andy said.

'Then obviously you haven't been doing any of the suggested research you were given when you chose to go with your mother on this call, young man.'

Despite his best efforts, the schoolmarm tone in Miss Dorothy's voice just wouldn't go away. When he'd first thought of a Wild West theme expansion for his veeyar, Andy had been tempted by a virtual version of the Long Branch Saloon. Then he'd considered what his mom would have said if she'd found out about it. The mental images hadn't been pretty.

'I'm only going to be there a couple hours,' Andy protested. 'Mom's working on a sick elephant. Once she gets the problem diagnosed, we're out of there.'

Sandra Moore was a veterinarian in Alexandria, Virginia and ran her own clinic. Andy helped her out and often nurtured some of the more needy animals at home.

'And how was it you ended up in the lions' den like some young Daniel?' Miss Dorothy glopped healthy portions of yellow dough into a biscuit pan.

'While we were talking to Mr Cservanka, Mom mentioned that I was really good with computer programming,' Andy explained. 'Then he told her the lion-tamer's act had a big case of DFB.'

'DFB?'

'Data flowing bad,' Andy said. 'I thought maybe it was something I could fix.'

'Was it?'

Andy snorted, thinking about the bareback riders and how they'd probably mercilessly rib him. 'Dunno. This time through I got eaten.'

'I'm guessing that wasn't a solution.'

Who'd have guessed Miss Dorothy would have had a sense of humor? Andy felt chagrined. That was part of the reason he hadn't already bounced back onto the Net and zipped out to the circus again. 'I haven't exactly figured out what the problem is, but I haven't given up on it yet.'

Thundering hooves sounded outside the door.

'That will be Jason,' Miss Dorothy said.

Andy turned and crossed to the narrow, X-shaped window that doubled as a defensive gunport. It allowed some air to stir around inside the building without being big enough for someone to enter through. Rifle barrels slid through easily, though.

Outside, a tall, thin rider forced himself out of the saddle of a sweat-streaked palomino and dropped to the hard-baked earth. Jason Rideout was one of the riders that frequented this Pony

Express station, part of the environment established by the veeyar's independent programming to make the operating system more interactive.

Jason shook his head as if trying to wake himself, then tied his horse to the corral and lurched toward the building. He took the rough-cut leather pouch from his shoulder, holding his rifle in his other hand.

One of the other riders emerged from the corral and took care of Jason's horse. Caring for the livestock was a big concern in the veeyar, and if Andy became too idle he invariably ended up with those duties. Feeding the horses wasn't so bad but he could definitely live without mucking out the stalls and paddocks. Virtual or real, it was unpleasant either way.

'Howdy, Miss Dorothy,' Jason said as he entered the room.

'Sit yourself,' Miss Dorothy replied. 'I'll get you a big plate of biscuits and gravy and a pork steak.'

'Yes, ma'am.' Jason dropped his pouch on the table then put his rifle in the rack next to the door. He unbuckled his holstered pistol and gunbelt and hung it on a peg beside the rifle. Miss Dorothy didn't allow firearms to be carried inside the station.

'Rough ride?' Andy asked. He'd been on a lot of them himself since he'd programmed the veeyar. Carrying the mail meant long hours in the saddle under a burning sun, crossing mountains with a winter wind pushing against horse and rider, and trying to find shelter from the wild blue northers that ripped dark clouds apart with white-hot lightning bolts. Matt Hunter and Mark Gridley had accompanied Andy a few times, but they had their own pursuits and didn't exactly care for the hard life of the Pony Express – other than as an occasional diversion.

Jason smiled as he washed his hands in a water basin. 'I thought Iron Deer and his braves were going to take my hair this time but that horse had better legs than any of theirs.'

Occasionally, after Andy got to know some of the riders, they were lost to the Indians or outlaws they had to be wary of at all times. Brice Campbell had even died from snakebite only a month ago. The veeyar environment was as realistic as Andy could make it. His history report had netted him an A, but not because he'd aimed at a high grade. School was generally boring. His interest had been fully awakened by the research and that was when he always did his best work.

'I've got letters for you.' Jason dropped onto the split log seat and shoved a fistful of letters in Andy's direction.

Andy took them and flipped through them. Embedded in the stamp was an icon that allowed them to open. He scanned the addresses, recognizing most of them.

Before Andy could open the first one, a shimmering rectangular panel suddenly formed in the air beside him. The Instant Message came from someone who had access to his private veeyar. 'Andy.'

Recognizing his mother's voice, Andy touched the screen, opening it into the veeyar. The screen cleared immediately and he saw his mother's face filling it.

Sandra Moore looked a little irritated. 'I was told that you'd been kicked out of the lion-tamer veeyar.'

'Yes, ma'am,' Andy admitted. He thought his mom looked really tired, too, a sure indication that maybe things with the sick elephant weren't progressing well.

'Mr Crupariu was getting worried that maybe something had happened to you,' his mom said.

'Bruised my ego,' Andy admitted. 'I was taking a moment to regroup.'

'Maybe you could regroup while getting a few things for me from town. I called in some prescriptions to a local drug store and they'll have the medicines ready in the next half-hour or so. I don't want to leave Imanuela, so I thought maybe you could get them.'

'Sure,' Andy replied.

His mom pursed her lips. 'When we get time later, we're going to talk about the lion cage episode, mister. Getting eaten by feline predators isn't something I'd okay on my watch.'

Andy's father, deceased in the South African Conflict when Andy was a baby, had been a Marine to the bone. Being a military man's wife, Sandra Moore had picked up a few military terms during their marriage. She only used them for emphasis. When she needed it to, her stern voice carried more authority even than Captain James Winters, the Explorers' liaison with Net Force.

'Okay,' Andy told her. 'I'll be right there.'

His mom closed the screen and it disappeared in a colorful pop.

'Take a look at the research material on circuses,' Miss Dorothy urged. 'I think you'll find it's interesting.'

Andy nodded to satisfy the veeyar's operating parameters, then crossed to the front door. When he stepped from the Pony Express station, he didn't step out into the yard looking toward the horse corral. He stepped directly into the Net.

Instead of hard-packed earth that barely supported a thin covering of grass, Andy flew above a multi-colored grid that represented the Net. He got his bearings quickly, marking the icons for big business and government installations. He could have simply logged off and returned to his body at the circus, but he wanted the brief trip through the Net to clear his head.

He flew above the cyber-representation of Alexandria toward the south-eastern quadrant outside the city where the Cservanka Brothers Circus was temporarily lodged. In seconds he hovered above the collection of tents and trucks that made up the circus.

Bright lights flickered within the circus, marking areas within it that held self-contained veeyars. Although he hadn't yet visited them and really didn't intend to, Andy knew the Cservanka Brothers Circus supported more than just the physical circus of real performers and animals.

The lion-tamer show was part of the holo-projector sequences built into the circus. His mom had told him that an ancient version of the circus existed in total veeyar immersion. If a visitor wanted to, he could visit an authentic eighteenth-century circus in Wallachia, Romania.

Andy preferred an online game of Space Marines or something equally adrenaline-raising. He flew closer to the circus and felt the trickle of the security field around the circus's online site. The pass Mr Cservanka had given him allowed him entrance to all parts of the circus.

However, Andy remained convinced that circuses were for kids. *Why settle for elephants and clowns when you can be facing down a battalion of Space Marines? Heavy-duty lasers and pocket nukes while running across broken terrain – now, that was entertainment.* Of course, a true gamer couldn't leave out the lure of brain-eating zombies.

Resigning himself, Andy logged off the Net and returned to his body.

The disconnect sensation registered as a brief buzz that rippled through the back of Andy's head and neck. He opened his eyes in the real world and the laserbeam contacts stopped tickling the subdermal implants that allowed him to merge with the Net. The circuitry under his skin that tied into his nervous system had been installed when he was a child.

Heritzel Crupariu stood peering down at him. 'You did not fix the lions,' he accused. 'They ate you.'

'I noticed.' Andy sat up in the implant chair and gazed around the lion-tamer's personal tent. At least he was allowed a little privacy but he figured the main tent where the lions' cage was located was full of carny folk yucking it up at his expense. 'But I'm getting back at them already.'

'How?'

'Trust me. They've got the worst case of indigestion you've ever seen,' Andy assured the man.

Crupariu laughed and dropped a heavy hand on Andy's shoulder. 'You make a joke. I like that.'

'Good,' Andy retorted. 'But you should see me when things are going my way.'

'Maybe. But this I know. Broken lions are no laughing

matter and jokes are not going to fix them. People come to circus, they expect to see clowns doing falls, elephants standing on two legs, a lion-tamer taming lions. They don't see that, maybe they don't come back again.'

Andy pushed himself out of the implant chair. It was an industrial-grade model that had seen a lot of use but it still remained serviceable and mostly comfortable. The isometric exercise program wasn't top of the line, but it was good enough to keep a user's body toned up during lengthy online sessions.

'I'll get them fixed,' Andy promised.

'How?'

'It's probably a code problem. Nothing major. This is something I'm good at. And if I can't fix it, I have a friend who is even better than me. Really. Trust me.'

'But I do,' Crupariu responded, puffing his broad chest out. 'Papa brought you to me, said you would fix lions. Papa is a very smart man.'

Papa was Anghel Cservanka, one of the two brothers who owned the Romanian-based circus. Andy had only met the man briefly.

Taking a blank datascrip from the small computer kit he'd brought with him, Andy slotted it into the implant chair. The two-inch square cube pulsed briefly as it absorbed the binary programming.

'What are you doing?' Crupariu asked.

'Making a copy of the program and the session I just took part in.' Once the upload was complete, Andy popped the datascrip out and put it back in his kit.

'Why?'

'So I can check it out when I get back home.'

'Why not check it out here?'

'I did,' Andy replied. 'That didn't work out so well. I want to isolate the program. Here at the circus, all the programming is set up to be interdependent. Maybe the problem is with the overall schematics based in that interdependency. The only way to figure that out is to isolate the core program for the cat act. I need to know.'

'The circus opens in two days,' Crupariu said. 'If we open without the lion-taming show there will be many unhappy people. People come to circus and want to see lions and lion-tamer.'

'Got that,' Andy assured him. 'I'm all over it. Maybe I'll have an answer tonight.'

'Good.' Crupariu clapped him on the back again. 'Papa said you were a very smart boy. I tell him I know you like a rocket scientist. Of course, the panthers were the ones who lunched you.' The lion-tamer's broad face split in laughter. 'See? I too can make with the jokes, no?'

'No,' Andy agreed whole-heartedly. He resented being brought to the circus again. He should have stayed home, gone over to Mark Gridley's house and tinkered with whatever the Squirt had going, or joined a Space Marine online game. Circuses were for kids and he'd stopped being a kid a long time ago. But his mom had made his duty clear to him.

'Once,' Crupariu admitted in a softer voice, 'I was a clown for Cservanka Brothers Circus. Can you imagine this?' He thumped his broad chest.

'Must have been a big clown.'

'Some people think maybe I wasn't so funny.'

'Some people have a limited appreciation of humor.' Andy knew that first-hand.

The tent flap yanked open and a blue-haired clown with a large rubber nose popped his head in. His gaze focused on Andy. Despite the festive white face and bright colors, the clown had a serious expression. 'Andy?'

'That's me,' Andy said.

The clown waved a white-gloved hand urgently. 'Your mom said to come quick. Imanuela's not doing very good.'

Andy bolted through the tent flap.

Chapter Three

Stepping from the lion-tamer's tent, Andy had to dodge quickly to avoid the bearded lady as she ran past him. He stood back against the tent and watched in disbelief as a brigade of clowns thundered by, their too-big shoes slapping the ground like a bunch of gaudy, frantic penguins. A bareback rider trailed them on one of the white show ponies, both decked out in pink feathers.

'What is wrong with Imanuela?' a fifteen-foot clown demanded. He took long strides, perfectly balanced on stilts, throwing his arms forward to move quickly.

'She is sick,' a woman in top hat and tails yelled out. She held her top hat on with both hands as she ran.

'I knew she was sick,' the stilt-man cried back. 'I just want to know what has changed. Has she gotten worse?'

'I heard she may be dying,' another man said. He was dressed in a red and green shirt with belled sleeves and carried flaming torches.

'Hey, bo,' a clown made up as a bum called out angrily, 'don't be saying that about Imanuela. You'll jinx her, eh? That lady, she's a-gonna be fine and that's that.'

Andy lost count of the number of circus performers that flowed by him through the narrow aisle between the tents. The Cservanka Brothers Circus was big, but he hadn't realized how many people were actually part of it. And he hadn't known so many of them cared so deeply about the elephant.

Crupariu stepped out into the traffic and threw out his arms. Everybody stopped in their tracks. 'Stand back. This boy's mother is the doctor tending Imanuela. She asked that he be there. He is needed.'

The crowd halted immediately, parting to make a path for Andy. They gazed back at him expectantly, waiting for him to move.

Andy couldn't even remember where the elephant was. Crupariu had guided him to his private tent, but the big man had enjoyed showing off the circus grounds as well, providing a narrative that Andy had paid only polite attention to. The path they'd taken had rambled.

'Go,' Crupariu urged Andy. 'You are younger and faster than I am.' He pushed Andy from behind.

Go where? Andy was used to action, and he didn't always have a plan when he did something, but at least he had a clue. He ran through the circus crowd, feeling really bizarre when they started cheering him on.

The harsh blat of a motorcycle engine drowned out the cheering. The motorcycle closed quickly, leading Andy to believe he was going to get run down.

Glancing over his shoulder, he saw a rider dressed in white leathers fringed with bold yellow stitching and yellow fringe on the jacket sleeves and pants legs. A white helmet and black face shield covered the rider's head. The powerful trail bike chewed across the soft ground, leaving a torn path. A show horse reared as the motorcycle shot past but its rider quickly got the animal under control.

Andy stepped aside as the motorcycle slipped fractionally sideways and came to a sudden stop beside him. He was still wondering how the machine had missed him when the rider threw out a leg to balance it. The rider turned toward him.

'Get on! Imanuela is on the other side of the circus!' the muffled voice commanded.

Andy hesitated only an instant. Turning the ride down wasn't something he could do no matter how dangerous the rider appeared. His ego was on the line. He stepped forward and threw a leg over the quivering motorcycle.

'Hold on tight!'

Andy wrapped both arms around the rider's waist, finding it smaller than he had imagined.

The rider twisted the accelerator and popped the clutch. The motorcycle's front tire cleared the ground but the rider didn't let off, expertly riding the machine back down and smoothly changing gears.

Andy hung on, grinning in spite of his nervousness. The ride was wild and frantic, ground-churning slide-turns around tents and circus trucks. They sped down the partially assembled midway where games and food booths were being set up.

The large, sectioned corral the circus animals were kept in occupied the gently rolling hill behind the Big Top. The rider brought the motorcycle to a skidding stop nearby and cut the engine.

Andy stepped off the machine and spotted his mom in one of the larger areas where Imanuela was kept. The elephant lay on her side. She was obviously in pain. Andy's attention immediately focused on the elephant, drawn by the natural empathy he'd always had for animals. He trotted over to the corral.

A couple of dozen circus performers already ringed the area. All of them looked worried, and all of them were watching Andy's mom.

Sandra Moore had blonde hair like her son and kept it cut almost as short as his. Her lightly freckled cheeks had pinked up from exposure to the spring sun the last couple hours. She wore work jeans tucked into boots and a Chambray shirt, her normal business attire.

More circus performers continued to join those already at the corral. The conversations escalated in volume and intensity.

'Imanuela's never been sick like this before,' someone whispered hoarsely. 'Is she going to be all right?'

Trotting forward, Andy caught the top of the chest-high corral and vaulted over easily. 'Mom?'

She looked at him, her poker face in place. That was when Andy knew things really were bad. His mom was always calmest in the middle of a storm.

'Hey,' she said. 'I'm going to need some help keeping Imanuela quiet.'

Andy glanced down at the elephant. Imanuela's huge ears marked her as an African elephant. They were much larger than those of her Asian cousins. Her ears flapped constantly, creating leathery smacks against her gray, wrinkled skin, but her head appeared to be too heavy for her to lift. The elephant was pawing at the ground and trying to force herself up onto her feet. Her huge brown eyes rolled and were edged in white.

'I'll be happy to, but doesn't she have a handler?' Andy asked. 'I don't want to make her any more uncomfortable than she already is.'

'If you're not going to help, I can do it.'

Turning, irritation filling him at once because of the challenging tone, Andy watched the motorcycle rider vault over the corral fence, rolling into a graceful flip and landing lightly. As the rider walked over, gloved hands released the catches on the safety helmet. Short-cut dark hair framed a really cute face and big chocolate eyes. She dropped the helmet to the ground and stripped off her gloves.

'Easy, Imanuela,' the girl urged softly as she neared the elephant.

Imanuela's trunk waved and she gave a little trumpet of pain. Her leg trembled as she tried to get to her feet.

'No.' Andy's mom caught the elephant's ear in one hand and laid her body weight across Imanuela's head. 'She's got to stay down.'

The motorcycle rider hugged Imanuela's face in her arms. 'Easy, Imanuela. You must stay down. You are sick.'

The elephant trumpeted again and continued her struggle to get up.

'She thinks you're playing with her,' Andy said, stepping up beside the girl.

'I know what I'm doing,' the girl snapped. 'And I'm willing to do what needs to be done.'

Anger flared in Andy. The girl had obviously marked his question as a reticence to handle the elephant. 'Look, you're not going to do any good here. Can't you see that?'

'Standing over there isn't going—'

'*Syeira!*'

Immediately, the girl's gaze turned to the man standing inside the corral with them. 'Yes, Papa.'

Papa Cservanka was in his early seventies but his voice still contained the iron whipcrack of authority. His Romanian heritage and a lot of exposure to the sun had darkened his skin to a deep bronze. His silver-gray hair was parted neatly on the left and held only a few black strands that indicated the color it once was. A fierce silver mustache covered his upper lip. He wore faded denim overalls, black and yellow rubber galoshes, and a bright blue tee-shirt that advertised the Cservanka Brothers Circus. The logo featured clowns, a man being shot out of a cannon, and Imanuela the elephant, crowned in all her glory in a feathered headdress as she stood on her two hind feet.

'You will not disrespect these people,' Papa said.

'I meant no disrespect,' Syeira replied. 'I am only worried about Imanuela.'

'As we all are, granddaughter,' Papa said gently. 'But you must leave her in the hands of the professionals.'

Still, Syeira appeared reluctant to move away.

'Your grandfather's right,' Sandra said, remaining on the elephant's head in an effort to keep her down. 'I know you want to help, but Imanuela only wants to stand when she's around you. Let Andy and me handle her.'

'He didn't seem interested in helping her,' Syeira accused.

Andy's face flamed. He didn't need his mom explaining his actions.

'He asked about her handler,' Sandra explained. 'If Imanuela had a regular handler, that person would be better suited for this. But Andy can do this job. He's good at it. You'll see.'

Without another word, Syeira turned from Imanuela. As the girl passed him, Andy saw the glint of tears in her eyes, but the set of her jaw was pure, stubborn challenge. She went to stand by Papa, folding her arms tightly.

Andy joined his mother, placing his body weight on the elephant's head. 'So what about her handler?' he asked.

'Not available,' Sandra answered.

'He left us,' Papa explained. 'It was shortly after this season started in January. He was hired away by another circus.'

'Imanuela's got to stay off her feet,' Sandra said to Andy, 'and I've got to get her started on some of the meds I brought with me.'

Andy smoothed his palms across the elephant's face, feeling the craggy, wrinkled skin. 'What's wrong with her?'

'Best guess, she's having premature labor. At least, that's my working diagnosis right now.'

'Imanuela is going to have a baby?' Papa asked in surprise. His eyes widened.

Sandra nodded. 'I'm pretty sure about that. I'll run some tests once we get her stabilized to make sure. The medicine I'm going to give her now shouldn't hurt her, and it might relax her enough to slow the labor.'

A surprised murmur ran through the circus performers. Nearly all of them seemed happy about the announcement.

'Imanuela's going to be a momma!' someone said.

'I thought she couldn't do that,' another one said.

Andy couldn't believe the depth of the reaction that went through the onlookers. As he strove to calm the elephant, he stared at the performers. Only one of them – a well-dressed, thin man who appeared to be in his early thirties, his hair swept back from his forehead above wraparound sunglasses – looked like he'd just been given bad news. He shook his head, his lips pursed into a thin line under his pencil-thin mustache.

'Okay, Andy,' his mom said with a slight smile, 'I'm going to need you to do that voodoo that you do so well with animals. I really need to give her a full examination. She can't get up or we'll be forever getting her back down. By then it could be too late for the baby. Maybe for her, too, if this gets really complicated.' Despite the calm way she spoke, Andy knew his mom was tense.

'Got it,' he replied, but he wasn't sure if he could pull it off or not. Imanuela was hurting *and* she was afraid.

He kept his weight on the elephant's head. He held her ear in one hand, knowing most elephants were trained for touch commands there that generally keyed off the hooked crop their handlers used. Quietly, he started talking to Imanuela, whispering words of encouragement.

Slowly, the elephant stopped fighting Andy, relaxing and placing her head on the ground. Imanuela moved her trunk restlessly, then curled it around Andy's waist, holding on tightly. Her rolling eye finally settled on him, then it closed slightly.

'That's right,' Andy said calmly. 'We're going to take care of you. I've got you.' He ran his palms over her head, tugging on her ear occasionally and pushing at her trunk.

His mom moved quickly and efficiently. She took an IV kit from her med bag and quickly set it up. Imanuela only flinched a little when the needle was inserted, then the drip bag started pushing the meds hanging in the collapsible rigging standing nearby into her system.

A long time later, Andy watched Imanuela's large eye flicker one last time, then completely close as the deep sleep caused by the meds claimed her. He sighed in relief but didn't immediately remove himself from the elephant.

'How is she?' Papa Cservanka asked quietly. He held a red checked handkerchief tightly in one gnarled fist.

Sandra kept her hand against the elephant's stomach and

Andy knew his mom was checking for the strength and frequency of the labor pains she was trying to stop. 'The meds are working. Her contractions have slowed down a lot. She shouldn't be in too much pain.'

'You have slowed the labor?' Papa asked.

Sandra stood and wiped her forehead. 'Yes.'

'Why?'

'Because I don't think Imanuela's at full-term. And if she isn't, neither the mother nor the baby are ready for this. If the birth didn't kill the baby, I don't think it would survive long.'

Worry lent an edge to Papa's features. 'The little baby would die?'

'Possibly. I want to run a few more tests on Imanuela and get a better idea of when she's actually due.' Sandra stripped off the elbow-length gloves and dropped them in a nearby bright orange biohazard waste disposal. 'Do you know when she became pregnant?'

Papa shook his head. 'No. She has never had a baby before.'

'Never?'

Andy pushed himself up from the elephant, knowing from his mom's tone that meant trouble as well.

'No,' Papa answered solemnly. 'Imanuela has been with our circus for almost forty years, since she was just a calf. My father and I purchased her and her mother from a failed circus.'

'If you didn't plan on this pregnancy,' Sandra said, 'that means you must have a male elephant with the circus.' She looked around. 'But I didn't see one.'

'We don't have one,' Papa corrected gently. 'Bull elephants are dangerous. They are more stubborn and likely to cause trouble than a cow or a calf.'

'Well, she's run into one somewhere along the way. Do you have any idea when this could have happened?'

Papa mopped his face with the handkerchief and shrugged. 'There is a possibility. We wintered down in Florida the year before last. Many circuses that tour the United States winter there.'

'Did any of them have bull elephants?'

'Dr Moore,' he said, 'the circus shuts down for the winter. That only means that we don't tour. But there are things to be tended to. New equipment. Repairs for old equipment. Breaking in new acts. Training our young people who have grown old enough to take part in the rings. I was a very busy man. If Imanuela is pregnant, there had to have been at least one bull elephant there. But I did not know of it then.'

'That's close enough,' Sandra said. 'it allows me to calculate how far along Imanuela might be.' She checked the IV bag and the drip rate automatically. 'The most she can be is eighteen months along. Elephants go to term—'

'In twenty-one months,' Papa said. He gazed worriedly at the sleeping elephant. 'I just did not know this had happened to Imanuela.'

'I'm guessing. We'll know for sure in a short time.' Sandra knelt and took a hypodermic from her medical bag. She switched the IV drip off and drew blood, then turned the drip back on.

'Will Imanuela be all right?' Papa asked.

Andy gazed around the circus crowd and saw concern in those faces as well. It was surprising, but he was glad it was there. Sometimes, in the clinic, people dropped their pets off like they were having a piece of equipment repaired.

'I think so,' Sandra answered.

'And the baby?' Papa asked in a quieter voice.

'I'm going to see what I can do. If I can delay delivery for even a few more weeks, the baby will have a pretty good chance of making it.' Sandra glanced at her son. 'Andy, I called in a few prescriptions that I'll need you to pick up.'

Andy nodded.

The corral bars clinked and rattled. Glancing over his shoulder, Andy saw the well-dressed man open a gate and step through. He fastidiously avoided stepping in poop spots

31

left by the elephant. 'Papa,' he called. 'Might I have a word with you?'

Despite the attempt to mask it, Papa couldn't quite cover the irritated look he got. 'I don't think now is a good time.'

The man looked at Papa and shook his head. 'Putting off trouble and sorrow doesn't make it go away.'

'I know this,' Papa stated with an edge in his voice. 'I taught you that, if you will recall.'

'I recall. That's why I step forward now.' The man turned his attention to Sandra and stuck out a hand as he stripped his sunglasses away. 'I'm Martin Radu, Dr Moore. I provide many services for the Cservanka Brothers Circus, not the least of which is transportation.'

Andy took an instant dislike to Radu. His mom shook hands with the man and he knew she didn't care much for him either. However, Andy was also certain that anyone who didn't know his mom well would never have guessed.

'What can I do for you, Mr Radu?' Sandra asked.

Radu glanced at Imanuela. 'In this present condition, can the elephant be transported?'

'It would be better if she wasn't.'

'Then I can assume that the elephant *can* be transported?' Radu pressed.

'Martin,' Papa said in rebuke. 'How can you even ask such a thing while poor Imanuela is lying there in such a state?'

'I ask, Papa,' Radu stated, 'because someone must. Would you have this circus die because of one elephant?'

Chapter Four

'How dare you ask that question!' Syeira strode angrily toward Martin Radu, obviously ignoring the fact that the man was head and shoulders taller than she was.

Automatically, Andy stepped forward, intending to intercept the young girl if he had to. Radu didn't look or act like the kind of guy who'd tolerate much in the way of a verbal assault.

Dark emotion flushed Radu's face. 'This is none of your concern, Syeira.'

'Imanuela is the concern of everyone at this circus,' Syeira retorted.

Radu looked over Syeira's head. 'Papa, I asked that you speak with your granddaughter regarding her manners.'

'I shall,' Papa agreed, 'but it will be later. At this moment, I would like to discuss Imanuela in greater detail. Perhaps you lack a little perspective regarding her.'

Radu glanced around the circus crowd self-consciously. Andy thought the man hoped someone would step forward in his defense.

'Imanuela is the heart of this circus,' the clown on stilts called down. 'She draws the audience that fill the Big Top.'

'And if she can't travel with us, Emile?' Radu demanded. 'What do we do then? Do we stay here in Alexandria while the rest of our bookings do without us and the coffers grow empty?'

'Imanuela is one of us,' Syeira said.

'Let her be one of us,' Radu replied, facing her again.

'When Taptyk fell from the motorcycle in the Cage of Death and broke his arm in Paris last year, the circus left him behind while the necessary surgery and therapy was performed. He returned to the circus when he was able. This is no different.'

Andy glanced at the crowd, noticing that some of them appeared to waver.

'Taptyk bought a plane ticket and caught up with us in a matter of days,' Syeira pointed out. 'Imanuela would need special transportation.'

'I could arrange that,' Radu said. 'But it would be expensive.'

'This is Imanuela,' Papa said quietly, patting the sleeping elephant on the head. 'Any expenses would be worth it.'

'Those new travel arrangements would require additional permits,' Radu said. 'That means further cost and further time spent.'

'All of which you can do.' Papa folded his arms across his broad chest.

Radu shook his head. 'I only ask whether this is all necessary and worth the additional cost. And caring for and training a baby elephant, Papa, is this really a task that we need to take on at this time? Already we are near the end of the funding that has kept us afloat for the last five years. Do we really want to risk losing that charter over special transit and another mouth to feed?'

'What are you saying?' Syeira asked.

'The baby elephant is already at risk,' Radu pointed out. 'If we terminate the pregnancy, then Imanuela is no longer at risk and we eliminate all of the additional costs.'

'We will not harm the baby,' Papa said quietly.

'And if Imanuela dies as well, Papa?' Radu asked. 'If we instead lose two elephants, not one, then what do we do?'

'That will not happen.'

Smoothly, Radu turned to Andy's mom. 'Could it happen, Dr Moore?'

Andy hated that his mom was put on the spot, but he knew

she had no choice except to answer honestly.

'It could,' she said. She started to continue speaking but Radu interrupted.

'Do you see?' Radu asked Papa, then shifted his gaze to the crowd around the pens. 'It's not just the show, the charter, and the circus that is at risk with the baby. Imanuela is also at risk. Do you want to stand by and let her die as well out of some mistaken nobility?'

The rumbling conversation that came from the crowd this time sounded confused.

Sandra Moore raised her voice. 'Imanuela is at risk, yes, but she was more at risk before I arrived here today. I'm pretty sure, judging by what I've seen so far, that I can stabilize her condition, and I think I have a real shot at saving the baby.' She kept focused on Radu. 'I know what I'm doing, Mr Radu, and I put my patients first. Before transportation problems, before inconvenience. I have two patients here, not one.'

'What if the baby cannot be saved? What if Imanuela is at risk as well?' Radu demanded.

'Then,' Andy's mom said, 'and only then, would I even consider terminating the pregnancy.'

'The baby threatens her now.'

'The baby is a reason for concern, yes, but Imanuela is responding well to the medications. This is no longer a critical situation.' Sandra shifted her gaze to the crowd, taking a step up beside Radu.

Andy recognized the move from one of the poli-sci classes he took at Bradford Academy under Dr Dobbs. By stepping up beside Radu, his mother stole the attention the man was getting. Andy had always respected his mom, for the way she'd raised him by herself as well as the way she took care of the patients that turned up at the clinic. She was showing the tough stuff she was made of now.

Radu snorted. 'You ask us to—'

'Enough, Martin,' Papa said in a stern voice. 'Stop before you embarrass us any further.'

'I'm not embarrassing—'

Papa held up a hand. 'No. Imanuela and her baby are in the hands of this fine doctor. There will be no more discussion about what we will do.' He raked the crowd with his gaze. 'There is a show to put on tomorrow night. What are you all doing standing around? Are you so close to finishing your tasks that you have all this time to spare?'

Sheepishly, the circus performers shook their heads.

'Then go,' Papa told them. 'Imanuela is in good hands. If anything changes, I will let you know.'

The crowd filed away. Andy marveled at them, watching how their worry seemed to evaporate as they returned to the canvas tents. Jugglers flipped brightly colored throwing pins back and forth while a bareback rider rode her pony at a canter around the crowd. The stilt clown strode overhead briskly.

'Papa,' Radu said hoarsely, his control obviously strained. 'I think you are letting your emotions overrun your good sense.'

Papa placed a hand lightly on the other man's shoulder. 'I carry this circus in my heart, Martin. Each person that works here is my child, as surely of my blood as Syeira and Traian. I will not fail any of them. Or you.'

Radu sighed. 'I know, Papa.'

Andy listened to the man's words, but he knew Radu still believed Papa was wrong.

'Dr Moore,' Radu said. 'Will Imanuela be able to perform tomorrow night?'

Without hesitation, Sandra said. 'No. The medication I'm going to give her will keep her relaxed for the next two or three days. And I don't want her upset or strained any more than is necessary.'

'Already, Papa,' Radu said, 'we are without the star attraction of our circus.'

'It will be all right,' the circus owner said.

'If the audience knows Imanuela isn't performing, they

36

may not come. She has drawn many of the crowds that have seen us for years.'

'I know, but not telling them would be wrong, Martin. Contact the media and make sure all the ads are changed.'

'Mr Cservanka,' Andy spoke up.

The circus owner turned toward him, interest flashing in the gray eyes beneath the gray eyebrows. 'Call me Papa. Everyone does.'

Andy nodded, but he didn't say it. Papa was too much like dad, and that word still held a whole lot of emotional impact for him. 'Maybe you don't have to do entirely without Imanuela.'

'What do you mean?'

'You could put together a holo performance of her based on past performances,' Andy said. 'The circus is set up to launch online as well as in real time. Already some of your acts, like the lion-tamer's, are online, not live.'

Papa scratched his chin thoughtfully.

'We don't have a holo of her performance,' Radu said, taking an interest.

'I could make one,' Andy volunteered. He wished he would just close his mouth. The circus was definitely lame, not something he wanted to spend any more time at than he had to. But he was working part-time at his mother's clinic for the summer and it was an easy bet that she'd be coming to check on Imanuela. At least working on a project of his own would be more interesting.

'You?' Radu asked. 'You're just a boy.'

'*He*,' Papa interrupted before Andy could say anything, 'is also the boy who is repairing Heritzel's lion-taming act.'

'Another problem.' Radu glanced at Andy. 'Have you fixed that yet?'

'I'll have your lions, tigers, and panthers online by morning,' Andy said with only a trace of irritation. 'I've been working on the problem less than an hour. And if I'm right, the glitch isn't due to just a little programming code error.'

'What do you think it is?' Papa asked.

'It acts like a virus,' Andy replied. 'Kind of complicated and tricky, but I'm positive I can handle it.'

'And still have time to put together a holo of Imanuela for the audience tomorrow night?' Radu said.

'If you can get me all the information I need,' Andy said, 'sure. Piece of cake.'

'What do you need?' Syeira asked.

Sandra took out her stethoscope and listened to Imanuela's heart. Then she rolled the elephant's eyelid back and shined a light into her eye.

'Get me access to your archived records regarding Imanuela's past performances,' Andy said, 'and I can take what I need.'

Radu scowled. 'Access to those records is—'

'—will be released to you before you and your mother leave tonight,' Papa stated. 'Martin, I will not have it any other way.'

'Those are protected,' Radu argued. 'We license those performances.'

'It will be as I say,' Papa said.

'That's another thing,' Andy put in. 'The online security you have around the circus needs to be upgraded. Net Force has recently released some free programs that are a lot stronger than anything you've currently got in place. I can do those upgrades in the next couple days.'

'See?' Papa beamed at Radu. 'This boy is amazing.'

'He can do it,' Andy's mom said as she checked the IV drip. 'Andy's good with Net interfaces and programming in general.'

Papa shoved a beefy hand Andy's way. 'We will discuss your fee at a later time.'

Andy grinned, feeling good. 'Most of this is free software. It won't take long at all to do the upgrades. I can't charge you for that.'

Papa raised his eyebrows. 'Oh, and you expect your mother to pay for your college? Or perhaps for your dates with those

38

pretty girls that must hang around you?'

Andy's face flushed and he glanced at Syeira. Her obvious amusement at his discomfort made him even more embarrassed.

'I thought not,' Papa said. 'We will talk soon. In the meantime, Martin will get access to the circus programming to you.'

Radu nodded stiffly and walked out of the corral.

'How's Imanuela doing?' Andy asked, wanting to turn the attention away from himself.

His mom stood. 'She's doing well. But I'm going to need those prescriptions I called in. Help me unload the other meds I have in the car in case I need them, then you can drive on into Alexandria to pick them up.'

'There's no reason to do that,' Papa said. 'Syeira can drive Andy into town to pick them up. There are a few items I need picked up as well. I'm sure Syeira would appreciate another strong back to do the loading.'

Glancing at Syeira, Andy kind of doubted that. The girl didn't appear to be any more excited about the pairing than he did. But duty called – and at least she wasn't bad to look at.

Andy sat in the passenger seat of the ten-year-old pickup and tried to ignore the smell of elephant dung that clung to his tennis shoes. He hadn't noticed stepping in any of it but that was generally how it went. Murphy's Law – The Veterinary Addendum: If there was animal poop anywhere, it ended up on your shoes. To his way of thinking, that was the worst drawback to working in the clinic.

He watched the street, finally noticing how effortlessly Syeira steered the vehicle. The male voice of the Net-linked global positioning satellite called out appropriate lane changes and turns as they drove through the south-western section of Alexandria.

'I like your mom,' Syeira said, breaking the silence that had filled the pickup cab since they'd left the Cservanka Brothers Circus. 'I really liked the way she stood up to Martin,' the girl said.

'I haven't seen her back down from too many things.'

'I think she surprised him.'

'Yeah.' Andy paused as Syeira whipped the pickup into an empty parking space near the shopping center that held the drug store where his mom had called the prescriptions in. Surprisingly, considering it was Thursday afternoon, the traffic was pretty dense. 'He's not a very likeable guy.'

'It's his job that really stresses him out.' Syeira crossed the parking lot, pulling on a lightweight green nylon windbreaker. The Cservanka Brothers Circus logo, featuring Imanuela the Elephant, covered her back.

'What does he do?' Andy asked. 'Besides arranging transportation for the circus.'

Syeira stepped through the doors leading into the shopping center. 'That is already a full-time occupation. You have no clue how much is involved in arranging transportation for a circus as big as the Cservanka Brothers.'

Andy fell into step at her side. 'I guess not.'

Syeira sighed. 'Sorry. I didn't mean to sound so critical.'

'It's okay,' Andy replied.

'No, it's not. I should really apologize for how I acted back with Imanuela, too.'

'Okay.'

Syeira looked at him. 'Okay?'

'Yeah.' Andy grinned. 'That you can apologize for. When it comes to animals, I know my stuff.'

'I liked you better when you kept your ego in check.'

'It's not ego,' Andy responded. 'My mom trained me, taught me everything I know about animals. That's kind of what I was thinking about at the time.'

'So the student defends his teacher.'

'And she's my mom.'

A smile spread over Syeira's face. 'Family is something I

definitely understand. I apologize.'

'And I accept,' Andy replied. 'Graciously.'

Syeira shot him a glance. 'Trust me when I say you're going to have to work on the gracious part.'

'You're not the first to tell me that.'

Laughter, genuine mirth, erupted from Syeira unexpectedly. It drew the attention of a few people standing in front of a department store display. Andy found he really liked the sound of that laugh, liked the sound of her accent, too.

'Somehow,' Syeira said, 'I can believe that I'm not the first.'

'So how about you?' Andy asked. 'You're Mr Cservanka's granddaughter—'

'Papa,' she corrected. 'Everybody calls him Papa.'

Andy nodded. 'You're his granddaughter, so you're in the circus, too?'

Syeira stopped in front of the store map display. The shopping center was three stories tall, packed with large and small shops catering to all kinds of products and services, from bed and bath décor to clothing to groceries. 'Is it so hard to believe that I'm in the circus?'

'No.' Then Andy shrugged. 'But maybe you being a motorcycle daredevil is a little hard to swallow.' He gazed at the shop layout with little interest. He'd been to the pharmacy there on other occasions for his mother when they didn't have time to wait on a delivery.

'Why? Because I'm so young? Or because I'm a girl?'

Andy glanced at her and answered honestly. 'Both.'

Syeira turned toward him and Andy was suddenly aware that she was as tall as him and standing less than two feet away. 'That's kind of narrow-minded, don't you think?' she asked.

'I like to think of it as old-fashioned.'

'Not attractive.'

'I wasn't working on being attractive,' Andy retorted. 'You asked how I felt. I answered honestly.'

'Which might take some real effort.' Before Andy could say

anything, Syeira went on. 'I apologize for that, too. It was a cheap shot. Like you, I know what I know. I am very good at my work. It's just that I don't like the idea of depending on you and your mom to make sure Imanuela is going to be okay.' Her eyes held a misty sheen.

'Hey,' Andy said softly, 'don't worry about Imanuela. She's in good hands. The *best* hands. Why is it so hard to depend on my mom, and even me? Your grandfather did, or he wouldn't have called us in.'

'It's hard to depend on you and your mom because you're not part of the circus. You're outsiders. If you travel with the circus for a while, you get used to the concept of "us" and "them." '

'Now *that* sounds narrow-minded.'

'Maybe, but it's true.' Syeira started on again, taking long strides that caused Andy to hustle to keep up. 'We go into a town or city and most people are glad to see us, but there's always that line between the circus and the citizens. They want us to entertain them, then after that they want us on our way.'

'Seems like it would be easier to do everything online,' Andy stated.

'A virtual circus?'

'Part of your circus is virtual now.'

'But not all of it.' Syeira slowed as she walked past a style shop and gazed inside at the seat filled with women and girls getting manicures and new hairstyles.

Andy's nose itched at the smell of the abrasive chemicals. He tried to figure out what emotion he saw in her face.

She glanced up at him and her face went cold again. She turned away from the shop and walked toward the fountain in the center of the mall. Colored lights shone on the spraying water, creating a rainbow in the center of the potted plants and trees that ringed it.

'Why didn't they just use a holo of the fountain?' she asked.

Andy gazed at the mothers seated around the fountain with

small children. Kids dropped pennies into the cistern and laughed when the misty spray hit them. Teens gathered nearby in clusters, talking among themselves.

'I don't know,' Andy said.

Syeira didn't stop walking till she reached the fountain. 'It would have been cheaper and easier to maintain if it was just a holo, wouldn't it?'

'Yeah.' *You don't need an accounting degree to figure that out,* Andy thought.

'Maybe it would have been even more fantastic,' Syeira pointed out. 'Instead of a ten-foot fountain, they could have designed a waterfall that tumbled over broken rocks at the ceiling. They could have sprayed it with laser lights, filled it with fish that swam upstream and down.'

Andy knew that was true. He'd seen the fountain for years while visiting the mall with his mother and friends but he'd never wondered about it.

Syeira extended her hand into the water. 'They put in a real fountain because you can touch it.'

'You can touch water in veeyar,' Andy argued. 'It feels the same.'

'Maybe it feels the same in veeyar, but you know it's not real. Papa says people like coming to the circus because they can sit on the benches and see a real show. Even though the circus and its acts are rehearsed, there's still an element of very real danger.'

'What danger?'

'Someone could fall from the trapeze,' Syeira answered. 'The clowns could actually throw a bucket of water over the crowd instead of confetti. And maybe the lions and tigers could escape the lion-tamer's cage.'

'But that doesn't happen all the time.'

'No, but it could. That's part of what draws an audience to a live circus.'

'Hoping that someone gets hurt?' Andy shook his head. 'I don't want to believe that.'

'Not really hoping that someone gets hurt,' Syeira said, 'but more being aware that the possibility exists. That's part of the excitement for some people.'

'Not for me.'

'Then what brings you to the circus?' Syeira faced him and asked the question directly.

'My mom,' Andy answered.

'When was the last time you attended a circus?'

Andy shrugged. 'Three or four years ago.'

'What did you go to see then?'

'A sick zebra.'

'When was the last time you sat under the Big Top and watched the performers?'

'I've peeked in online a few times.'

'Did you find anything interesting?'

Andy hesitated, but as he stared into the girl's dark eyes he had the distinct feeling that she would know if he was lying. 'No.'

'I see.' Syeira took her hand from the fountain. 'It's getting late. Why don't you get the prescriptions from the pharmacy while I get Papa's shopping done? We'll meet back here when we're done.'

'Maybe,' Andy replied, feeling very dismissed. But his answer only met her back. Irritation burned inside him. He was beginning to think there was nothing he could say right. 'I've got a better idea. When you get done, you can find me in the arcades.' He turned and walked in the other direction, not looking back.

Chapter Five

'Increase magnification,' Andy ordered.

Immediately, the letterbox-shaped heads-up display inside his helmet pulsed. The bridge spanning the turbulent river he waded through became clearer, showing the heavily armored cavalry units positioned across it.

'Warning,' a gentle feminine voice stated. 'Water is streaming in through stress fractures from earlier damage sustained in this firefight.'

Andy tapped a control inside his left cyber-augmented glove. The HUD pulsed again, overlaying a schematic of the forty-foot tall Space Marine battlesuit he wore. He wore cyber-augmented boots as well that allowed him to move the battlesuit's legs like they were his own.

The schematic showed the various stress fractures from the earlier missiles that scarred the battlesuit's legs. It also showed that the crown of the battlesuit's head that held the cockpit remained two meters below the river's waterline. A periscope jutting from the battlesuit's head provided the screen's video feed.

The battlesuit was definitely taking on water, rising to nearly a two-foot depth in both legs.

Andy had felt the resistance as he'd moved, but he'd guessed that it was from the thick mud that covered the river bottom. 'Deploy snorkel.'

'Snorkel away.'

Vibrations echoed through the battlesuit as the snorkel

jettisoned from its left shoulder. The battlesuit had an onboard oxygen supply that Andy had been using for the last twelve minutes. It was good for another eighteen minutes before it was exhausted. He planned to begin the attack on the bridge before then, but securing his legs would have used that supply up in seconds.

On the bridge, the enemy units occasionally shifted. They still didn't know he was so close. Andy tried to relax in the command seat but he was finding it difficult. From all his hours of play in Space Marines, he was accustomed to the safety straps around his chest, arms, and legs. But the game scenario itself was better executed than he'd believed. Some of the guys he normally gamed with had talked about the newest operation available in the mall arcade center but, being true gamers, they hadn't gone into much detail about the contents. The excitement lay in overcoming the obstacles and enemies on one's own, not following the path someone else had blazed.

Tapping another control in his right glove, Andy brought up the weapons menu and remaining ammo inventories. He still had his lasers, but the heavy machine guns and all but two of the missiles were gone. Still, he carried the Inferno Warhead in the battlesuit's belly.

All he had to do was destroy the bridge running supplies across the river to the Phraxite troops and take their command center offline for a few crucial minutes. He'd lost his six teammates along the way, never knowing for sure if they were veeyar constructs or real people in other cockpits scattered throughout the mall arcade.

Of course, some of those fellow players in the mall served the Phraxite troops as they tried to turn Damgora into their last expansion conquest.

The snorkel reached the river's surface and floated.

'Snorkel in place and operational,' the feminine voice stated.

'Engage,' Andy commanded. 'Equalize the pressure inside

the armor to meet the depth pressure.'

'Meeting those parameters will increase the pressure of the atmosphere inside the battlesuit,' the onboard computer said. 'Before you exit the battlesuit you may need to decompress.'

'Acknowledged,' Andy said. 'Get it done.'

'Snorkel engaged.'

Andy waited patiently. Patience wasn't one of his strengths but he'd learned during his gaming that it was as necessary as any weapon available to him. He watched the enemy forces with his long-range scanners.

'Pressure equalized.'

Andy shifted restlessly in the cockpit chair. Despite the attention the game required, Syeira Cservanka remained in his thoughts.

After she'd left him standing at the fountain, his irritation had grown stronger. Once he'd gotten the prescriptions his mom had called in, he'd bailed for the arcade center, intending to release some pent-up frustration. Then he'd realized that he was acting like a kid, finding something amusing to do while the more responsible partner had continued on with the actual business at hand.

The thought hadn't set well with him.

'Continue increasing pressure,' Andy instructed.

'Warning, the increased pressure will definitely require some decompression before you leave this unit.'

'Understood,' Andy replied. 'Get it done.' Even a well-meaning program that questioned his authority wasn't something he wanted to put up with at the moment.

'Interior pressure increasing. What PSI do you want to establish?'

'I'll let you know.' Andy adjusted the HUD, then moved his feet, getting underway again. The screen automatically split, keeping the periscope view as well as adding the infrared view that swept the riverbed.

The infrared capability revealed the geography of the riverbed in a dozen shades of green. The battlesuit's huge feet sank into the mud as he started forward but the onboard gyros kept him level. The river had eroded a deep channel in the center that was much deeper than the side Andy walked along. The steep grade was treacherous but the battlesuit's huge, splayed feet kept him on track.

He watched the schematic overlay. Gradually, the increased air pressure inside the battlesuit forced all of the water from its legs.

'Warning,' the computer voice interrupted. 'Due to the weakened hull this unit's integrity may be breached. Suggest jettison of all personnel.'

Andy glanced at the HUD and saw the warning grids flare to life. If the legs blew, his position would be revealed. And the Phraxians didn't take prisoners as a general rule.

He moved his arms and legs inside the cyber-augmented gloves and boots, urging the battlesuit to go faster. If the Phraxians had sonar detectors mounted in the water near the base of the bridge, he was sunk – literally.

Mud squished underfoot and slid away in great clods. Fish darted before Andy, their bodies glowing neon-green in the infrared light. 'Retract snorkel.' In the schematic overlay the snorkel quickly retreated into the battlesuit's shoulder.

The enemy forces along the bridge shifted suddenly, their attention centered on the swift-moving river.

Andy knew he had been spotted. All he had left on his side was time. He had learned to be incredibly quick with the Space Marine battlesuits. He toggled the controls in his left glove as he threw the battlesuit's arms forward. The onboard gyros responded immediately, leveling the battlesuit in a horizontal position.

In the next instant, lasers sizzled through the river, igniting the dark water in a haze of red, blue and green columns of super-heated light. Warheads crashed into the river's muddy bottom, killing fish for dozens of yards around and ripping huge craters in the mud. Debris and dead creatures littered the water and obscured Andy's view.

Working through the onboard gyros, Andy tilted the battlesuit to a fifteen-degree angle and kicked in the leg thrusters. The battlesuit shivered, seemingly on the verge of shattering, but the leg thrusters powered the huge battlesuit through the water. Even as large as it was, the battlesuit tried to skip like a stone against the river current.

Andy concentrated on the battlesuit's sensor array feeding into him through the HUD. Target-lock was impossible. He didn't have a GPS satellite-feed and he had lost visual confirmation through the periscope. He worked from memory, angling toward the river's surface, aware of the way the water got lighter.

A warhead exploded only a few feet away, spraying a series of concussive waves over him. Despite the combat harness that held him in place, he slammed back against the console. The impact momentarily took the HUD offline and left only gray fuzz dancing in his vision.

Hoping that he hadn't been too badly knocked off course, Andy brought his remaining missiles online. He checked the automatic-mapping program and knew he had covered over half the distance to the bridge. In the next instant, bright light flooded his vidscreens.

Andy found that he was bearing slightly to the left. He corrected instantly, swinging the battlesuit around. Automatically he brought up the targeting screens and watched as the crosshairs vectored in on the bridge. A warhead crunched into the battlesuit near the main forward sensor array, temporarily blinding the vid relay, but the targeting programming remained locked on.

Triggering both remaining missiles, Andy felt the shiver of their release just as the vidscreen cleared. Less than a heartbeat later, the missiles detonated against the bridge supports. The audio dampers filtered most of the destructive crescendo but the roar of the twin explosions still echoed within the battlesuit's control console.

Even as the bridge's main supports collapsed, one enemy

weapon found target-lock on Andy. The warhead threw a convulsive wave throughout the battlesuit and tossed him into the air. Temporarily out of control, Andy watched the river surface come too close, much too close. The battlesuit hit the water going the wrong way and way too fast. For a moment, Andy felt like he was riding a loose-limbed puppet instead of a top-of-the-line war machine.

Instead of backing off, Andy poured more power to the leg thrusters. The battlesuit cut through the river, not like a knife, but like a wedge. Waves thirty feet tall spumed up and crashed back down in his wake.

Flying debris from the bridge peppered the battlesuit but caused little damage. Andy recovered control only a few short feet from the wreckage of the collapsing bridge. He folded the battlesuit's huge arms around its head protectively, hoping the command console would remain intact. If it didn't, he would be automatically jettisoned, and it would be game-over.

The Space Marine battlesuit slammed through the falling bridge like a battering ram. Forward momentum all but stopped and Andy experienced momentary vertigo as the restraining straps pulled tight around him. His head felt like it was going to snap off.

Then he was through.

Using the HUD's backward-looking sensors available on the letterbox screen, Andy watched as the bridge's infrastructure came apart. Struts and beams tumbled and fell, mixing with falling enemy battlesuits, armored cavalry and men. If there were any survivors, and he knew they would be few and far between, they would not be able to stop him.

Andy had only a nanosecond to enjoy his victory. In the next instant his sensor vidscreen filled with three images that rose from the river. The Phraxian battlesuits showed scars from past engagements. None of them appeared to be in good shape but they didn't have to be.

Water cascaded down the three grim shapes and steam belched from the weapon ports as they brought their guns to bear on his suit and fired at almost point-blank range. The missiles detonated against Andy's chest armor.

With a deafening roar, the explosions ripped his armor away like orange peel.

Inside the command console, Andy watched the schematic overlay flash red. None of the systems, from the hydraulics to the powerplant exchanges, remained unaffected.

'Systemwide failures,' the computer voice said. 'Unit shutting down. Prepare to jettison.'

Feeling the unresponsive controls in the cyber-augmented gloves and boots, Andy knew the mission was over. The restraining straps pulled at his body even more tightly, holding him securely in the command control chair. Resolutely, he stared at the HUD's vidscreen, knowing how close he'd come to finishing the operation. There, just over the shoulders of the three enemy battlesuits, he saw the command center communications sat-links.

Desperately, Andy strove to trigger the Inferno Warhead, before the three enemy troops fired on him again. The sensor vidscreen went flat gray as the battered battlesuit shivered under the strain. Too late. On autopilot, the battlesuit shoved its head skyward, its arms extending straight up as well to provide protection for the escape module.

The HUD helmet faceplate cleared, no longer connected to the sensor array. Andy stared up at the blue sky above when the jettison match popped free. When the command chair blew free, the increased G-force pushed him deeply into the cushions. The command chair module flew into the air, and the parachute released from the canopy caught the wind overhead.

Andy felt the comm band pulse on his wrist. Two selections scrolled across the miniature vidscreen, bright green letters against a black screen. RETRY MISSION? CONTINUE WITH ESCAPE PLAN?

Either selection, Andy knew, would require more money for rented game time. The mall arcades weren't part of the online game provider he subscribed to. He chose to log off.

The sky turned dark purple and blood-red letters scratched across it. YOU LOSE, SPACE MARINE!

Another five seconds and he'd have won this round. Feeling frustrated, Andy pushed himself up from the mall arcade Mockpit. He glanced outside the arcade and spotted Syeira descending an escalator near the fountain. He also spotted the group of teenaged boys trailing close behind her.

The boys wore denim and leather, typical skater garb. Andy was certain they carried streamlined, collapsible skateboards in their backpacks. Criminal groups often used skater gangs as couriers within the metro area. Kids on skateboards could escape police pursuit by dodging through traffic and narrow alleys.

Obviously, Syeira didn't know the danger she was in.

Andy moved quickly, arriving at the foot of the escalator just ahead of Syeira. She carried a half-dozen packages that definitely drew the interest of the gang behind her.

Syeira gave Andy a tentative smile. 'Look, I didn't mean to come across as rude. I was thinking maybe we could just—'

Andy grabbed her by the hand and pulled her with him. 'Come on. We've got to get out of here.'

Syeira yanked her hand back and stood her ground. 'What's wrong with you?'

Andy glanced up the escalator. The skaters jostled other shoppers as they wove between them, hurrying to get to the bottom of the escalator. 'Trouble's coming,' Andy said, nodding at the group of boys.

Then it was too late. The boys surrounded them, gliding, constantly moving, giving the impression they were never truly at rest.

Without thinking, Andy faced the largest of the skaters, putting himself in front of Syeira. The other shoppers flowed around them, acting like they didn't see anything out of the ordinary.

Andy searched the mall in vain for a security guard or rent-a-cop. *Nobody handy. But drop a chili-covered cheese fry on the floor and one would be all over you.*

'What are you doing?' Syeira demanded.

'Trying to avoid this,' Andy said.

The lead skater stood almost six feet tall and was built like a football tight end. His short-cropped hair stood up like porcupine bristles, dyed electric blue. A black skull with flaming eyesockets was printed on his pullover leather vest. His fingernails matched the electric blue hue of his hair, each with a black skull inlaid on it.

'Hey, man,' the skater said, 'don't try going tough guy on us. We're the Skulls, and nobody messes with the Skulls.'

Andy spread his hands and spoke softly. 'We aren't looking for trouble.'

'That's the neat thing about trouble, man. Sometimes it finds you all by its ownself.' The skater grinned.

'That's telling him, Razor,' one of the other gang members said. Hooting jeers echoed the comment.

Andy turned, following Razor's movements, knowing the boy would lead whatever action took place. As a Net Force Explorer, Andy had taken several martial arts classes. Maybe he'd never be as good as Megan O'Malley but he knew how to take care of himself. His own tendency to be the class clown, usually at the expense of himself and others, had brought him into his share of conflicts in the past. He'd had more practice than he liked to think about with this kind of thing.

'We're not afraid of trouble either,' Andy stated.

Razor broke out into a gale of laughter and the gang followed suit. 'How much trouble does it take before you start getting afraid?'

Andy met the skater leader's gaze. 'Your pockets aren't that deep.'

Before Andy knew it, Syeira took him by the arm and pushed him forward. 'Let's go,' she said. 'If you stay here, there's only going to be trouble.'

Andy resisted. Surely she could see that trouble was already on them. He wasn't about to turn his back on any of the skaters. Stubbornly, Syeira released his arm and started forward by herself. Andy felt torn; any movement on his part was going to be perceived as weakness, leaving him open to attack.

Before Syeira had taken three steps, Razor nodded to one of his buddies. The skater member grabbed Syeira by the shoulder and spun her around. Packages fell from her arms and one of them shattered inside its box when it hit the floor.

'Who said you could leave?' Razor demanded.

Syeira faced the skater leader with a blank expression. 'I haven't done anything to you.'

Razor raised and dropped his shoulders in an exaggerated shrug. 'So? That doesn't mean we won't do anything to you if we get the chance. That's just the way the world works.'

The skater kept his hand on Syeira's shoulder, holding her in place.

'What do you want?' Syeira asked.

Razor circled around her, making a production of looking her up and down. 'Cservanka Brothers Circus? What's that?'

'It's a circus,' Syeira replied in a neutral tone. 'If you can read that, surely you can understand that.'

Andy started forward.

Syeira glanced at him, said, 'Don't,' and returned her attention to Razor.

Razor concentrated on Syeira. 'You're not from around here, are you? You're some kind of carny trash, aren't you?'

Syeira faced him calmly. 'One scream from me and you're going to be covered over in mall security guards.'

Razor's hand darted up under his leather vest. When it emerged, he was gripping an open switchblade knife. The razored edge gleamed in the daylight streaming through the overhead skylights. 'Screaming might not be such a good idea.'

Andy moved suddenly, taking the skater gang by surprise. He shrugged through the first gang member's attempt to grab him and shot out a foot that caught the guy on the side of the leg. The kick wasn't hard enough to break anything but Andy knew from experience it was painful.

The skater fell backward, screaming and trying to hold his knee.

Razor shifted and brought the switchblade around in a glittering arc, pointing it at Andy.

Chapter Six

Andy blocked the slashing blow of Razor's knife-hand with the back of his right arm. He looped his arm around Razor's, controlling the other boy's wrist. Locking his free hand under his elbow, he wrenched up violently and pinned the skater leader's arm behind his back.

Before the other skaters could move, Andy levered Razor's arm up between his shoulder blades. The leader's hand opened automatically and the switchblade clattered to the floor. Andy kicked the knife away, sending it under a jewelry booth.

Razor bellowed fiercely and swung his free fist at Andy's face.

Andy dodged away but didn't completely escape the blow. Razor's fist crashed into Andy's cheekbone, igniting bright colors that flashed through his vision.

'Now you're going to get yours,' Razor promised.

The mall crowd around Andy evaporated. He barely got himself set before the first skater launched himself into the air and kicked at his chest. Andy grabbed the boy's ankle in one hand and yanked, pushing the kick off target, pulling the kicker off-balance. Fighting in real-time wasn't the same as fighting in veeyar. Real-time meant real hurts and real bruises. Not letting go of his attacker, Andy kicked the skater in the side, driving the air out of his lungs.

Razor threw himself at Andy, his arms whipping like windmills.

Andy defended himself, knocking Razor's blows away. Still,

his arms were badly bruised in seconds. Without warning, someone kicked him in the back, knocking the wind out of him and shoving him into Razor's waiting fist. For a moment, Andy thought he had been knocked out. His vision filled with a rainbow explosion and a cacophony of ringing bells deafened him.

The skater gang howled in triumph and urged Razor on to his certain victory.

Blows rained on Andy as he struggled to hang on to consciousness. He pulled his arms in tightly around his head to protect himself.

Suddenly, Razor flew backward, throwing his arms out to the sides as he tried and failed to remain on his feet.

Andy had thought mall security had arrived – until he saw Syeira standing there. She rotated explosively, rolling her hip to get all of her weight into a roundhouse kick that missed Andy by inches and thudded into the face of the skater holding him from behind.

Regaining his balance and his composure, Andy whirled to face the skaters. They descended on Syeira and him like carrion-eaters dropping on roadkill. He blocked blows with open hands, pushing them away from his face, taking them on the shoulder or the back if he had no way to escape them entirely.

Syeira moved gracefully; her blocks, parries, punches and kicks were flawless. As good as Megan O'Malley was, Andy felt she'd have been hard-pressed to have kept up with Syeira. In seconds, it became apparent that the skater gang feared Syeira more than they did Andy.

'Hey, you kids!' a man's deep voice thundered. 'Break it up!'

'Security!' Razor yelled. 'Get out of here!' He stripped off his own backpack and reached inside. Grabbing the collapsible skateboard while running for the nearest exit, he pulled the board to its full length, snapped it into place and rolled it ahead of him. In three short strides he caught up with the skateboard and leaped on top of it. A heartbeat later, he weaved his way through the mall crowd and made his escape. The other skaters were hot on his heels.

Breathing hard, Andy looked over at Syeira. 'Are you okay?' he asked.

'Yes,' she snapped. 'No thanks to you.'

'What are you talking about?' Andy asked incredulously. 'If I hadn't stepped in that guy would have cut you.'

'You like the idea of playing the hero, don't you?'

Andy could not believe it. How could she turn what just happened into his fault? 'This wasn't about being a hero. Those guys had locked onto you. You didn't even know they were there until it was too late.'

'I knew they were there. I also knew they didn't have to be dealt with like that.'

'There wasn't any other way.' Andy couldn't believe that either. How could she be so narrow-minded?

The four mall security guards that had responded to the fight surrounded them. One of them, a beefy man with a military style haircut, gave them an icy stare. 'Somebody here owes me an explanation.'

Andy reached into his pants pocket and took out his foilpack. He flipped it open to his Net Force Explorer ID. It wasn't exactly a get-out-of-jail-free card but a lot of police and security organizations respected what the Net Force Explorers were all about.

He related the story quickly, satisfying the security guards. But the look on Syeira's face told him that she wasn't happy at all.

'There's nothing like a first impression.'

'Some first impression.' Andy shook his head at Mark Gridley's words. 'I've met nicer drill instructors at Net Force Explorer camp.'

Dressed in one of the virtual crashsuits designed by Mark, Andy flew after the younger boy. The crashsuit looked like a silver suit of armor that appeared to be completely made up of small angles that intersected. The helmet was formed of a huge crystalline polyhedron that constantly flowed into new shapes.

In veeyar now, they sped along the computer programming that made up the lion-tamer's act. The lines of programming code took on the aspects of a three-dimensional maze cube that continuously flowed and reshaped itself, making mapping almost impossible.

Mark Gridley, called the Squirt, was hands-down the best guy in programming Andy knew. Although only thirteen years old, the Squirt was often called on to consult in regular Net Force missions. His father was Jay Gridley, present head of Net Force, and his mother was Net Force's top computer tech.

'Careful,' Mark cautioned.

'What?' Andy stared deep into the channel to the maze cube they presently followed. Even with the crashsuit's infrared capability and high-tech sensor array he couldn't see much. The maze cube had a habit of blasting nasty surprises into their path. Andy had already destroyed two crashsuits during the last forty minutes. Both times he'd been kicked offline and had to fight to return.

Ahead, Mark rocked his crashsuit to the left. The twin booster jets on his backpack flared to life briefly, spraying twin fiery blazes.

The next instant, a snakelike creature exploded from the maze wall. It looked long and hard, bigger in circumference than Andy's thigh, topped with a barracuda's wedge-shaped head. Sharp teeth filled the thin-lipped mouth. The gray-green skin was dark and mottled with scars from past battles.

The serrated teeth gnashed only on air, missing Mark by nearly a foot. Then the creature turned its attention to Andy.

Andy pressed the jet controls inside the crashsuit's right glove. The jets fired immediately but he knew it was going to be too late. The creature was too quick. For one terrifying moment, the wedge-shaped head filled with jagged teeth streaked for his face. The creature's impact against the crystalline helmet knocked Andy sideways, driving him into the tunnel wall with the jets flaring. For a moment, he thought he could still get away. Then the creature struck again, clamping its teeth around his right calf.

Doubling his fists, Andy hammered the wedge-shaped head to no avail. The powerful jaws closed inexorably, quickly bringing enough pain to threaten triggering the automatic log-off failsafe.

'Don't panic,' Mark called out. 'Use your lasers.'

Andy twisted his left wrist and popped the laser free of the crashsuit. He grabbed the creature's snarling jaws with his empty hand and pulled himself around. Pointing the laser at the bulbous eye, as big as a dinner plate, looking deep into the slick, liquid metal blackness, he fired the laser.

The ruby beam lanced through the huge eye with a liquid hiss. Gray steam roiled up from the creature's head. The crashsuit's programming automatically adjusted for the laser flare, preventing damage to Andy's optic nerves as well as maintaining his vision. The creature shivered in its death throes, shaking its prey like a terrier shaking a rat.

Although he wasn't physically hurt and the pain remained well within the program's tolerances, Andy wasn't having a good time. Only charred gore remained where the eye had been. He shoved his fist forward and triggered the laser again. This time the creature's head erupted.

The creature writhed in agony, at last releasing the hold on Andy's leg. A heartbeat later the creature fragmented into bright yellow diamonds and disappeared.

Andy took a deep, shuddering breath and wiped residual creature-slime from his helmet. He popped the laser back into hiding.

'That was close,' Mark observed. 'I thought you were toast for sure.'

'I appreciate the vote of confidence.'

Mark glanced down the tunnel they were following. 'This virus is a lot nastier than I'd thought at first.'

A bit more cautiously now, Andy trailed after his friend. 'How nasty?'

'I don't know.' Mark approached a juncture where the tunnel they followed split into a Y. He hesitated, looking in both directions. 'You could always blow this off and tell Syeira that you couldn't purge the virus.'

'No way,' Andy responded vehemently. *Giving up definitely isn't an option.*

Mark fired his jets again and flew down the new tunnel. 'She might understand.'

Andy checked the sensor panel on the inside of the crystalline helmet. It pulsed bright orange, automatically mapping the new direction three-dimensionally. The latest turn put them on track for the maze cube's center. 'Syeira is pig-headed and cocky. And those are her good traits.'

'Some people might think the two of you had a lot in common.'

Only a few feet ahead, another of the barracuda-like creatures representing the computer virus in the lion-tamer's module leapt from the tunnel overhead. Rubbery flesh pulled back tightly over the widely distended jaws that dripped scarlet ichor as the creature lunged at Mark.

Andy popped the laser free of its housing again and fired as soon as he had a target-lock. The ruby beam slashed the wedge-shaped head free of the thick neck. The amputated head bounced from Mark's back, then fragmented into yellow diamonds with the rest of the body.

'Thanks,' Mark said. 'I didn't see that until it was too late.'

'No prob.'

'Actually, it is. That attack proves this virus isn't a linear one. It's capable of learning from its mistakes.'

'You don't think this was some hacker having a good time? You think someone planted a nasty custom bug in this module?' Andy realized that put a different twist on things.

'Maybe,' Mark said. 'Get set.'

The end of the tunnel came into view only a hundred yards ahead. For a moment it looked like the tunnel's mouth opened onto empty space. Then Andy noticed the squirming mass that resembled a small planet ahead. He cut the crashsuit's jets and grabbed hold of the tunnel's side by triggering the anchors mounted in his left glove. The anchors drove inches-deep into the silvery metal, then flared their triangular heads.

'The virus could still have come over the publicity file data feeds,' Mark said. 'Most businesses that rely on marketing over the Net also include up-to-date security countermeasures to filter out any incoming viruses. The Cservanka Brothers Circus doesn't have decent programs. But you already knew that.'

Andy watched the squirming, wriggling chaos in the center of the maze cube. The creatures endlessly circled the tumbling Mobius strip that represented the lion-tamer module's AI. The module's artificial intelligence capabilities were limited, ancient by current standards. Andy spotted at least six blue-green memory cells that had been grafted onto the Mobius strip.

'The virus is thicker than I thought, too,' Mark commented.

'Are you trying to tell me it's impossible to defeat it?' Andy asked.

'Not impossible,' Mark replied, 'but definitely tricky.'

Andy pulled up a chron readout and checked the time. It was almost ten P.M. There was still plenty of time to finish the virus purge before the next day – *if* it could be done. 'I'm ready to be amazed, Houdini.'

Mark nodded. 'The real problem is that I'm not sure if the module memory can survive the security upgrades we need to install. If we try to force them we may crash the module's integrity.'

'We could always download another copy of the program from the circus,' Andy pointed out.

'I don't really like the idea of starting over,' Mark said. 'It's taken us nearly an hour already. Even if we save our progress this far, we won't be able to upload it into the next copy. Everything we've gained will be lost.'

Andy wasn't happy with that possibility either. The lion-tamer module's security systems prevented any tampering on that magnitude. Unfortunately, it still remained vulnerable to viruses like the one presently inhabiting it. Frustration chafed at him.

So, too, did the memory of Syeira's accusations back at the mall. The mall security guards had released them after only a few moments. But the ride back to the circus in the pickup after they had gotten the things Papa had sent them for had been long and quiet.

Mark held his gloved hands in front of him about a foot apart. Violet lightning sizzled and crackled between his palms. 'Here's the plan. The first thing we do is download the module memory, tuck it away someplace safe. Then we go after the virus. Got it?'

Andy nodded, then watched as the lightning between Mark's palms grew stronger and faster, till it became a solid bar of lavender light that pulsed waves into the darkness surrounding the virus creatures and the module memory.

Abruptly, Mark slammed his palms together. A thunderous crescendo reverberated throughout the module, instantly drawing the attention of the virus creatures slithering around the memory. Nearly twenty of them sprang forward, arcing toward Andy and Mark.

'You have to hold them off,' Mark said, 'and give me enough time to set up the memory download.'

Andy retracted the finger anchors and kicked himself forward. He fired his jets, wishing he was in Space Marine armor instead of the crashsuit, and set himself on an interception course with the virus creatures. He released the lasers from both arms and started firing.

The ruby beams sliced across the darkness and burned into the ranks of the virus creatures. They sizzled and popped, hissing for a moment before they fragmented into the yellow diamond shards. Still, there were too many of them for Andy to hope to hold them all back.

Then the violet light column blazed past him, incinerating the virus creatures it touched. When the violet beam connected with the memory module, the module glowed with the same incandescence.

'The download's started,' Mark informed him. He jetted to the right, helping catch more of the virus creatures in a vicious crossfire of laser fire.

Less than ten seconds after the download had been initiated, the virus creatures swarmed Andy and Mark. Andy lost sight of his friend almost at once. Sinewy, gray-green bodies covered in leathery scales wrapped around him. He felt the pressure of their tightening coils even inside the crashsuit's reinforced exo-skeleton.

Andy fired his jets, hoping to dislodge some of the creatures. One of the grinning barracuda faces lunged forward, snapping its fanged maw over his left laser. Andy triggered the laser and watched the virus creature's head explode in a ruby cascade. Nice kill – but the laser was destroyed with the virus creature.

'Keep them away from the download,' Mark yelled.

Familiar with the crashsuit's operating system from past runs with Mark, Andy closed his fist and summoned up a secondary weapon to replace the lost laser. A steel rod shot through one of the virus creature's eel-like bodies. Then the heavy-duty blades of the broad ax formed and sundered the creature in half.

The crashsuit's warning system pinged as damage reports scrolled into Andy's vision. If the crashsuit broke down he knew he'd be logged off the Net automatically. Using the crashsuit's jets and leverage he gained from holding onto his opponents, he swung his ax and split the wedge-shaped head in front of him. The virus creature shattered into yellow diamonds and winked out of existence.

'The download is completed,' Mark said. 'Standby to go nuclear.'

Still in total brawl mode, Andy blasted another creature with his surviving laser. Even as the creature fell to pieces, another creature zoomed at Andy like it was going to drill right through him.

Andy pushed off against the creature next to him, barely avoiding the streaking attacker. Reacting quickly, he stabbed his right glove into the creature's midsection and triggered his fingertip anchors. The anchors ripped into the creature's leathery flesh, then locked down. The creature's momentum ripped Andy free of the snarling boil of attackers.

Then it seemed like a sun was suddenly born in the maze cube's center. Harsh, bright light ignited the semi-gloom and burned all the darkness away. Even the crashsuit's visual protection couldn't match the fiery display.

Instinctively, Andy shielded his eyes with his free arm. His sight returned in blurred shadows first. The first thing he could clearly see was the burning body of the creature he had anchored to. He retracted the finger-anchors and kicked free. He keyed the comm as he stared around the emptiness where the memory module had been covered over by the virus infestation.

'Mark, are you still here?'

'Yeah.'

Andy searched the sensor screen. There was Mark to his right. He fired his booster jets and brought himself around to face his friend. 'That was a little more intense than I expected.'

'I haven't ever tried something that big in an environment this small,' Mark admitted.

Andy scanned the surrounding space, checked the crashsuit's sensors again, but found nothing. The virus creatures had been exterminated. The memory module had been erased as well. 'Well, at least they're gone.'

Mark agreed. 'Yeah, but so is everything else. Let's see if we can rebuild this program version without the virus recurring.'

Chapter Seven

'How's it going?'

Andy glanced up from raiding the refrigerator. He held a grape-flavored sports drink gelpack in one hand and a bag containing microwave pizza slices between his teeth while he rummaged more deeply, desperately seeking something chocolate.

His mom continued through the living room and entered the kitchen. She carried an overfilled laundry basket toward the utility room.

Andy dropped the pizza from his mouth and caught it with his empty hand. 'How's what going?' Suspiciously, he followed his mom to the washer and dryer.

His mom dumped the laundry basket on the tiled floor and quickly separated the contents into two loads. She put the jeans in first, then added soap and started the cycle. 'Your project,' she said.

Andy shrugged. 'Mark and I have already finished with it.'

'Have you let Papa know you've finished?'

'I sent the corrected program to the Net address he gave me. I assume someone got it.'

'That's good.' She glanced at the grape gelpack and microwave pizza slices he held. 'You're planning on calling that dinner?'

Andy smiled, feeling more at ease. 'Actually, I was planning on calling it a snack.'

'You're not calling *that* a snack after the way you picked at the dinner they served at the circus. I've never seen you eat so little. Are you sick?'

'I feel fine. I just didn't feel like eating then.' The confrontation with the skaters at the mall and the displeasure Syeira had shown had left him without an appetite at the time. But purging the lion-tamer module had put his appetite right back on track.

His mom took the bagged pizza wedges from him and walked back into the kitchen. She deposited the pizza in the refrigerator, then conducted her own raiding expedition. She took out the lettuce, a tomato, a bell pepper, pickles, and an onion Andy had deliberately avoided. She added a small packet of shaved ham, cheese, and a container of leftover chicken soup.

'I can make my own sandwich,' Andy protested.

Ignoring him, his mom popped the soup container into the microwave and set the timer. She took out a cutting board and quickly sliced the veggies. When the timer went off, she took the soup container out and poured two bowls.

'A sandwich and soup will be better for you than pizza.' She took a loaf of French bread from the pantry and sliced half off. She split the half, decorated the bottom with the chopped vegetables, covered those with ham and two different kinds of cheese, zapped it for a few seconds to melt the cheese, smothered it all in mustard and salt and pepper, then covered it with the top of the loaf. 'I could use the nutrition myself.'

Andy placed the two bowls of soup on the table and sat. When his mom fixed a meal for the two of them she generally expected to talk.

'Papa seemed really concerned about the lion-tamer act,' his mom said. She sliced a third of the foot-long sandwich off then put both pieces on plates before joining him at the table. 'He said they had never had trouble with it before.'

Andy picked up his sandwich and took a bite. His stomach growled in anticipation. 'With the shape their security system is in, I'm really surprised they're not having more problems.'

'But you think you and Mark can fix that?'

'Sure.' Andy blew on his soup to cool it, then slurped the noodles up. 'Why are you so interested?'

'Papa mentioned that the circus was going through some rough times. I just didn't want to see that happen to them.'

'I can fix the security,' Andy said.

'Good. I'm sure Papa will appreciate that. He's a nice man.'

Andy nodded. 'Did everything go okay with Imanuela?' He knew his mom had planned a visit out to the elephant's corral earlier via the Net, intending to use the holo-projector Papa had set up for her.

'The labor pains stopped after I gave her the stuff you brought back for me. Everything looks normal for both mother and infant. Neither are showing any signs of distress.'

'That's good.'

'What about you?' she asked. 'Did you get a chance to talk to Syeira? Am I going to have to worry that she might convince you to run away to join the circus?'

'That,' Andy said with real feeling, 'is probably the last thing I'd want to do.'

His mom raised her eyebrows in teasing speculation. 'She *is* cute.'

'When she opens her mouth to speak,' Andy said, 'especially when she opens it to tell you what she doesn't especially care for you, the cuteness factor experiences a total meltdown.'

'You seemed aware of her cuteness while she was around tonight.'

Andy blushed. Despite their disagreement at the mall, his attention *had* been drawn to the girl after their return to the circus and the awkward dinner Papa Cservanka had invited them to. He was a sixteen-year-old boy. What did his mother expect? That he wouldn't look at a pretty girl? 'Yeah. I was aware. Aware the same way a mouse notices a cat crouching to pounce.'

'Did you two have a disagreement? I thought even

short-tempered Andy Moore would be okay for a quick trip to the mall.'

'I was,' Andy replied.

'So she was the malefactor.'

Guilt stung Andy. Syeira hadn't done anything wrong; not really, anyway. 'No. Some stuff happened. There's just some fundamental differences between us.'

'Usually those only serve to make things even more interesting.'

Andy glanced up at her. 'Maybe we could talk about something else.'

'Okay, truce,' his mom responded. 'It's just that every now and then I like knowing I can still make you squirm. And when I saw the obvious chemistry—'

'Chemistry?' Andy shook his head. 'We're talking more along the lines of fissionable materials.'

'—I thought I'd bring it up.' She tore off a piece of bread and chewed it distractedly.

Andy was glad for the break. In all the years between them when they'd talked about all kinds of things, he'd never once thought about discussing girls with his mom. And now that the subject had been brought up, he *really* didn't care for it. Still, it would have been maybe easier if he could have understood why Syeira had gotten irritated with him so easily. Usually he knew why people had that reaction. And usually he didn't care, because he knew they'd get over it.

But he couldn't help thinking that Syeira would be gone in just a few days and he'd probably never see her again.

'I'm going to be taking care of Imanuela over the next few days,' his mom said. 'I thought if the security upgrades are going to take you a little while, I could visit her in holo and you could handle the onsite physical treatments for me.'

'Why would I be there?' Andy asked. 'I could do the upgrades from here.'

'It was just an idea. Papa was generous enough to comp us both passes to the circus. I thought maybe you'd like to spend some time there while it's in town. And it would save me a trip out there. Most of what Imanuela needs is maintenance.'

Okay, that's what I need. More guilt. Andy barely resisted sighing heavily. But that was a trick that had stopped working nearly five years ago. Might as well give in gracefully. 'Okay, I'm going to be busy for the next couple days working on the security upgrades. I could do them from the circus and take care of Imanuela.'

'I appreciate that,' his mom said. 'And while you're there, keep your eyes and ears open. You usually don't miss much.'

'Miss much?' Andy repeated. 'Like what?'

'Something in the computer systems. Papa mentioned this wasn't the first problem they've had with the circus's veeyar sector. I'm thinking there's somebody out there who may not like circuses much.'

'We're running a dust-off,' Matt called out. 'A hit-and-git maneuver to deploy troops.'

On the Net, Andy sat in the cockpit of the V-22 Osprey and spotted Matt ahead and to the left in his own craft, flashing silver against the bright blue sky. Andy wore a tan and gray flight suit, the United States flag embroidered over his left breast. He heard his breath echoing in the oxygen mask overlapping the helmet.

'Where?' Andy asked.

'Pull up the mission ops through the onboard computer,' Matt replied. 'I've got everything configured.'

Releasing one hand from the V-22's yoke beside the control stick, Andy pressed his thumb against the onboard computer's scanner. The screen flashed green beneath his thumb for a moment.

Black letters scrolled across the scanner screen above his thumb. ACCESSING. The green glow winked out of existence. IDENTITY CONFIRMED. MOORE, ANDREW. STATUS, PILOT.

Andy was impressed. As usual, Matt remained detail-oriented even in veeyar, especially when it came to extra credit reports for school. Andy watched the files containing maps of the target area and vid showing confirmed targets move across the screen.

'I based the scenario on the Balkan terrorist capture of Terrence Hulburdt,' Matt said. 'He was the British industrialist kidnapped by the Albanian Serbs in 2006. I don't know how much you remember about the area at the time.'

Andy adjusted his course, losing speed and trailing along at Matt's right wing. 'The Balkans were, and are, a mess – a bunch of nations who were crammed together after the First World War. They've never been happy about it. There's a lot of unrest due to political and religious differences.'

'Actually,' Matt said, 'the cramming together was done pre-World War I. The term *Balkanization* was coined in 1912. But you're right about the rest of it.'

Andy flew east along the steep and rocky coastline of the Adriatic Sea. The GPS sat-relay put him in the north-western reaches of Montenegro. Further out to sea, the colorful sails of fishing boats splayed against the deep green-blue of the sea.

Matt turned further inland, only a few hundred feet over the craggy mountaintops. 'You are checked out on the Osprey, aren't you?'

'Sure,' Andy replied. 'But I'd rather pilot a Space Marine battlesuit or a Nirfanik tri-wing. They go a lot further and outperform this tub.'

'Gripe, gripe, gripe,' Matt taunted. 'The exercise is designed to give a first-hand account of how well the Osprey performs under these conditions. You're carrying a fully equipped ten-man special ops team. We're going to streak into the target zone and deploy the troops. Standard TRAP op.'

The TRAP acronym, Andy remembered, stood for Tactical Recovery of Aircraft and Personnel.

'Exciting,' Andy said. 'Why don't you wake me when you're done?'

'The terrorists we're after have gun emplacements, a few armored trucks, and air support.'

'And we're in these,' Andy complained. 'Are the weps operational?' He studied the weapons array, refamiliarizing himself with the setup. The MV-22 was the United States Marine Corps version of the Osprey and carried two cabin-mounted .50-caliber machine guns and a 20mm cannon mounted in the nose turret.

The Ospreys looked like conventional prop-driven aircraft except that the twin props were oversized for the craft's dimensions. The Osprey was a little over fifty-seven feet long but the props were thirty-eight feet in diameter.

'I could freeze the scenario,' Matt offered. 'Set you up in a nice Apache gunship with all the bells and whistles. But I can guarantee you won't make it back to the aircraft carrier based in the Adriatic.'

Andy knew that. As a tiltrotor craft, the Osprey would fly several times further than conventional helicopters and had the advantage of helicopter-like strike and hovering abilities.

'I'll pass,' Andy replied. He checked the altimeter and saw they were staying within a hundred feet of the ground, rising and falling with the terrain. The twin Allison 1107C engines vibrated smoothly, answering every feathery touch on the controls.

The craggy land below was bare in most areas, but clumps of trees and vegetation stood proudly in others. A narrow road wound through the trees and over the broken ground. The road looked abandoned, a way that had been lost.

Idly, Andy wondered if Syeira ever trolled the Net, and what she would make of experiences like piloting a military aircraft on a rescue mission.

'Hey,' Matt called.

Andy suddenly realized he hadn't been paying attention to the radio, flying by instinct. 'What?'

'Are you with me?'

'Right behind you, Blue Leader,' Andy cracked.

'I'm recording this for my report. A little less levity might be in order.'

'Understood,' Andy replied.

'What has you so distracted?'

'Nothing.' But Andy sounded guilty even to his ears.

'Could it be the girl you met at the circus?'

Andy frowned unhappily. 'The Squirt talked.'

'Maybe a little,' Matt said. 'But he's never known you to be thrown off by a girl.'

'I'm not.'

'Come to think of it,' Matt said as if Andy hadn't said anything, 'I haven't either. She must be something.'

'I'm not distracted or thrown off. And she's not a girl; she's an irritation.'

Matt banked to the right and dropped the cruising altitude to fifty feet. 'Tell me about her.'

'What's to tell?'

'All right, don't tell me about her.'

Andy felt torn. Of all his friends, Matt Hunter and Leif Anderson were the ones who knew most about the opposite sex. Unless he asked Catie, Maj, or Megan – which he was definitely not going to do. It was bad enough that Mark and now Matt knew. 'There's really not much to tell.'

'There's got to be something if she's rattled you this much.' Matt streaked across the treetops. A cloud of birds erupted to the right, streaking south in panicked flight.

Andy watched the birds. It was like Matt to include little touches like that. 'Her name is Syeira. She's kind of a daredevil. She performs in the family circus. Rides a motorcycle like a holofilm stunt star.'

'Ah, now there's something about a girl that would catch your eye.'

Andy ignored the jibe and gave his instruments another pass-through. Everything looked okay. 'She's cute, too. Dark hair, dark eyes. And, um—' *Oh, geez, how to put this!* – 'athletic looking.'

'Sounds good,' Matt commented.

'Not after she opens her mouth,' Andy grumbled. 'She's arrogant and opinionated, and she has a lot of attitude.'

'You guys have a lot in common.'

Andy thought he heard Matt laughing but the sound was so slight he couldn't be sure. 'The one thing I know we have in common, she doesn't like me and I don't like her.'

'At least you can agree on something. That's a start.'

'Oh, it's not a start,' Andy disagreed. 'It's a finish. The circus is only going to be in Alexandria a few days then it's off for who knows where.'

'They probably have schedules.'

'Schedules?' Andy threaded through the narrow valley that cut through the harsh land and verdant pocket of forest. He knew Matt had chosen the approach route to blind them from enemy radar.

'Yeah. You could always see her over the Net.'

'Why would I want to do that?'

'Maybe you wouldn't,' Matt said.

'You're darn right I wouldn't,' Andy agreed. 'You haven't met this girl, Matt. You don't know what she's like. She's a real pain in the—'

'Andy, you have a call.' The computer voice from his own workspace quietly integrated with Matt's workspace. A glowing blue phone icon formed in the air to his right.

'Who is it?' Andy asked. In the distance, he saw morning fog hugging the end of the valley. The tall peaks seemed to melt away, opening onto a barren tablerock cobbled over with huge boulders.

'Syeira Cservanka of Cservanka Brothers Circus,' Syeira answered in her own voice as the computer forwarded the announcement.

'That's kind of unexpected,' Matt said. 'I think.'

'It is,' Andy assured him. 'Hang on a minute and I'll get rid of her.'

'That's rude,' Matt told him.

'We're kind of in the middle of doing your homework,' Andy pointed out.

'My homework can wait a couple minutes.'

Andy wanted to argue. Syeira was an unwanted interruption. But he found himself saying, 'Okay. How far away is the target zone?'

'Long enough for you to handle this call.'

Hesitantly, straightening in his seat, Andy tagged the phone icon. Instantly a rectangular window opened, revealing a head and shoulders shot of Syeira.

She'd changed out of the biker leathers and into a red blouse that set off her dark good looks. Confusion settled into her features. 'Andy?'

'Yeah.' Andy waved a hand. 'I'm online.'

'Am I interrupting?'

Yes. Only Andy found himself shaking his head. 'No. It's okay. I'm just helping a friend with some homework.' The valley's end in the distance seemed to be holding its position and he realized Matt had paused the timeframe.

Syeira grinned unexpectedly and Andy found himself grinning too. He was glad he was wearing the flight mask and helmet.

'I never had homework like this,' she said.

Andy shrugged. 'Bradford Academy. You wouldn't believe the things they require sometimes.'

'You actually go there? I mean, not just holo?'

'Sure.'

'I've never been to any school physically except for the classes in the circus.' Syeira gazed around the cockpit with interest.

Feeling very uncomfortable with any hint at silence between them, knowing Matt was listening in and getting an earful, Andy asked, 'Did you get the lion-tamer module?'

Syeira nodded. 'That's why I called. I received it, but for some reason I can't open it.'

'There shouldn't be any problems with it.'

'All I know is that the program keeps pushing me out. I've checked the coding and everything looks okay, but I can't get in.'

'I can pop over and take a look,' Andy offered. With all the tinkering he and Mark had done with the program there was a possibility the circus' OS simply wasn't recognizing the module anymore.

'I don't want to take you away from anything you need to do.'

Andy was thinking, *okay*, but his voice betrayed him and asked, 'Ever flown before?' And suddenly he felt like he stepped out into empty space over a Bengal tiger pit. He knew the feeling because he'd actually done that once while accompanying Leif on a virtual safari.

'Sure, I've flown,' Syeira answered with a smile. 'Lots of times. Eurorail doesn't quite make it all the way to the United States.'

Now that sounded real geekoid, Andy chastised himself. 'Right.'

'But I've never ridden in a cockpit,' Syeira said. 'Looks like it's probably fun.'

Andy's stomach flip-flopped, and before he could stop himself, he asked, 'Like to try it out?'

'Why not?' Syeira reached for him.

As soon as Andy's fingers made contact with hers – with what he felt certain was a stronger jolt of electricity than he was accustomed to feeling – she was in the cockpit. He deleted the co-pilot that had come with the scenario, then instructed Syeira how to belt into the empty seat.

'So what are we doing?' she asked. Her eyes were still smiling behind the helmet's tinted bubble shield.

'Hostage rescue,' Andy said, and he quickly filled her in on the parameters of the mission. He also introduced Matt and Syeira to each other. 'If you want, you can upload some borrowed skills from the archived files.'

'Do you need a co-pilot?' Syeira asked.

Is that a dare or a regular question? Andy didn't know for sure. 'No,' he answered. 'I've flown missions like this a lot.'

'Okay, then I'll just watch.'

The declaration sounded harmless, but it sure didn't feel that way. Andy gave her a tight nod. 'Okay. Matt?'

'Yeah?'

'Any time you're ready to re-engage,' Andy called out.

'Now,' Matt replied.

And the sky around the Osprey came to life again. The MV-22 hurtled toward the end of the valley, barely skirting the steep walls.

Without warning, an anti-aircraft missile streaked from one of the hillsides and arced for Matt's Osprey!

Chapter Eight

'Bogey!' Andy yelled in warning, knowing he was going to be too late. 'Brake hard to starboard!' The instinct to cover a mission partner's back was automatic. However, of all the people Andy had ever known, Matt Hunter was the only one who was born to live in the skies.

Matt rolled the MV-22 Osprey hard starboard and the earth-to-air missile missed him by scant inches.

'I can't get a target lock on the warhead,' Andy warned.

'No praw,' Matt commented. 'That bird is a heat-seeker and it won't find a hot enough signature here. The Allisons are running too cool for it to find us.'

Andy watched, breathing a sigh of relief as the missile stayed on course and exploded high in the puffy white clouds above. 'Go, I've got your back.' He scanned the countryside as Matt sped through the valley mouth. The trees remained thick along the valley floor and most of the way up the mountains on either side, leaving only the thrusting peaks unprotected.

Another earth-to-air missile blew a dark hole in the sky a little over a hundred yards in front of Andy. The concussion buffeted the tiltrotor, rocking it from side to side.

Small arms fire from scattered ground troops rattled occasionally against the MV-22's sides. Armor plating under the cockpit seats protected the pilot and co-pilot from armor piercing 7.62mm rounds, and the composite materials making up the tiltrotor's body were resistant to ballistics.

Andy banked around the valley mouth, glancing briefly at the co-pilot's seat. 'You okay?'

Syeira's expression was noncommittal. 'It's more violent than I expected.'

'History homework,' Andy replied. 'Battles, wars, what can you expect?' He felt guilty for feeling just a little smug that she was uncomfortable, but when he thought of the way she'd made him feel in the mall, that quickly passed. 'Violence is kind of a universal language.'

'No,' Syeira replied quietly, her voice out of place amid the thunder of the props. 'Papa taught me that a lot of people believe that but they're wrong. People sometimes fight for reasons they don't understand, just as they fight people they don't understand.'

Andy shook his head. 'They understand enough. From the time the first caveman picked up a rock and threw it at a neighboring caveman, they've understood.'

'And you think that's how communication started?' Syeira asked.

Andy made himself remain quiet. From the tone in the girl's voice he knew she'd never agree. He concentrated on following Matt, closing the distance.

Matt started the conversion that changed his Osprey from plane to helicopter. The wing nacelles swung on their pivot points, pulling the huge propellers up from a vertical position to the ground to a horizontal one. During the twelve seconds the conversion took, the tiltrotor became a stationary target for the ground units.

'Laughter,' Syeira said, 'that's what Papa told me was the universal language. People understand everything from the sappy grin of the half-witted tramp clown to the painted-on tears of a clown in white-face.'

'Look,' Andy said, 'if this is bugging you, you could always leave.'

She looked at him. 'Do you want me to leave?'

Andy met her gaze. *Yes.* 'No.' *Why did I say no? Yes is such an easy word to say.*

Syeira pointed. 'Take out the Humvee over there before it blasts Matt out of the sky.'

'What?' The unexpected command caught Andy offguard. He scanned the terrain and spotted the Humvee skidding to a stop in front of the palatial estate that was ground zero for the mission. A ten-foot-tall stone wall ran around the main house, the outbuildings, and the huge garage. Trees and cultured gardens cut patterns and designs into the landscaping.

The Humvee crew fired at Matt's Osprey, knocking sparks from the sides. Matt expertly dropped the converted MV-22 to hover less than three feet above the ground in full helicopter mode. Black-clad special ops troops jumped from the Osprey's belly clutching assault weapons. Ground troops from the sprawling house engaged them at once.

Andy swung the Osprey around and targeted the Humvee. He hammered the vehicle with the 20mm cannon, reducing it to an orange and black ball of exploding fire.

'Move!' Syeira ordered. 'Up!'

Andy reacted to her command instinctively, gaining altitude at once. A rocket streaming smoke cut just under the Plexiglas nose. 'That was close.'

In the next instant Matt's twin 7.62mm machine guns blasted the guard house near the front gate, ripping it to shreds. 'Drop 'em and stay low,' Matt called out. 'I've got the upper deck.'

'Do I have weps controls over here?' Syeira asked as Andy descended.

Weps controls? Andy tried to stay focused on handling the Osprey, but he couldn't help looking at Syeira in fascination. 'Yeah. The Osprey is an exercise in redundancy. It's designed so if one system goes down a backup system is already in place.'

Syeira leaned her head back for a moment. By the time Andy locked down into hover, she was opening her eyes again. She reached for the controls. 'Let me manage the weps.'

What?! But he could use the help. He nodded, then opened his throat mike, addressing the special ops crew in the Osprey's belly as he brought the tiltrotor into place over the main house's roof. 'Captain Rogers, deploy your team. Do you read? Over.'

'Reading you five by five, sir,' the special forces officer replied.

As the soldiers deployed, running out grappling lines that caught the peaked roof, the MV-22 shifted from side to side slightly. Andy adjusted the pitch of the rotors automatically, holding the Osprey steady. 'Syeira, you have the weps. Are you sure—'

The Osprey shivered when Syeira opened the twin machine guns up. Andy tracked the tracers and watched the two streams of 7.62mm bullets rip through the guard house by the front gate.

'Left,' Syeira ordered. 'Now.'

Andy shifted, bringing the MV-22 around, catching the armored transport carrier rolling out of the garage a hundred yards away.

Syeira fired once, putting the 20mm cannon round in the ground thirty yards in front of the advancing M-2 Bradley. She adjusted aim in an eyeblink, then fired a half dozen shots directly into the armored transport carrier. The reactive armor blew, throwing shards skyward as smoke coiled around it. By the time the destruction stopped, the Bradley rolled to a stop, the engine dead.

'Wow,' Andy breathed. 'Where did you learn to shoot like that?'

'I uploaded skills from the Net,' Syeira answered, her eyes roving.

'Skills are one thing but the confidence to use them is another.'

Syeira shrugged. 'Maybe a few dozen sessions of Space Marines helped.'

Andy grinned, not believing it. 'Space Marines is one of my favorite online games.'

'When I get the chance to play,' Syeira said, 'it's one of mine as well.' She spun the machine guns around, breaking a line of resistance made by ground troops.

Andy watched the main house as windows along the second and third floors blew out, ripped to pieces by bullets or a grenade's concussive blast.

'We've got our target, sir,' Captain Rogers radioed. 'Ready to make exfiltration.'

'Roger that, Captain,' Matt said. 'Andy, you've got the back door. I'll take care of the arriving troops.'

Powering the Allisons up, Andy climbed briefly and twisted to come around behind the house. 'We've got to make the back door.'

Syeira shifted the 20mm cannon instantly, then spaced out four quick blasts. The stone wall crumpled inward, unleashing a smoky haze that drifted out over the yard.

'Captain,' Andy called out. 'How's that back door looking?'

'Through and through, sir. Give us a green light.'

'Go.' Andy dropped the Osprey to within a couple feet of the ground, expertly swinging it around so the nose faced outward. He glanced over his shoulder, watching the black-clad special forces unit rush pell-mell from the hole blown into the main house.

'We've got company,' Syeira said.

Facing forward, Andy watched three Humvees streak from the treeline. 'These guys were more ready than we thought.' The Osprey shifted slightly as it took on the weight of the arriving troops.

'I'm done here,' Matt said. 'I can't hold position.'

'Roger that,' Andy replied. 'Give me a minute to batten the hatches and we're away.'

Syeira opened up with the machine guns and the 20mm cannon. This time she deliberately raked the ground in front of the advancing vehicles, throwing earth and expensive landscaping over them.

Bullets slapped the Osprey's nose. Even though it was veeyar, Andy felt himself dodge before he caught himself.

Captain Rogers called from the cargo space. 'Get this bird into the wind.'

Andy powered the props and rose straight up quickly. He heeled over hard to port, kicking in the conversion sequence to shift from helicopter mode to plane. When Matt sped by him, he followed close on the other plane's tail fins.

'We did it,' Syeira yelled triumphantly.

Andy looked at her, noticing the smile in her eyes, and couldn't help grinning himself. 'Yeah, I guess we did.'

'Growing up in a circus doesn't mean I've led some kind of cloistered life.' Syeira Cservanka leaned against the corral in Andy's Pony Express veeyar and watched the horses prancing around the ring. 'I've played veeyar games before. I just don't have a lot of time for them.'

'You've got to excuse Andy.' Matt stuck a hand in the feed bucket he'd brought over from the main building's porch. 'He sometimes has a tendency to leap first and look later. It's his special talent.' He fed grain to a young colt that had at first pretended to be too haughty to eat from his hand.

Andy blew out a mock sound of disgust. Actually, he felt pretty good. Syeira was turning out to be more interesting than he had initially thought. At least, more interesting than he'd thought after the mall run.

'But I haven't exactly had a normal childhood either,' Syeira said, glancing at Andy. 'Maybe I'm guilty of being pretty quick to leap as well.'

'Your parents are in the circus?' Andy asked.

She shook her head. 'Not now. They were. My dad's an accountant in Bucharest and my mom operates a bakery.'

'I guess you didn't feel like being an accountant or a baker,' Andy said.

Some of the brightness in Syeira's smile faded. She kept her attention on the horses. 'My parents,' she said quietly, 'tend to be complete all by themselves.'

That's it, Andy, why don't you seek out the sore places and jab them with a sharp stick. 'Sorry.'

'I chose to live with Papa when I was small,' Syeira said. 'I tried living with my parents but they're always too busy working at their careers. They don't even notice they don't make time for each other anymore.'

'I used to feel that way about my mom,' Andy admitted.

'What about your dad?' Syeira asked.

'He's dead,' Andy answered neutrally.

A hurt look flashed on Syeira's face. 'Oh, guess I'm the clumsy one now.'

'He died before I was born,' Andy said. 'I never got to know him.' *Not if you don't count building a near-AI sim of him.*

'But your mom's not that way,' Syeira said. 'You can tell how much she cares about you.'

'Oh, you think so?'

Syeira turned and leaned back against the corral fence. She'd chosen to wear jeans, a blue-checked Western shirt, and a red kerchief tied loosely around her neck, emulating the Pony Express motif. She also wore two Colt .45s tied down low on her thighs. Andy figured she was about the cutest girl he'd ever seen at the Pony Express station.

'You can tell, Andy,' Syeira answered. 'The way your mom looks at you, the way she trusts you. Even the sound in her voice.'

Andy blushed furiously. No matter whether he was earning her ire or being friendly, Syeira seemed to have the ability to keep him constantly off-balance.

'Am I embarrassing you?' she asked.

Matt was grinning over her shoulder but thankfully he wasn't looking at Andy.

'No,' Andy said.

'I thought maybe I had and I wanted you to know I didn't

mean to.' Still, a mischievous gleam flickered in her dark eyes. 'I know about families. A circus is one of the biggest families around. You saw how concerned they were about Imanuela.'

'I thought it was partly because Imanuela is billed as the star of the show. Martin Radu seemed more concerned about the advertising.'

'He's under a lot of pressure, and he also does all the twenty-four-hour man prep himself. The circus performers love Imanuela. She's been with the circus longer than all but three of them.'

'Your grandfather,' Andy said.

Syeira nodded. 'Papa, Traian, and Elsa, our fortune teller. No one can imagine what the Cservanka Brothers Circus would be like without Imanuela.'

Hearing the note of worry in the girl's voice, Andy automatically said, 'Nothing's going to happen to Imanuela. My mom's going to see to that.'

'What's a twenty-four-hour guy?' Matt asked.

'Circus slang,' Syeira explained. 'In the old days, the twenty-four-hour guy preceded the circus into town by twenty-four hours, got all the permits, paid off any necessary bribes to local officials, figured out how to lay out the site, and put up all the signs to guide people to the Big Top. These days, he still handles all the advertising, but the job isn't all about hanging handbills. It's done much farther in advance, through the Net mostly. But he still gets the permits and marks out all the places on the lot where the tents will go. And sets up the advertising. It's a tough gig.'

'Sounds like it.' Matt dipped another fistful of feed from the bucket and fed the colt more.

'You should see more of it,' Syeira said.

'More of what?' Matt asked.

'The circus.' Syeira answered Matt's question, but Andy noticed she was looking at him. 'I mean, before you start leaping to conclusions about how boring it is.'

85

Andy colored again. *What is it about her?* He glanced helplessly at Matt. 'When?'

'We could do it now,' Syeira said. 'We could check out the lion-tamer module at the same time.'

Andy hesitated. 'I don't know. We could have more homework to do.'

Matt shook his head. 'All I've got left is the editing and voice-over stuff. I'll have to do that by myself.'

'Maybe you're too tired,' Syeira said. 'I was just thinking that since school was out you could stay out late. I mean, you're not actually *out* when you're on the Net.'

Andy thought quickly but there wasn't a single reason to refuse her offer that didn't sound lame. 'Okay. You coming, Matt?'

Matt looked at him oddly for a moment, then said, 'Sure. If I'm invited.'

'You are.' Syeira pressed a palm flat out and a shimmering silver doorway materialized in thin air. She stepped through, disappearing from sight at once.

Matt gazed at Andy as if fascinated. 'Well, are you going?'

'It sounds like a trap.'

Matt smiled. 'Paranoid?'

'No. I just remember how she treated me earlier. She wasn't exactly thrilled with me.'

'Maybe the feeling was mutual. How do you like her now?'

Andy squared his shoulders. 'If you leave, I'm leaving.'

Matt laughed openly. 'Boy, she sure does have you worked up.'

Ignoring his friend's comment, Andy squared his shoulders, slid down from the corral fence, and said, 'Wrong. I'm wearing her down.' Then he stepped through the silver doorway.

Chapter Nine

'Tickets, please. Get your tickets ready. See one of the finest shows on earth, ladies and gentlemen. And all for one thin dime. Where else can you get entertainment like this for ten cents?'

Andy gazed at the fiercely mustachioed man in tails and top hat standing at the podium in front of the big canvas tent in front of him. The man held his hand out, obviously waiting.

'Do you have a dime, young sir?' the man asked. 'For the price of one thin dime you can have memories of the Cservanka Brothers Circus for the rest of your life. Regale your family and friends with tales about the most fearless trapeze act ever held under the Big Top. Hold them in the palm of your hand as you tell them about brave Crupariu the Lion-Tamer. And the clowns, young sir? Why, the Cservanka Brothers Circus is home to the finest clowns in the world.'

Syeira was nowhere to be seen.

'I don't mean to rush you, young sir,' the ringmaster said with edged pleasantness, 'but there are a lot of folks behind you who are convinced they're in the right place.'

Before Andy could make an angry retort, Matt stepped up beside him, fishing his hand in his pocket and coming out with two ancient silver dimes.

'Thank you,' the ringmaster said. 'Now just step right in. Step right on in and see how many wonders are there for the partaking all for the price of one thin dime.'

'Let's go,' Matt suggested, stepping through the tent flaps. Andy lagged behind, staring in awe at the city streets around them. European-styled cottages and buildings stood two and three stories tall, clumped closely together. Men and women walked along the cobblestoned roads and the ironbound wheels of carts and wagons rattled sharply. Somebody had done a nice job on this sim, right down to the small details that most users wouldn't even notice.

Passing through the tent flaps, Andy almost ran into a clown in white-face and a ragged red wig waiting to hand him a flyer.

'Welcome, welcome,' the clown said. Then he took out a handkerchief, pretended to sneeze, and honked the big red nose he wore. The garish red wig flew up on the sides.

A little blonde girl no more than two or three sitting on one of the bleachers at the side squealed in delight. She clapped her hands, then took the bright red paper flower the clown presented her.

'Walk this way,' the clown requested. He spun on one floppy foot and performed an exaggerated march between the stands. 'We have special seats for you.'

Matt followed, his gaze on the aerialists flying across the center ring on the trapeze bar. They performed without a net, and the crowd's attention followed the young man flipping through the air. He seemed to make a death-defying grab at another man hanging upside down from a trapeze bar. One of his hands slipped.

The crowd took in a gasp of disbelief. Then the young man secured his grip and landed on the narrow ledge on one of the main tent poles. Applause and cheers filled the tent as the audience showed their appreciation.

The smell of popcorn overlaid everything, thickening the air. Bright pink, blue and purple tufts of cotton candy stuck up from paper cones in the hands of several kids. The candy's heavy, sweet scent competed with the smell of candied apples and an occasional wiff of the wild animals offstage to give an undertone to the smell of circus.

The clown led Andy and Matt to the front row of seats in front of the lion-tamer's act. Crupariu, dressed now in white pants and a bright red leather vest left unbuttoned, his wrists wrapped in thick gold bands, stood just outside the cage.

Andy recognized the lions, tigers and panthers from his previous experience with them. The clown showed them to their seats.

A harsh scream burst through the tent. Two clowns carrying mop buckets suddenly appeared from around the end of the bleachers. They got into an argument, each of them shaking their forefingers in the other's face. Then one of them upended his mop bucket over the other one's head, drenching him completely. The wet clown shivered theatrically while his tormentor took off. Then the wet clown took off in pursuit, carrying his mop bucket in both hands with a kamikaze expression.

'No!' the clown who'd guided Andy and Matt to their seats cried, throwing his hands up. 'These people are special guests!'

The dry clown darted and dashed, elbows akimbo, trying desperately to escape. But the wet clown seemed to be twice as fast.

Andy watched, a grin on his face. The dry clown was definitely about to get paid back.

The dry clown squawked and headed for the stands.

'No!' the clown cried, reaching for the dry clown. The wet clown drew back his water bucket as the dry clown came to a skidding, one-legged stop in front of Matt and Andy.

The smile and the humor dropped from Andy. Veeyar or no veeyar, he wasn't looking forward to getting wet.

Abruptly, the clown guide and the dry clown both ducked, removing whatever protection they might have offered from the coming deluge. Andy tried to get out of his chair but there was no time. The wet clown drew the mop bucket back and let fly.

Andy covered his face and head helplessly, intending to have a word with Syeira. Then a shower of silver confetti poured down over him.

Matt laughed uproariously.

'Very funny,' Andy commented, brushing the confetti from his shoulders and lap. It just now registered that Matt hadn't moved at all. 'You knew there wasn't any water in the bucket.'

'How long has it been since you've been to a circus?' Matt asked.

'One that wasn't online?' Andy shrugged. 'Years. I was little. I learned early not to trust clowns.'

'And spent the rest of your formative years trying to become one.'

Andy was working up a biting retort when the lights inside the tent dimmed. Considering that the light appeared to come from lanterns and torches situated under the tent, he figured that was nothing short of amazing.

'Ladies and gentlemen,' a thunderous voice announced. 'For your edification and petrification, Cservanka Brothers Circus proudly presents the honorable Baron Crupariu, the master of fearsome beasts.'

A spotlight fell on the ringmaster standing at the center stage. He held his top hat in one hand and swept it toward the cage filled with big cats.

'Baron Crupariu,' the ringmaster called out.

Crupariu bowed deeply, then hitched up his pants, coiled his whip, and entered the cage cautiously. The cats shifted slightly, as if in anticipation. Napoleon, the big male lion that had recently chased Andy with single-minded intent, loosed a couple of impressive growls.

The audience quieted even before the ringmaster spoke again, obviously drawn into the tableau of a man stepping into an enclosure filled with so many dangerous creatures.

'Ladies and gentlemen,' the ringmaster managed to blare out while somehow seeming to appear quiet himself, 'we'll need participation from you for this next act. Although Baron

Crupariu has worked with these animals before, none of them have ever been far removed from the wilds where they were born and raised. Please refrain from making any sudden movement or loud noises.'

Napoleon stood on the blue and white striped barrel where he'd lain. As Crupariu got closer, Napoleon lifted a paw and swept razor-sharp claws at him. Crupariu dodged swiftly out of the way, raising his whip in warning. Then he went into his act.

Distracted, Andy glanced around, searching the audience. 'Do you see Syeira?'

'Shhhh,' Matt said.

'Hey,' Andy protested, 'it's not like there's any real danger in there. I worked on that program myself.'

'*Shhhhhhh!*' the crowd behind Andy hissed.,

Andy shook his head in disbelief, resigning himself to watching the lion-tamer program he'd worked through earlier. As he watched, though, he had to admit that Crupariu was much better at putting the big cats through their routines than he'd been. But Andy took pride in the way they moved and acted. If he and Mark hadn't debugged the program they'd still be fighting and talking back.

'And now,' the ringmaster announced in a quiet, deep voice that carried throughout the big tent, 'assisting Baron Crupariu in a feat of derring-do and chance that is the very heart of the circus is the lovely . . . *Syeira!*' The ringmaster quickly faded back into the shadows as her name echoed.

When he looked back to the lion cage, Andy spotted Syeira wearing a red shirt with belled sleeves and cream-colored jodhpurs. The shirt gleamed from hundreds of tiny sequins sewn onto it.

Syeira opened the lion cage and stepped inside. She carried a whip as well, quickly putting the big cats through their paces. At the end of a short routine, she commanded Napoleon up onto a barrel in the center of the cage. The big lion swiped at her a number of times, but she managed to just avoid the ripping claws.

It was obvious that she was having trouble working with the male lion.

'Is something wrong with the program?' Matt whispered.

Andy shook his head vehemently, setting off a fresh cascade of silver-glitter confetti. 'Mark and I went over that module from one end to the other. By the time we reconfigured it, none of the virus was left.'

'Maybe it got contaminated again after the re-installation.'

'I put it back together with the latest anti-virus scanners Net Force has issued.'

The audience grew steadily quieter.

In the lion-tamer's cage, Syeira batted Napoleon on the nose with her coiled whip. The lion snarled angrily and snapped at her. Only inches separated his sharp fangs from the girl's tender flesh.

Despite his own certainty, Andy felt himself grow tenser.

Incredibly, Napoleon finally gave in to Syeira, sitting on his rump, his forelegs extended. The big cat opened his mouth, holding it wide.

'Is she going to do what I think she's going to do?' Matt asked in a hoarse whisper.

Andy couldn't answer. Paralyzed by a sudden chill, he watched as Syeira tossed her whip aside and seized the upper and lower jaws of the lion's mouth. In disbelief, Andy saw her stick her head inside the big cat's maw. Syeira smiled and waved without concern.

Then the lion's massive jaws snapped closed.

Concerned cries rang from the audience.

Incredibly, Syeira's headless body pulled back from the lion. Her hands groped for her missing head as she stumbled around blindly.

'Oh, feek!' Andy groaned, rising out of his seat. What could have happened here? Things couldn't have gone more wrong.

'You should have seen the look on your face.' Syeira howled

with laughter, drawing the attention of the families dining in the small German restaurant a few blocks down from the Wallachian circus. She slapped her arms together in an exaggerated fashion, like the slamming together of a lion's jaws. '*Chomp!*' She totally lost it again.

'That,' Andy said with more than a little rancor, 'was a very *evil* thing to do.' He didn't like being the butt of a joke, and Syeira's scheme to add a proxy of her headless self into the lion-tamer module wasn't very funny to him.

'I didn't think it was evil,' Matt said. He held his glass up in a toast to the girl sitting across the booth from them. 'I think it's the best I've ever seen Andy Moore taken down. Maybe the first time I've ever seen him truly speechless.'

'Thank you, Matt.' Syeira clinked her glass against Matt's.

'It wasn't funny,' Andy argued. 'It was sick and twisted—'

'*And* truly inspired,' Matt interjected.

Andy ignored the comment. '—way over the top, but nowhere even near the zip code of humor.' He'd also discovered the presentation was a bubble on the actual Net presentation of the circus. The real audience attending the circus virtually hadn't seen any of the act containing Syeira losing her head.

'Maybe I should tell Syeira about some of the pranks you've pulled,' Matt suggested.

'No,' Andy said, giving Matt a warning glance.

'Oh?' Syeira raised her eyebrows with obvious interest.

'But I won't,' Matt finished. 'Not out of the kindness of my heart, but because nearly everything Andy did pales by comparison to tonight's production.'

'You shouldn't say that,' Syeira said, looking at Andy. 'I get the feeling that Andy is a very competitive person. If he's motivated properly I don't think I'll ever have a safe moment.'

'No,' Matt agreed. 'You'll be watching your back from now on. You should be safe for a while, though, because Andy won't try anything unless he's sure he can top you.'

93

'You'll get maybe a day or two of rest,' Andy told her.

'While you recover from your fright?' Syeira asked.

'No,' Andy admitted grudgingly, 'because the gag was that good.'

'Well, then,' Syeira said, eyes shining, 'I look forward to the payback. However, I must tell you – speaking as a professional entertainer – that an audience must first be lulled into a false sense of security before being thoroughly *surprised*. And I don't think I'll ever feel secure around you again.'

A middle-aged man with a paunch and a silver and black goatee approached the table. His waxed hair lay back and glistened. He smiled unctuously. '*Domnisara, domns*, will there be anything else?'

Syeira looked at Matt and Andy. 'They make a really great Mocha layered cake that they garnish with sliced almonds.'

'Sure,' Matt agreed. 'It's veeyar. All the taste and none of the calories.'

Andy threw up his hands in surrender.

Syeira ordered three pieces of cake.

'This place isn't exactly Wallachia of the eighteenth century,' Matt said.

'No,' Syeira said. 'It isn't supposed to be. This village is based on the Wallachia of that time, but it's been *improved* on. Like including modern restrooms. Not that people need them in veeyar, but they expect to find them here, so they're up-to-date instead of what was actually used then. Another feature that kind of fades into the background is the improved lighting provided by the lanterns and torches.'

The waiter arrived with three pieces of cake and passed them out. Andy picked at his, even though the taste was incredible. Veeyar experience felt as real as the real thing, but had no substance – which meant food adventures could be programmed that would, in real life, court heart attacks and instant obesity.

'When Papa agreed to a Net presence for the Cservanka

Brothers Circus,' Syeira went on, 'he knew what he wanted. Stories are passed down through circus people. Tales of bravery, of sadness, of friendship and undying enmity. Those things don't change. But Papa was nurtured on stories of the Old Country, of the farms and the villages the original Cservanka Brothers Circus came from.'

Andy sipped water and watched Syeira speak. Despite the fact that he was very upset with her, he liked the way the lamplight made her skin glow warmly. The passion she had for the risks she took showed on her face now.

'My native country has never known peace,' Syeira said. 'Signs of habitation have been found there from the Paleolithic period. Hunters, gatherers and farmers settled there, only to be attacked by the Thracians. Then Greek cities rose there and the Romans after them. Christianity, brought by the Roman legions posted there to preserve trade routes, was quickly accepted by the Thraco-Dacians. Then the Romans took over, only to be driven from Romania some years later by barbarian migrations.'

'I've ridden with a couple of those hordes,' Andy put in. 'They were tough, vicious little guys.'

Syeira nodded. 'For the next eight centuries there was no rest in Romania. After that, my country became the front line of demarcation between the Ottoman Empire and the nations supporting Christianity. Religious battles still go on there. Romania was involved in both world wars. Then there was all the unrest in the 1980s that still causes problems today.'

'Gypsies came from Romania, right?' Andy asked.

A hard look took some of the softness from Syeira's face. 'What are you saying?' she asked a little coldly.

'Nothing,' Andy replied. 'It's just that the gypsies are often called Rom. I just figured Rom, Romania. And the early circuses were started by gypsies, right?' From the look on her face he knew he'd said the wrong thing.

'That's not correct.' Syeira tabbed the bill with her thumbprint.

'They charge you for this?' Andy asked.

'For the experience,' Syeira said, 'yes. It's like any number of things you sign up for on the Net.'

'Let me pay my part,' Andy said, tracing the icon that tapped into his e-money. Matt was already summoning up his own icon.

'No,' Syeira said. 'You are here by my invitation.' She looked at both her companions. 'I expect no arguments.' She paused. 'Or I will summon the lions.'

Andy nodded, not daring to say anything else that would make her mad at him. *How can I keep saying the wrong thing to her?*

Matt only grinned. 'Okay.'

Syeira pushed up from the booth. 'Let's continue this conversation outside. If that's okay. I'd like to show you more of the virtual world the circus offers.'

'I didn't mean to get angry at you back in the restaurant, Andy.'

Andy shrugged. 'It's okay. You won't believe how many people can be angry with me in one day.'

'Or irritated, annoyed, aggravated, or incensed,' Matt added. 'And there are interesting variations and combinations on all of the above.'

The steady clop-clop-clop of ironshod hooves rang on the cobblestone street. Andy sat in the horsedrawn buggy on upholstered leather seats and gazed out at the shops and homes that lined the streets.

Virtual Wallachia constantly moved. Women hung laundry out, cleaned house and tended children and small gardens beside their homes. Wooden boxes and clay pots filled with beautiful flowers filled window eaves and narrow stairs that led to the upper floors. Men worked in blacksmith shops, livery stables and hardware stores, and carpenters and stone masons added to the village architecture. Children ran through the streets, whopping and hollering, drawing occasional stern words from the adults.

It felt like a hometown.

'Do you like it?'

Andy looked at Syeira and sensed that the question was important to her. 'Yeah. It's a great place.'

'Papa spends a lot of time here when he can,' Syeira said. 'He used to bring me here all the time when I was little. He planned this village, laid it out, and saw to it that the veeyar additions were just like he imagined. He used to buy me ice cream in that little shop there all the time.'

Andy followed the line of her pointing finger and spotted a small building that advertised Old Fashioned Confections. It was painted white and gilded with pink gingerbread.

'Papa spoiled me so much when I was a child,' Syeira admitted. 'I loved it. My parents were too busy finishing school and starting their careers to pay much attention to me. My mother actually learned a lot of her baking skills in the bakery here in the village. Most of the people you meet here are near-AIs but some are real people Papa hires to act out their parts. Besides going to the circus, you can learn to blow glass, weave baskets, make barrels and wagon wheels, or any number of skills.'

'Sounds like a great place for people with hobbies,' Matt commented.

'Those people can get this at any number of places on the Net,' Syeira said. 'But Papa has created an atmosphere that they like to return to.' She paused. 'That's why I became so angry when you thought we were gypsies, Andy.'

'I didn't mean any disrespect,' Andy said. 'I just thought it was interesting.'

'I know. The whole idea of a gypsy sparks images of a roving band of thieves getting rich by rickety carnivals and rigged midways.'

'Or fortune tellers in horror holos,' Matt said.

'Usually snaggle-toothed old crones.' Syeira shook her head.

'Those are the scariest kind,' Andy pointed out. 'I mean,

who'd be afraid of a gypsy girl who was cute?' Syeira looked at him oddly and he found his face turning hot. He gazed back out the window.

'The Romani,' Syeira said after a moment, 'aren't from Romania originally. Though some of them now are. They've been known by other names than gypsies. Like Tsigani, Tzigane, Cigano, and Zigeuner. And some more names, given to them by outsiders, that are completely foul. They're also cursed – and don't comment on that poor word choice, Andy—'

Andy pulled off an innocent look that he thought was successful.

'—by the stereotypical image that I just talked about,' Syeira continued. 'The real heritage of the Roma is much different than the one the public holds of them. The Roma came from the Far East, and were believed to have been from Turkey, Nubia, or Egypt, which is actually where the name gypsy comes from. A few of the Romani helped that belief along by saying they were from Egypt.'

'But they weren't from there?'

'No. Language studies indicate that the Romani were from India. In the eleventh century, the Muslims under General Mahmud of Ghazni struggled to push Islamic beliefs into India. At that time, India was thought to be ruled by Aryan invaders.'

'The same Aryan race Adolf Hitler tried to build up in Germany during World War II?' Matt asked with real interest.

Syeira nodded. 'They were supposed to be barbaric hordes of East Europeans, with light-colored hair and light eyes. They started the caste system in India, separating the social structure by *varnas*. That's Sanskrit for colors.'

'I didn't know that,' Matt said.

'Ask your history teachers,' Syeira suggested. 'If they're any good, they'll know.'

'How did you get to know so much about history?' Andy asked.

Syeira waved a hand toward the buggy window. 'Papa. Before he got onto the net, Papa read books on countries and people. He said if you really want to understand life and your place in it, it's best to know about those who have gone on before you.'

'He sounds like a smart man,' Matt said.

'He is. And he read to me when I was small. All kinds of stories. Only he changed them so I could enjoy them, embellishing events till they became like fairy tales.'

Andy listened to her, watching her dark eyes drink in their surroundings even though he was certain she'd seen this place hundreds of times. He'd never met anyone like her.

'Anyway,' Syeira said, 'the Aryans didn't want to fight the Muslims because they didn't want to die at Islamic hands. They considered the Muslims to be inferior. So they gathered an army from populations everywhere, made them honorary members of the Kshattriya, the warrior caste, and allowed them to wear their weapons and their own emblems again.'

'But that army was destined to be cannon fodder,' Andy said sourly. His mind filled with images of the warriors, confused, lost, and so far from the homes they'd left.

'Exactly. Among other big problems the army was made up of dozens of different peoples with a variety of languages and dialects.'

'Must have really made communication hard,' Matt stated.

'That army,' Syeira said softly, 'had several things working against it. Different languages were only part of it. They worked together enough to come up with a verbal language but not a written one. It was based on the Indian language they'd all at least been exposed to, but it was added to a lot.'

'The Romani language,' Matt said.

Syeira nodded. 'The war didn't go well for them. The Muslims met the Indian army in Persia, then drove them into Europe by 1300.'

'They fought for two hundred years?' Andy asked.

'And more. But they reached Europe by 1300. When they

reached Romania they were enslaved. The battles over that continued for another two hundred years.'

'Battles that included the Crusades,' Matt said.

'Yes.'

'And the Crusades brought an even more volatile mix of cultures and languages into Romania. All of Europe and the East fought over trade routes and sea lanes.'

'As well as religious differences,' Syeira said. 'You can't forget that.' She glanced at Andy. 'Our family carries Romani blood but we are not gypsies. The Cservanka Brothers Circus has always been a family-owned business. Even with the help we are receiving from the international arts support groups, Papa still runs the circus the way he wants to run it.'

'I really didn't mean any offense,' Andy offered.

'There's none taken, really. But I wanted you to know the difference. There are gypsy bands out there who do everything they can to keep that bad image of gypsies alive, but we are not them. We are just a family, Andy, doing what we can to make a future for ourselves, and to share our past with all who can enjoy it.'

Andy nodded, not at all sure what to say.

Syeira poked her head out the window on her side of the buggy. 'Hey, the marketplace is just ahead. Do you want to stop?'

With the exuberance she was showing, Andy knew there was no way he could say no.

Booths and kiosks lined the dead-end street. Rugs, vases, foods, jewelry and livestock stood on display. Hawkers, from small children to old men and women, cried out their wares, competing with everyone else for attention.

Syeira knew many of the sellers by name and she dragged them into the thick of things. Matt was momentarily diverted by a booth attendant selling kites made of bamboo and brightly colored silk.

'These are beautiful,' Matt said.

'They're just kites,' Andy groused, looking for Syeira through the crowd. Some of the market attendees were in traditional dress but a lot of them were in modern clothes, marking them as veeyar visitors. The wares displayed here were definitely for sale, and would be shipped to the buyer in real life upon completion of the Net purchase.

'Yeah,' Matt said, lifting one of the kites with a silver dragon painted on a red field, 'but the Chinese invented kites like these. Lawrence Hargrave of Australia used them to lift himself from the ground and set the whole invention of the airplane into motion.'

Yak, yak, yak, Andy thought, looking round. Then he immediately felt bad. Matt was a good friend, though a tad finicky at times, especially when Andy was feeling hyper. But Syeira had been out of sight a long time. Where was she?

'A guy named Samuel Franklin Cody flew across the English Channel in 1903 on a vessel towed by kites,' Matt went on.

'Sails on strings?' Andy asked. 'Big deal.'

'Your enthusiasm is overwhelming.'

'Kind of hard to be excited about kites.'

'Your attention wouldn't be deflected by something, would it? Say, someone pretty and vivacious.'

'Say someone insufferably arrogant and irritating, and I might agree with you.'

'Oh?'

'Yeah.' Andy glared at Matt. 'Look, she's just a girl with a sick elephant.'

Matt nodded, his attention riveted on the kite he held. 'Yes, she is.'

'She's nothing to me.'

'I totally understand that.'

'And she's been gone long enough I'm beginning to think she left us.'

'You're not stuck here,' Matt said. 'You could log off the Net at any time.'

'And give her the satisfaction of stranding us here?' Andy made a face. 'No way. If she's still here, I'm going to find her. If you buy that kite before I get back, feel free to go fly it.'

'Sure.'

As he made his way through the thronging crowd, Andy felt Matt's grin burning into his back between his shoulder blades. *I should have stayed home. Even if Syeira had meant well, I can't talk to her without requiring a United Nations diplomatic team to clean up the fallout afterwards. Gypsies, I didn't have to say anything about gypsies.*

'Boy,' a voice said with some urgency.

Andy turned to face the speaker, a quick rebuttal on the tip of his tongue. He wasn't in the mood to take anything off of anybody.

The woman waved at him from a nearby booth draped in black cloth. Her hair looked like an upended gray-fringed mop with the handle cut off. Even from the distance Andy could see that several teeth were missing and she looked ancient. She wore a shapeless black dress that still somehow managed to emphasize her sticklike figure.

'Yes, boy,' the old woman said again. 'It was you I was talking to. You come here. Madam Ziazan can give you protection from the evil beast that ravages our countryside during the shadows that drape the night.'

Andy shook his head. 'No thanks.'

'Boy,' Madam Ziazan called more sternly, 'would you rush so foolishly into death's embrace?'

Drawn by the woman's words, Andy stepped over to her booth. 'What are you talking about?'

The old woman lowered her voice and looked about as if she suddenly didn't want anyone to hear. 'I'm talking about the Beast of Wallachia, boy. The blood-drinker. The soul-stealer.'

Despite his unwillingness to believe her, Andy started to feel a little creeped out by the hoarse, whispering voice. 'Who?'

'Some call him Vlad, boy,' Madam Ziazan spoke furtively.

'Others call him the Warlord-Prince. His name is Vlad Dracolya, brother to Radu the Handsome and Mihnea. All know him as the Impaler.'

Andy's eyes widened and he felt his heart beat just a little faster. 'You're talking about Dracula?'

The old woman put a finger to her lips and hissed. 'Quiet, boy. His spies lurk everywhere. No one is safe. At night, when the wind blows right, you can hear the screams of his tortured victims coming from his castle.'

Andy followed her pointing finger, trailing it up to the castle set high on the forested hills surrounding Wallachia. His brain fired, filling with legends he'd gotten off the Net as well as horror holos. A solitary trail wound through the dark forest in the foothills before the outer walls.

'Here, boy,' Madam Ziazan urged, 'with these few things you can make yourself safe. A vial of holy water. A wooden stake. A necklace of garlic cloves.' She took his hands and filled them.

'Look,' Andy said, looking at the strange collection of items he held, 'I really don't think—'

Then a flash of red caught his eye. Upon closer inspection, he spotted Syeira standing beside a tent and a small corral containing a dozen goats.

'How much?' Andy asked. He quickly agreed to the price, spending only a couple dollars, thumbprinted the charges, and cut through the crowd toward Syeira.

'Hey,' the old woman called. 'Don't you want a map of the castle?'

'No,' Andy replied, trying to keep his mind from thinking about what kind of map it could possibly be. As he got closer to Syeira, he noticed that she was already talking to someone. An unfamiliar anger ignited inside Andy, bringing just a hint of hurt with it. He wanted to know who she was talking to.

Upon closer inspection, gleaned through the shifting crowd, Andy saw that the man talking to Syeira was tall and dark, dressed in funeral black, and wore a black greatcoat that hung to the middle of his calves.

The man had a high forehead and looked like he was in his mid-twenties. His coal-black hair was swept straight back and a thin mustache stained his upper lip. Tall and well built, he was half a head taller than Syeira.

'You must listen to me, Syeira,' the man said in a harsh voice. 'You know what I say is true.'

Tears glittered in Syeira's eyes as she faced the man. Andy stared at her, feeling some of the anger ebb inside him. *She's not talking to this guy because she wants to.*

'No,' she said quietly. 'I don't know that at all.' She turned to walk away.

The man sighed in exasperation and grabbed Syeira by the shoulder, spinning her around. 'You *will* listen to me, Syeira.'

Before he knew it, Andy was in motion, striding straight for the man, and ready to rumble.

Chapter Ten

Andy dropped a hand on the man's shoulder and pulled him around. Andy didn't know who looked more surprised: Syeira or the man. And maybe he was just as surprised as any of them.

Dark rage filled the man's face. He brushed Andy's hand aside. 'Who are you?'

'I'm a friend of Syeira's,' Andy said. Despite the fact that he was in veeyar and a physical confrontation wouldn't really harm him, he wasn't looking forward to it.

The man grinned, his eyes narrowing to thin slits. 'Such an insolent little whelp. Still, he bares his teeth rather convincingly, doesn't he?'

Syeira stepped quickly between them, facing Andy. 'What's wrong with you?'

'Me?' Andy couldn't believe it. 'He was the one who grabbed you.'

The man shook his head. 'And you would champion her honor so quickly?' He folded his arms. 'Syeira, why haven't you told me of this boy who holds you in such high regard?'

'I only just met him, Uncle Traian,' Syeira said.

Uncle? Confused, Andy stepped back.

Syeira frowned. 'He tends to react first and think afterward.'

'Thanks heaps,' Andy muttered dryly.

'Don't you think if I'd needed help I would have called you?' Syeira asked. 'And I could have always simply logged off and filed a report.'

Andy sensed the frustration seething within her and knew that not all of it she was directing at him was because of him. Uncle Traian had his fair share coming, too. 'If I did anything wrong, I apologize.'

Syeira remained silent.

'Nonsense,' Traian said, waving it away. 'You did nothing wrong. Some men follow their hearts first and their heads second. I like a man who is passionate; he always has something to live for, something to strive for.' He offered his hand to Andy.

Andy took it, feeling the smooth muscular control.

'I am Traian Cservanka,' the man said. He tipped his head forward in a short bow, never losing Andy's gaze. 'At your service.'

'Andy Moore.'

'Had I known you were with my grandniece, I would have acted in a different manner. Sometimes I forget she is no longer the child I continue to think of her as. I did not know you were watching over her.'

'He was with me,' Syeira said. 'I wasn't with him. And he's not here to watch over me.'

'It is not a question of whether you can look out for yourself,' Traian said with a smile. 'This has to do with a man's honor, the way he chooses to see himself, and to present himself. Your young companion acts on this whether he knows it or not.'

'He's a friend,' Syeira said.

The way she said it, however, left Andy wondering if that was true.

'As you wish.' Traian shrugged. 'I did not mean to interrupt your evening but I did wish to speak to you about Imanuela. There are times when it seems Anghel will listen to no one but you.'

'I'm not going to ask Papa to leave Imanuela here,' Syeira declared.

Traian became more somber. 'My brother must be made to

listen to reason, Syeira. The future of this circus depends on this year. If we break engagements, we may well lose our funding for the next contract. Decisions should be made that benefit us all. Not for one old and ailing elephant.'

'That's not how Papa sees it,' Syeira said in a low voice. 'And that's not how I see it either.'

Traian shook his head. 'You have been too long with that old fool, Syeira. His soft heart has softened his head, and it will be the ruin of this circus. Managing a circus takes a firm hand and clear vision.'

'Papa has always said that a vine may bear bitter fruit for a season or two,' Syeira replied, 'but that will pass as long as its roots remain true.'

'Fah! Those times have changed, and this circus needs to change with them.' Traian waved at the marketplace and village around them. 'This is evidence of those changes.'

'And we have changed with them.' Syeira kept her voice steady with effort. 'This place is also proof of that.'

'More changes have to be made.'

'Talk to Papa. Please.'

Traian looked like he wanted to say more, but he let out a tense breath and nodded. 'Of course. Will I see you tomorrow?'

'Yes.' Traian's gaze moved to Andy. 'It has been a pleasure meeting you, young man.' He touched his forehead in a salute. 'Until we meet again.' He turned and walked through the crowd, quickly disappearing.

'Now that,' Andy said, 'is an intense guy.'

Syeira nodded, clearly unhappy. Then she noticed the vial, stake, and necklace of garlic cloves in Andy's hands. 'What are you doing with those?' she asked.

'Dracula lives up on the hill,' Andy explained.

A smile suddenly brightened Syeira's face. 'Did you buy the map as well?'

'No. I left before we got to the map part.'

'Raiding Count Dracula's castle is one of the adventures that runs in this system.'

'And he's really a vampire?'

'Of course. What fun would it be if he weren't? If you find the Count and stake him, and if you find his secret treasure, you win a prize.'

'A lifelong dental plan, maybe?'

Syeira laughed and walked through the marketplace, speaking to people she knew.

Andy converted the stake, vial, and garlic necklace into icons and stored them in his personal veeyar. If he needed them later – if the Count happened to put in an appearance – he could easily access them. 'Do you want to talk about—' He hesitated when she gave him a look. 'Okay. Maybe not.'

Unexpectedly, Syeira reached back and squeezed his hand. 'It's not you, Andy. You're pretty okay.'

'That's a relief. Because for a few minutes there today, I really didn't know.'

'Things are hard at the circus right now. I've never seen Papa so worried. I thought the idea of Imanuela and the baby was going to drive him over the edge. There are other problems, too.'

'Like being up for contract renewal?' Andy nodded. 'I know how that is. Mom used to do a lot of contract work when she first opened her business. Every year when it was time for contract negotiations it got weird. I got to where I hated it.'

'But she doesn't have to do that anymore.'

'No. She worked really hard to get her business going and it did. We're not rich or anything but we live comfortably.'

'In the same house all your life?'

'Mostly. We lived on base when I was a baby but I don't remember that. Mom wanted a house to raise me in after Dad was gone. It took a while, but she made it work.'

Syeira looked around, ducking under a low cloth awning. 'Papa always said home is important. I was raised here, and under the tents of the real circus. Sometimes I wonder if I missed anything as we moved about the world.'

Andy shrugged. 'Parent-teacher meetings. Mowing the lawn. Maybe a few other things. Probably not much. Home is really more about people who love you than it is about a place.'

'True. Still, many of the circus performers have grown up around the circus. As a result, most of them remain very loyal to their circuses.'

'But that's not happening now?'

'A few of the performers are losing faith in our circus, and in Papa. They're afraid that the funding contract isn't going to be renewed.'

'Is that so bad?'

'Not to me. I love the circus, Andy, and it doesn't matter whether we tour or not. The Net gives us access to the whole world. Further, even. I could be happy for the rest of my life with that. But we've traveled through most of Europe and the United States over the last five years. Some of the performers will accept no less in their future.' Syeira looked up at the perfectly blue sky. 'It might not look like it, but it's getting late. I've got to get an early start if I'm going to work on the trapeze with Uncle Traian tomorrow.'

'You're in the trapeze act?'

'Not officially. I'm trained to do most of the stunts but I've never been featured in the act. I've always been an understudy. But if Klaus and Marie quit, and that's possible, I'm going to be up there in the spotlight.'

'Are you ready for that?'

Syeira's eyes sparkled. 'Yeah. Papa is hesitant about it. The risks, you know. But he supports me. Traian, however, thinks I need a lot more practice.'

'Maybe he's being a little hard on you because you're family.'

'No. When it comes to the trapeze, Traian knows everything there is.' Syeira peered around. 'Do you see Matt?'

Andy looked around, then pointed at Matt, who was still talking to the kite dealer.

'I want to tell him goodbye.'

'Sure,' Andy said, suddenly seeing the flower booth nearby. 'I'll be right there.' As soon as Syeira left, he stepped over to the booth.

'A flower for the lovely girl, *domn?*' the young woman tending the booth asked. 'As you can see, we have many colors, many varieties. Though none may touch her beauty.'

'What do you think she would like?' Andy asked, suddenly realizing he'd never bought a flower, real or veeyar, for any female other than his mom.

The woman reached for a basket. 'A rose, *domn*. Roses touch the heart.'

'We're just friends,' Andy hastily explained. 'I just want something she could keep to remember the night by.' *At least maybe it will be something she can remember favorably.*

'Of course, *domn.*' The young woman pointed to a basket of golden flowers. 'Then you should give her a daffodil, which means respect. Perhaps a carnation? It stands for joy.' She plucked a white carnation from a basket, adding it to the daffodil she'd already picked up. 'To signify that you have had a good time. If you have had one.'

'I have,' Andy said.

'And perhaps you should add a daisy, for innocence.' The woman added a spray of tiny yellow and white flowers. 'And a touch of heather, which indicates admiration.' She bundled a sprig of tiny amethyst flowers with the others, then added baby's breath to pull them all together. She wrapped them in delicate green paper, making a cone shape.

All of a sudden the couple of flowers Andy had intended to buy looked like a blooming garden in the young woman's fist. He felt really nervous. 'You don't think this is too much?'

The young woman laughed. 'Oh, *domn*, you worry about nothing. I saw her with you. She will appreciate this show of affection.'

'*Affection?*' Andy shook his head. 'No, not affection. See, I was going more for appreciation. You know, for bringing me to see the circus.'

'*Domn*,' the young woman grinned at him, 'either way, it is too late. Here she comes.'

Andy let the young woman guide his thumb to the payment scanner as he turned. Matt and Syeira spotted him at once. Matt was much too amused, and although he tried to hide it, he couldn't. Syeira looked as uncomfortable as Andy felt.

'You bought a kite,' Andy said to Matt.

'Yeah,' Matt replied. 'And you bought a bouquet.'

Andy gazed at the cone of flowers in his fist as if they'd erupted there without him knowing it. 'Yeah.'

Everyone stood there with nothing to say for a moment.

'Well,' Matt said, 'are you going to take them with you or are you going to eat them right here?'

'I'm not eating the flowers.'

'Oh.' Matt raised his eyebrows.

Feeling sick to his stomach and noticing his hand shaking – *Oh, feek, where did this idea come from and why did I have to act on it?* – Andy extended the flowers to Syeira. 'These, uh, are for you.'

Tentatively, Syeira took the flowers, acting like she didn't know what to do with them. 'For me?'

'Unless you don't want them,' Andy told her.

'Of course I want them,' she said. 'I'm just surprised.'

'They're to say thank you for the dinner and for bringing us to the circus,' Andy said.

'Oh.'

The note of disappointment in her voice was so tiny it almost escaped Andy. Any other time it probably would have, but he was hypersensitive at the moment. He didn't know what to say, couldn't figure out what he'd done wrong, but suddenly Syeira was as quiet as she'd been back when they were at the mall after the confrontation with the skaters.

'I need to be going,' she said. 'You're welcome to stay if you want and look things over a little more.'

'Sure,' Andy said. 'But I think I'm going to go home. I'm working with Mom. There will be a lot to do at the clinic.'

Syeira nodded.

'We'll be coming out to the circus tomorrow to check on Imanuela,' Andy said.

'That would be good.'

'Maybe we could talk. Unless you're too busy.'

'No,' Syeira said. 'I'd like that. Bye.' She waved, then disappeared in a haze of prismatic color as she logged off the Net.

Andy pressed both hands against his face and took a deep breath.

'Are you going to be okay?' Matt asked with genuine concern.

'If I don't throw up, sure.'

Matt laughed. 'You're making this too hard on yourself.'

'Making what? I'm not making anything. It was just a bunch of flowers. *Veeyar* flowers. Jeez, I could have sent her a card and thanked her for the trip.' Andy looked at Matt. 'Do you think I should have sent her a card instead?'

'No. The flowers were a nice touch.'

'A nice touch of what?'

'Whatever.' Matt shrugged. 'Want some advice?'

'No. Do I look like I need advice?'

Matt gave him a quick once-over. 'Maybe.'

'Well, you're wrong.' Andy paused, taking an easier breath. 'And another thing, if this gets out about me giving her flowers, especially if it's twisted so that this was some kind of *nice touch* thing, you're going to hate your next year of life.'

Holding his hands up in mock surrender, Matt said, 'I wouldn't do that to you. I just wanted you to know you could talk to me. If you decided you ever needed to.'

'I don't. Have fun with your kite and I'll talk to you soon.' Andy logged off before Matt could say anything else, certain he didn't want to hear whatever it was. And he regretted the impulse to buy the flowers. That was just so . . . geekoid. What *had* he been thinking?

But it was too late to take them back now.

Andy's mom didn't accompany him out to Cservanka Brothers Circus the next day. She'd checked in virtually, and was constantly monitoring her patient online. But somehow, virtual visits weren't enough for Andy today. Besides, his mom needed him out there, or so he told himself. He arrived at the circus about noon and checked on Imanuela. The man that had stayed with the elephant throughout the night thought she'd rested well.

His mom guided him, via her presence online, through the injections of meds the elephant needed.

As Andy put away the gear he'd used, his mom said, 'Why don't you take a few hours to yourself there at the circus?'

Andy decided to take her up on it. Most of the circus performers appeared to be up and about, finishing the raising of the various smaller tents around the Big Top. But he hadn't seen Syeira yet. He thought maybe she was avoiding him. Maybe she felt as uncomfortable as he felt after last night. He'd had nightmares all night long of being stalked by flower bouquets – surely the oddest dreams he'd ever had.

Andy lifted his medical bag and headed for the corral fence.

Papa stood at the fence, resting his arms on the rail. 'Your mom is a good lady. She's taking good care of Imanuela.'

'Yeah,' Andy said, dropping on the other side. 'She cares a lot about her patients and what she does for them.'

'So you're going to be with us a while today?'

Andy nodded. 'If that's okay.'

Papa smiled. 'Of course it's okay. This is a circus, one of the best. What is there not to like?'

'Yeah.' Andy looked out across the tents. It seemed like a miniature city had risen from the empty lots the city government had leased to the circus. The circus had nearly doubled in size since he'd seen it yesterday. 'I guess Syeira hasn't gotten up yet.'

'She was up with the sun this morning, my young friend.' Papa waved toward the tents. 'You can find her in the Big Top. She and Traian are working on the bars.'

Andy looked at the big tent, watching the proud Cservanka Brothers pennant waving from the flagpole.

Papa smiled. 'I'm glad she's taking time to get to know you. Usually all she has is the people in the circus, and there aren't that many her age here anymore. Most of the other children her age are in schools or have different interests. Syeira loves the circus. You go along now. And if you're here when we have dinner, consider yourself invited.'

'I will. Thanks.' Andy set off through the tent city.

Handlers used the circus's other elephants to pull massive tent poles into place. Almost hypnotized, Andy watched the massive animals pull against the heavy yokes tied to the ropes secured to the poles they raised. In all the circuses he'd attended in veyar, he'd never seen this side of the business.

'Kind of awe-inspiring, isn't it?' a high-pitched, creaky voice asked.

Andy turned and followed his gaze to the small man only half his size.

'Sorry,' the little man said. 'Didn't mean to startle you.' He stood less than three feet tall and was nearly that broad. He wore white-face and a clown suit, his face framed by a bright red wig. He looked like he was in his late forties or early fifties. 'I'm Petar Jancso, known as Shakespeare the Clown.'

Andy introduced himself.

'I already know who you are.' Petar grinned. 'Everybody knows who you are.'

Andy felt the tips of his ears burning and tried to ignore it. Maybe stopping to see Syeira wasn't such a good idea. Maybe she'd told everyone about him giving her flowers. Thankfully Matt hadn't had any more to say about it.

'You've never seen a circus going up before?' Petar asked,

gazing out at the working elephants and crews.

'No.'

Petar sighed. 'There's nothing in the world like it. Nothing that makes a heart gladder. You know what the saddest thing is? Watching it all come back down. It's like the rise and fall of an empire. A glorious, wonderful empire of make-believe and happiness. And Papa's responsible.'

'Because he manages everything?' Andy asked.

Petar pursed his lips and blew. 'Piffle. Anyone can manage. No, Papa's special gift is that he lets us all be what we want to be here. We find out own place in the Cservanka Brothers Circus. How many dwarf clowns have you seen?'

'Not many,' Andy admitted.

Petar smiled hugely, the expression made larger than life by the makeup around his mouth. 'And how many of those clowns do magic?' He threw his arm out and a flash of smoke and a crash of thunder erupted from the ground near Andy.

'None that I can remember.'

'Clowns and magicians usually don't mix. Magicians don't wear rubber noses and clowns don't do hocus pocus. But Papa didn't see a problem with that and let me do my act the way I wanted to. Otherwise, I would have been relegated to the freak sideshows. Between you and me, those are kind of hard to pull off and still remain politically correct.'

Andy laughed before he realized it might not be appropriate. However, Petar laughed with him. 'There's one other job that I do around here that I take seriously.'

Andy looked at the clown and noticed some of the humor had drained from the man.

'Papa's the father figure around here,' Petar went on, 'but I've nailed down the big brother spot for myself. If somebody here at the circus has a problem, I try to help out. And I look out for people, be their friend when they need one. I like that job.' The dwarf clown hesitated as if trying to figure out how to say best what he wanted to say. 'One thing you're going to learn early, Andy, there's no real privacy in a circus. Everybody knows everybody else's business.'

Andy understood that but didn't say anything. He also didn't have a clue where Petar was going with his speech.

'I don't know much about you,' Petar stated. 'That's kind of bald-faced for me to say, but that's how it is. What I do know is that I want Syeira to be okay.'

'Why wouldn't she be?' Andy asked.

Petar stared at him for a moment, then a smile took away some of the seriousness in his features. He shook his head in amazement. 'You don't know, do you?'

'What?' Andy let the irritation he felt show in his voice.

'Never mind,' Petar answered. 'Forget we ever had this conversation.' He thought about that, cocking his head to one side. 'Actually, don't forget about it; just keep it in mind. But don't think about it a lot.'

Andy felt more confused than ever.

'I'm glad we had this little chat,' Petar declared, extending a hand.

I wish I knew what you were talking about, Andy thought as he took the little man's hand.

'See ya.' Petar wandered off to watch the elephants, his tiny hands clasped behind his back.

'No. Arc your body higher, Syeira. You need to go faster, generate more speed and height if you're going to do this.'

Stepping through the tent flaps, Andy recognized Traian's voice from the previous day. He stood just inside the Big Top and waited for his eyes to adjust from the brightness outside.

High above the safety net stretched across the center ring, Syeira swung from a trapeze bar, arching her legs to go faster and higher. She wore a shimmering blue and green ensemble that looked like a bikini. Clusters of silver strands hung from bracelets around her wrists and ankles.

A few circus performers stood around the center ring,

gazing up anxiously. Nearby, a half-dozen ponies stomped restlessly.

'She is going to fly,' someone muttered.

The tent was so quiet, the heavy canvas muffling the outside noises so well, that Andy heard the words easily.

'I don't think she's ready,' someone else said. 'See how tightly she's gripping the bar?'

'She has her grandmother's blood in her,' one of the bareback riders said. 'She was born to fly. She and Traian.'

Somehow mention of Traian's name dampened the excitement clinging to the crowd. They watched Syeira swing, and they became more anxious.

Gazing upward, his vision mostly clear now, Andy saw Traian standing on a pole platform. Traian had his arms crossed over his chest and looked disapproving. Another man in blue and green tights that matched the ones Syeira had on stood beside Traian, holding a trapeze bar ready.

'Higher, Syeira, higher,' Traian urged. 'You have to get the correct speed and height to make the distance.'

'I can make it.' Syeira sped toward the top of the tent again. 'Send the bar.'

'You're not high enough,' Traian told her.

Syeira hung from her arms at least thirty feet above the ground. 'I can make it.'

Traian shook his head, then he motioned for the man beside him to let the bar loose. The bar swung outward, matching Syeira's swing perfectly.

Andy watched, his breath catching in his throat, as Syeira raced toward the bar.

High above the center ring, at the apex of her swing, Syeira released her bar and tucked herself into a double somersault. She opened like a spring snapping, arms flying out, fingers stretching.

But she was inches short of the bar. As Andy watched, horrified, she fell like a rock.

Chapter Eleven

Andy sprinted toward the net, unable to stand by while Syeira fell even though he'd never reach her in time. Even if he did get to her, there was nothing he could do.

Incredibly, Syeira didn't scream during the nearly thirty-foot fall. Still silent, she hit the springy tension of the safety net and bounced high, her arms and legs pinwheeling for a moment before she went limp. When she hit again, the bounce was much lower.

Grabbing the net, Andy flipped up onto it and got to his feet just as Syeira stood.

'What are you doing here?' Syeira asked.

Andy thought she didn't look happy to see him. 'I wanted to make sure you were okay.'

'I'm training to take falls like that.' Syeira stomped for the other side of the safety net away from Andy.

'If you were a stunt person for a live-action holo,' Traian's deep voice thundered under the huge Big Top, 'perhaps you'd be in training to take such falls. But you're not, Syeira. You're in training to fly.'

Andy glanced up in time to see Traian step off the high platform above. He braved himself, knowing the man's impact against the safety net could throw him from his feet.

Traian dropped straight down, not bothering to fall back into a relaxed position. Only a handful of inches from the safety net he came to an abrupt stop, standing on air.

He's a holo, Andy realized.

118

'Take it easy on her, Traian,' Emile the stilt clown said. He stood taller than the safety net, swaying on his inhumanly long legs. 'She is learning.'

'I thought she looked very good up there,' one of the bareback riders enthused. 'Nice form. Clean moves. So pretty.' Other performers stepped up to Syeira's defense.

'A flower is pretty,' Traian countered, 'until it is wilted and broken. Is that what you wish for Syeira?' He stared at the other performers till they broke eye contact.

'You are too hard on her.' The performers stepped away, making an aisle for the old woman dressed in midnight blue. She strode through them regally, brushing away two attempts the bareback riders made to turn her away from the confrontation. Her gray hair was pulled back, leaving her features severe. Her dark eyes looked like two holes burned into her face.

'Mind your own affairs, Elsa,' Traian warned. 'You may run the sideshows but when it comes to the flying trapeze, I am the recognized master.'

'You unfairly push your own ambitions onto your great-niece.' Elsa came to a stop within arm's reach of Traian.

The name rang a distant bell in Andy's mind. Only three people had been at the Cservanka Brothers Circus before Imanuela had arrived: Papa, Traian, and Elsa, the fortune teller. Papa and Elsa easily looked old enough for that to be true, but Traian glowed with youthful good looks. Of course, the holo image floating above the safety net could be a proxy, a carefully tailored image that suited Traian's preferences for presenting himself.

'It's okay, Auntie,' Syeira interrupted. 'I can handle this.' She started up the pole.

'When would you have her learn?' Traian demanded. 'The show is performed without the safety net.'

'It doesn't have to be performed that way,' Elsa said.

Andy watched, as silent as the other circus performers

around them, and felt uncomfortable.

'The show has always been done that way,' Traian declared. 'Our audiences would expect no less.'

'No,' Elsa argued quietly. 'Our aerialists performed with a net for many years. You were the one who changed that, Traian. Because of your own vanity and need for danger.'

Traian strode angrily in the air a few inches above the safety net. 'The danger draws them, Elsa,' he stated passionately, waving toward the bleachers. 'They fill those seats with the anticipation of seeing blood.'

'They come here to forget their daily worries and live in a fantasy world with their children. They'd prefer not to see someone fall to their death.'

'Pah!' Traian roared. 'The circus is a place where the audience can face death vicariously.'

'Real death?' Elsa smiled and shook her head. 'Against trained lions in my day and computer-generated ones now? I don't think so.'

Traian curled one hand into a fist, then shot it at the flying trapeze. 'The risk remains! It is my domain!' His words cracked inside the tent.

Elsa faced him, unflinching. 'And do you still face that risk, Traian? Do you still live with it every day?'

Pain wracked Traian's features, and for a moment Andy felt sorry for him. The man's emotion was too raw, too strong to be contained. He evaporated in a haze of crimson sparks, taking himself from the holo-environment.

'Traian,' Syeira called from halfway up the pole.

Elsa looked up at her, tenderness in her voice and on her features. 'Syeira, come down from there. You've had enough for today.'

'Auntie, you shouldn't have done that.' Syeira dropped to the ground and walked toward the old woman. 'Training new flyers is what Traian lives for.'

'Don't argue with me, dear child,' Elsa said. 'I would like

to see you full grown if I should live so long. Not broken or six feet in the grave.'

'He was only trying to help. I *can* fly.'

'Yes. You have the blood and talent of your grandmother in you, just as well as Traian.' The old fortune teller took a towel from one of the thick hawser ropes supporting the safety net and draped it around Syeira's neck. 'Traian needs to find more to live for than training flyers. But that is not your problem.'

'If I had only listened to him,' Syeira said, 'I would have caught that bar and you two would not have argued.'

Elsa smoothed her hair. 'Traian and I have been fighting since we were children together. When we were young and first married, I lived for those fights. It brought such passion to us. Now it seems that I am the only one who is willing to stand up to him, besides Papa.'

Andy saw tears streak Syeira's cheeks. She mopped at her face with the towel.

'You've been at this since early this morning,' Elsa said softly. 'I know for a fact that you didn't get much sleep. You should go outside the shadows of this tent and walk in the sunlight. Your new friend is here.'

Andy's ears burned when the old woman glanced at him and smiled.

'You are only young once, Syeira, and you should enjoy every day of it.' Elsa gestured toward Andy. 'Come here, boy, and take her away from this place, for she has her great-uncle's stubbornness as well.'

Unwillingly, Andy walked to Syeira's side. 'Maybe we could grab a soda.'

'Sure,' Syeira answered. But she looked long and hard at the platform where her uncle had stood before she finally let him draw her away from the tent.

'It happened over forty years ago. Back in the 1980s. Traian and Grandmother Mavra were the main draw of the circus.

People came from all over Europe to watch them perform.'

For the first ten minutes after they'd left the Big Top, Andy had wished nonstop that he'd seen to Imanuela and simply left. But now he was glad he had stayed. After Syeira had walked off some of her anger at what had happened back in the tent, he found she really needed to talk.

They'd wound through the circus and ultimately made their way back to the holding area where the animals were kept. Once they'd headed that way Andy wasn't surprised to see that they ended up at Imanuela's pen.

Andy had been amazed by the way the other performers seemed to know to leave them alone. It was like someone had made a public address, only he hadn't heard it. He sat on the corral fence, his feet hooked in the rails.

Syeira sat comfortably beside him, her eyes on Imanuela as she talked. 'Grandmother and Traian knew no fear, Andy. You should have seen them. If you have watched any documentaries on circuses, I'm sure you've seen flatfilm footage of them.'

Andy nodded. One thing he'd learned about girls was that when they were emotional and talking, as long as they weren't yelling at him – because there had been times like that as well – everything was going about as well as could be expected. He sipped the grape soda he'd gotten back at a concession stand they'd wandered by.

'Grandmother loved Papa like no man she'd ever met,' Syeira went on. 'Aunt Elsa told me about them, just as she told me about her relationship with Traian. Aunt Elsa traveled with a gypsy caravan till she met Traian at a show in Budapest. They got married soon after.'

Andy found he liked listening to her voice, especially now that the tension in it had disappeared.

'It was like that for Grandmother and Papa, too.' Syeira finally cracked her lemon tea gelpack open and took a small swallow. 'But as much as she loved Papa, she also loved the thrill of performing. She was a flyer with another circus. Papa tried to hire her away but she refused. It took nearly two years, but he saved his money and bought the other circus out, incorporating it into the Cservanka Brothers.'

A smile touched Andy's lips. A persistent man, Papa.

'Ten years later, the accident happened.' Syeira's voice chilled.

Andy's neck prickled.

'It was in Munich, in West Germany. The Berlin Wall hadn't fallen then.' Syeira rolled the drink in her hands. 'The weather had been bad, a lot of rain. They had trouble putting the tents up. But even though the rain was miserable, the crowds came.' She paused. 'They shouldn't have performed that night.'

'But they did,' Andy said.

'Yes. Aunt Elsa told me that they had enough money put back to tide them over a few days of bad weather, but Papa, Traian, and Grandmother wanted to perform. They felt the show had to go on. International media people from a dozen different countries were covering the show.' Syeira took a deep, shuddering breath. 'During the trapeze act, there was a blowdown.'

'A blowdown?' Andy echoed.

'Circus term. It's what it sounds like. High winds toppled the center pole. All the rain had made the ground too soft. When the center pole fell, it pulled down all the quarter poles and side poles that supported the Big Top. The flying trapeze was the first to fall, and with it Traian and my grandmother.'

A sick feeling twisted in Andy's stomach.

'Several people were injured when the tent fell,' Syeira whispered. 'But only Grandmother was killed.'

'They were working without a net.'

Syeira nodded. 'As always. Traian wouldn't have it any other way.'

'And Traian?' Andy asked.

'He fell, too. Papa never speaks of that night – I don't think he can – but Elsa told me that Traian tried to save

123

Grandmother by diving after her and hoping he could drive them toward one of the guy wires supporting the trapeze so they could catch hold. He couldn't. The accident paralyzed him from the neck down.'

'So that's why he's in holo-form all the time.'

'When Traian isn't at the circus, either through the holo-projectors or in the veeyar version, his life is spent in a hospital bed in Bucharest. A machine breathes for him and he's fed through a feeding tube because he can't even swallow. He and Elsa never had any children. Papa and Grandmother were lucky to have had my father before the accident, but because of the tragedy my father wanted nothing to do with the circus once he got old enough to leave. If I leave here, Papa will have lost his entire family.'

'But that's not why you stay at the circus?'

'No. I love it here, Andy. It's the only real home I've ever known.' Syeira looked at him, her eyes wet with unshed tears but showing excitement as well. 'And I want to fly. More than anything, I want to fly in front of an audience and know that they're holding their breath because of me.'

'Mr Moore.'

Andy paused, one hand on the handle of the pickup he'd borrowed from the clinic to make the circus run. Glancing behind, he saw Martin Radu hurrying over to him.

'I've been trying to find you for the last twenty minutes,' Radu said.

Andy stowed the medical gear he'd brought. Before he'd left Imanuela and Syeira, he'd given her a shot of the hormones that continued to curb her premature labor.

'I've heard about the work you did on the lion-tamer module,' Radu said. 'Mr Crupariu seemed very pleased.'

I guess he didn't hear about Syeira getting her head bitten off. It was a little private joke, but still . . . Andy nodded. 'I'm glad.'

'I have a proposition for you.'

Curiosity had always been one of Andy's weaknesses. 'Sure.'

'Have you got a few minutes?'

Andy shrugged. It never hurt to listen. 'Let me call my mom to tell her I'll be back a little later.'

'How familiar are you with the midway area of the circus?' Martin Radu strode briskly through the stands that lined the path to the Big Top's front entrance.

'Not very.' Andy studied the booths containing confections and drinks, trying not to trip over the thick power cords lying across the ground. The cords were marked in yellow and black hazard colors and looked reflective enough to glow at night. A row of lanterns was spaced strategically along the way.

The booths held candied apples, caramel apples, popcorn, caramel popcorn, cotton candy in bright neon colors, sodas, hot dogs with chili and sauerkraut, hamburgers, corndogs, nachos, pretzels, funnel cakes, and a broad selection of ice creams. Then there were pushcarts with soft drinks, snowcones and juices. It was a smorgasbord of junk food that Andy's mom definitely didn't keep stocked in the Moore home. His stomach rumbled hungrily.

Other booths mixed in with the foods, offering games of skill and chance. Old standbys including dart throwing, ring tossing, water machine pistols, knocking milk bottles from a stand, plucking floating ducks from a water trough and others stood side by side with veeyar games that had limited playability like skeet shooting, paintball, home-run derby and golf.

Radu stopped in the center of the midway. 'Are you familiar with these veeyar games, Andy?'

'Yeah.'

'And what would you say about them?'

Andy tried to figure out a way to answer politely. 'They've been around for a while.'

'You don't have to be nice,' Radu said. He looked at them and blew out a disgusted breath. 'They're antiquated.

Obsolete. Museum pieces that are absolutely worthless.'

Silently, Andy agreed.

'Still, Papa refuses to upgrade. He insists that the circus be about the performers and the sideshows. He's a stubborn, stubborn man.'

Andy didn't comment.

'How familiar are you with gaming?' Radu asked. 'Would you say you're well-versed?'

Andy struggled to keep the smirk from his face. The circus's twenty-four-hour man regarded him intently. Andy finally decided to give it to him straight. 'You'd be hard-pressed to find many people outside the electronic gaming business that know as much as I do. I'm better with games than I am with animals.'

'Good.' Radu clapped him on the shoulder. He waved at the midway. 'What I would like, Andy, is to know how much you would charge me to design some new veeyar games that could be run by our current operating systems.'

'It takes months, sometimes even a couple years, for a full-production gaming studio to produce a single game,' Andy said. 'And they have a ton of resources, and lots of people working on them.'

'The games also cost much more than our budget would bear, especially for something that would be ours exclusively.' Radu strode down the midway again, waving Andy to follow along beside him. 'I've been thinking about this for some time, and I believe that what Cservanka Brothers Circus needs is an original veeyar game. A game that will remind audiences that have been here of who we are. Possibly something that we could spin off and sell ourselves.'

'Then you'd want someone other than me to handle it for you,' Andy pointed out.

'You did a good job with the lion-tamer module, and I trust that the security upgrade installation you plan to do will be more than satisfactory.'

'Yeah, but those were things I'm familiar with.'

'As I said,' Radu went on, 'I've looked into this matter for some time. I know that different gaming companies license old game engines for other designers to use. If I were to license one of those game engines, would you be able to build a game around it?'

Andy thought about it. The old game engines Radu was talking about weren't cheap but they were much more reasonable than new and original games. 'Yes. If I started with an existing game engine, I couldn't do it overnight but I could do it.'

'Could you do it in two weeks?'

The timeframe surprised Andy. Obviously Radu had been thinking about the project for quite some time. Why the sudden urgency? Still, he could always use the work, and the money. If Radu needed the game crashed into production, maybe he was prepared to pay pretty well for the privilege. 'If I didn't work on anything else, and if I had access to a lot of gaming resources, maybe.'

'I know you're working for your mom for the summer,' Radu said. 'I overheard her talking to Papa while you and Syeira went to the mall yesterday. Perhaps I could talk to your mother and explain the job opportunity here and she could free you up for the next couple weeks.'

Excitement filled Andy. It hadn't been that long ago that he was in Los Angeles at the annual gamers' convention when Peter Griffen had unveiled *Realm of the Bright Waters*, the new online fantasy game that was the current gaming world hit.

Maj Green, Matt Hunter, Catie Murray, Leif Erikson and Megan O'Malley – his friends and fellow Net Force Explorers – had all gone with Andy to the game convention in hopes of finding work or a market for their work in the gaming world. In the course of the adventures they'd had at that convention, they'd made several useful contacts. Peter Griffen had helped Maj license the Striper flight-sim she'd written to some top-flight gaming areas. Maj wasn't making a fortune from it but she was earning some nice college money.

Andy had been gaming as soon as he'd put his head back in his first implant-chair. When he had the opportunity, he lived, breathed and ate games. Getting a chance to design one that would be played by a number of other people was a dream come true for him. 'I don't know what my mom would say.'

Radu nodded. 'I understand that. What I need to know is how you feel about doing the project.'

'Me?' Andy blinked. There was only one answer he could give. 'I'd love to do it.' But at the same time he was a little afraid. He'd already designed game scenarios before with the build kits online. And Space Marines had an addition that allowed the creation of original terrain scenarios for battle, something he did regularly. He'd beta-tested for lots of his friends. But to build an actual game for real, even if it was of limited capacity, that would be out for public display and consumer use – it would be a solid rush.

'When would you feel it would be convenient for me to call your mother?'

'The sooner the better,' Andy replied. 'I've never been much good at keeping a secret around her, and trying to keep a secret when it's something I'm excited about would just about kill me. Why don't you call her now?'

Chapter Twelve

'You'd be gone for two weeks?'

Sitting across the dinner table from his mom, Andy nodded. 'Maybe a little more.' His mom didn't look happy about the idea, but she hadn't said no yet either.

She put down her salad fork, though. Usually a definitive *no* required the use of both her hands. Andy felt like he was losing ground.

'How much more?' she asked.

Still not a no *in sight.* Andy stifled a shrug because shrugs could be yes-killers. 'If I can get the game up and running in two weeks, which is going to be hard enough, I'll need some time to work on any programming bugs and system incompatibilities that might turn up. I'd need to be on hand a little while after it went online.'

'I don't know, Andy.'

Andy curbed his impatience, glancing at the homemade sausage pizza and the garden salad he'd made. His mom had gotten home later than he had. He was responsible for making some of the meals they shared, but she had known he was plotting something when she saw the chocolate frosted bake in the refrigerator. Chocolate was one of his mom's weaknesses.

He picked at his salad. 'I've been away from home that long before for Net Force Explorers training.'

'Yes, but you haven't been traveling with a circus. You were with Captain Winters or men he trusted. You were probably

129

safer in their hands than you were at home.'

'I'm not denying that.'

She cut a piece of her pizza slice with her fork and hesitated. 'You really want to do this, don't you?'

'Yeah. I like the circus. It's all new and interesting to me. And they are going to pay me for it. That way I can repay the money you lent me to go to that gaming convention I went to in Los Angeles.'

'You're already set to work that off by helping me in the clinic.'

'I know.'

'But I guess working on a game would be more interesting than washing cats and walking dogs.'

Andy caught himself just before he shrugged; he even maintained eye contact, another big factor in discussions with his mom. 'Yes.'

'So tell me this, Game Guy, do you want to do this more to design the game or because it gives you the chance to see Syeira every day?'

The question came completely out of left field and Andy felt his face burn with embarrassment. 'Hey.'

'Hey, what?'

'That's kind of personal.'

His mother gave him a small grin. 'So the answer is yes.'

'I didn't say that.'

'You wouldn't get all red-faced over a game.' Triumphantly, his mom popped the pizza piece into her mouth.

'I can see Syeira online if I want,' Andy argued.

'You could attend the circus tomorrow night by holo,' his mom pointed out. 'I see you're accepting ticket comps from Papa.'

Oops. He'd left those on the kitchen counter. 'Okay, part of the reason I want to go is because of the chance to see more of Syeira.'

'You like her?' his mom asked.

'I like being with her,' Andy countered.

His mom returned her attention to her salad. 'Why does Mr Radu want you to accompany the circus? You could design the game from home.'

'The game is going to require a lot of programming,' Andy said, explaining Radu's reasoning as he'd been given it. 'I'm also going to have to import a lot of design tools into the circus OS. Mark's going to help with that. Even despite the new security firewalls I've been installing and the work I've done so far, he thinks there's a chance that I could import a virus or crash the system. He feels like having me there in person gives him more control. He doesn't want to risk shutting a crucial part of the circus down at the wrong time.'

'Doesn't he trust your skill?'

'Yeah, but he's got a point. It is easier to contain OS integrity working on-site.'

'Why not design the game here and then go there to add it into the circus programming?'

'I could,' Andy admitted, 'and I told him that. But like he said, importing a large cache like that into the circus could cause other problems with programming conflict. The circus OS has limited resources. Even installing the new security programming – which the circus had to have – was tough because of the limitations of the existing program. Space and memory aren't issues because the Net is so big, but having the OS manage so many programs at one time – including the veeyar circus – is going to be tricky. He just wants me handy in case something goes wrong.'

'I see.' His mom returned to her meal.

'I'd really like to go,' Andy stated quietly, knowing he was pushing the envelope because he was asking for an immediate answer. But he had to know.

'Not thinking of making this a permanent change? The lure of the open road and no responsibilities can be attractive.'

Suddenly sensing where her real concerns were, Andy said, 'Mom, I've got a room full of half-finished models and hobbies. Let's face it, my attention span leapfrogs everywhere. Me, I'm not a circus kind of guy. The only thing that I've ever really been constant about is being here with you. Besides, I don't think Net Force would be interested in making an agent out of a circus clown or Toto the Dog-Boy.'

His mom nodded. 'Sometimes you can act so grown up that you scare me.'

Andy grinned. 'Did I mention there's a chocolate cake in the refrigerator?'

'Yes.' She smiled. 'You even showed it to me.'

'I don't know what else to say, Mom,' Andy said. 'But I'd like to try it. The first time you want me back home, I'll be back.'

His mom cut another piece of pizza. 'Having you on hand for Imanuela could be useful.'

'She can travel?'

'I wouldn't think about allowing it if you weren't going to be there with her. But if you were along to monitor her condition and treatment . . .'

Me? Along? Andy struggled to keep the excitement from his face. He resisted the impulse to say anything.

'I also don't like the idea of keeping Imanuela behind when the circus goes. Elephants are herd animals. Being around the other elephants is be good for her.'

Andy nodded, unable to hold back anymore. 'So I can go?'

His mom looked at him for a moment. 'Yes.'

Andy stifled a cheer by clearing his throat.

'On the condition,' she said, 'that you and I spend time together every day virtually and you leave the circus when I say you leave.'

'I can live with that,' Andy said. He could barely keep from shouting with glee. 'No problem.'

Andy sat in the bleachers and felt the hard planks beneath him. The smell of buttered popcorn swirled around him, mixing with the misty night air thick with the promise of rain.

The crowd oohed and ahhed around him, making it hard to hear anything else sometimes.

Out in the center ring, the four bareback riders performed with their mounts. They ran in practiced synchronization, the riders' bare feet touching the ground for an instant as they knotted their fists in the horses' manes, then leaped lightly to their broad, muscled backs. They lingered there for just an instant, then rolled to touch down again the other side of their animals. They came up from touching lightly and laid on the horses' backs, draping themselves like blankets over the galloping horses that never missed a beat as they circled the ring.

'Syeira is a bareback rider?'

Andy glanced over at Matt sitting beside him. Matt was there in holo-form, but he looked real and, with the holo-projectors interfacing in the circus OS, he even felt real.

'No,' Andy replied. 'Syeira's just filling in for one of the other girls tonight.'

Syeira spun around on the horse and got to her feet, standing on the animal's broad back. Her arms swept out to her sides and she seemed to dance as she balanced perfectly on the running horse. She looked great atop the horse, and smiled brightly for the crowd.

'Did you know she could do this?' Matt asked.

'Not until tonight,' Andy said. 'But she told me that all the circus performers are cross-trained in as many different acts as possible. She's working on mastering the flying trapeze. That's what she hopes will be her specialty.'

'It's dangerous.'

Andy nodded. The flying trapeze act had already done their set. During the time the trapeze flyers had been airborne without a net, the crowd had been uncharacteristically quiet. Then the clowns had come out and sparked the audience again, getting them ready for the bareback riders.

'What else does she do?' Matt asked.

Andy could only shake his head. 'She rides a motorcycle and can program a computer, but I don't know. Maybe just about anything.'

Out in the center ring, Syeira launched into a tumbling dismount, landing easily on her feet. She ran across the sand and vaulted onto a passing horse.

'Ladies and gentlemen,' the ringmaster called over the PA system, 'presenting Lord Byron, horseman extraordinaire!'

A man standing astride two matched stallions galloping side by side bolted out from behind the tent flaps and into the Big Top's spotlights. He and his horses ran into the center ring quickly. Syeira stepped onto the outside horse when it passed close enough to hers. Another girl joined them a moment later.

Nimble as a monkey, Syeira climbed to the horseman's shoulders as he balanced atop the two gleaming horses. Syeira reached down and helped the second girl to the horseman's shoulders as well. Then they stood, each with one foot on the horseman's shoulders, and held hands so they could counteract each other's weight. They balanced there, pointing their toes prettily in the air, as steady as though they weren't moving around the ring so fast their hair was streaming out behind them, their feet planted on a man's shoulders, the man standing without visible means of support on a pair of galloping horses who wore neither bridle nor saddle.

Thunderous applause came from the crowd.

A moment later, Syeira and the other girl leaped to the center of the ring. They landed only inches from each other, arms up and spread toward the crowd. The horseman thumped onto the sand an instant later, dropping immediately into an exaggerated bow. All the horses kept circling the ring, two of them ridden by the other two bareback riders.

'Ladies and gentlemen,' the ringmaster thundered, 'Cservanka Brothers has long been proud host to the Fellani Riders. Their skills are unsurpassed in equestrian prowess. Join me in giving them a big hand to show your appreciation.'

As the audience broke out in applause, Syeira and her two companions sprinted for the riderless horses, coming up behind them and vaulting onto their backs like flatfilm cowboys. A low and broad flaming hoop at the back of the center ring was lit and the smoke coiled up toward the top of the tent. One after another, the horses and riders leaped through the flaming hoop and disappeared behind the tent flaps.

'You really picked one,' Matt commented.

Andy looked at him. 'What are you talking about?'

Matt nodded toward the disappearing horses. 'Syeira. I think you've found a girl who's going to keep you on your toes for a while.'

'I didn't pick her.'

'Whatever.' Matt shrugged and grinned. 'At any rate, while you're with the circus, you're going to have your hands full.'

'It's nothing I can't handle.'

'Uh-huh.'

'Ladies and gentlemen,' the ringmaster called, 'please direct your attention to the left ring.'

The spotlights obediently followed the ringmaster's pointing finger. The spotlight touched only empty space. Then a rough voice rang out. 'Not over there, over here!'

The ringmaster made a show of being surprised and looked to the right ring. The spotlights followed him, playing over a white-faced clown in baby pants and floppy shoes in the right ring.

'Sheesh,' the clown said, 'give you instructions and you still can't get it right.'

'I got it right,' the ringmaster objected. 'It was left.'

'Left was wrong,' the clown countered. 'How can it be left when that's not right?'

'What do you mean *not right*?' the ringmaster argued. 'It's plain to see you're standing in the right ring. If it's not right, you should be in the left. Left is right.'

'Left is left,' the clown yelled. 'Right is right. Left is only left when it's not right.'

'Left is never right.'

'Sometimes it is,' the clown responded. 'If left is right then it's not wrong. Now left is wrong so it's right.'

Andy only halfway paid attention to the ringmaster and clown as they argued. In the back of the right ring, shadows moved quickly, setting up an impromptu stage. A moment later the clowns started assembling a few stage pieces.

In the next couple moments the clowns assembled a fire department scene, complete with Dalmatian, and went toward a 'burning house' high in the Big Top. The spotlight followed the clowns' expressions as they looked up at the tent pole.

Twenty feet above, a clown victim spread his arms wide and waved frantically while he stood on a platform and pretended to be trapped by the fire. The smoke streamed from a small pail containing dry ice, Andy figured, or maybe the effect was totally computer-generated.

The clown fire brigade quickly got their safety net out and raced to the rescue. The clown-victim teetered precariously to the left only to pull himself back to the right. The rescuers hauled their safety net back and forth, yelling directions and gesturing wildly.

The clown-victim finally pulled out a small purple parasol and jumped from the platform. The parasol came apart on the way down. When the clown-victim hit the safety net, he dragged all his rescuers to the ground. The crowd roared in laughter.

'Hi.'

Andy glanced up as Syeira joined him, now dressed in street clothes. 'Hi, yourself,' he said. She and Matt exchanged hellos as well.

'Are you enjoying the show?' she asked.

'You were terrific out there,' Andy declared.

'Trick pony riding.' Syeira shrugged. 'Any Pony Express

rider could probably do better.'

'Trust me, the outfit you were wearing wouldn't suit them.'

The clowns continued cavorting in the center ring. Now that the victim had been 'saved,' the clown fire chief – dressed in a fireman's hat that splayed his red curly hair out in all directions – kept trying to bill him. Only the victim kept insisting that he'd saved himself.

Syeira glanced around the crowd. 'The audience seems to be having fun, and there must be a lot of them physically here instead of just by holo-projection. The butchers appear to be doing good business.'

'Butchers?' Matt asked.

'The guys selling concession stuff,' Andy informed him. He'd picked the term up over the last couple days. 'They're called butchers.'

The concessionaires passed through the crowd barking out wares. Bags of peanuts, popcorn, and cotton candy were snapped up by the circus crowd, as well as soft drinks and snowcones.

The clown act drew to a close in a whirlwind of confetti and noisy horns. They chased each other back to the tent flaps.

'And now,' the ringmaster announced, 'for your edification and amazement, the astounding Turrins!'

The spotlights followed the ringmaster's grand wave to the center ring. Workers rolled a huge globe formed of steel bars into the ring. As they began securing the globe by guy wires to the stakes driven deep into the ground, three riders on miniature motorcycles thundered into the ring. The motorcyclists leaped the ring's side and landed, scattering sand in a half-circle toward the audience.

'Something's wrong,' Syeira said over the thunderous roars.

'What?' Andy asked.

'The Turrins weren't supposed to go on next. The Great Stanislas was scheduled.'

'The magician?' Andy asked. 'The guy with the trained monkeys who make him think his magic is working?' He'd seen bits and pieces of the act as Stanislas worked with his three-member troupe over the last couple days. He'd thought the act was a riot.

'Chimpanzees. They're apes, not monkeys,' Syeira corrected.

'Okay.'

Concern darkened Syeira's features as she pushed up from the bleachers. 'I've got to find Papa.'

'Wait up,' Andy called out. 'I'll come with you.' He scrambled through the crowd and vaulted through the bars at the end of the bleachers, landing beside Syeira.

Syeira led the way to the RVs and converted buses the circus performers lived in while on the road. Each vehicle bore colorful markings that advertised not only the Cservanka Brothers Circus but also whichever act they housed.

The logo on the Great Stanislas's RV showed the magician as well as the three chimps in the act. It was parked only a few feet short from the converted school bus in front of it. Night had fallen and even the bright and festive lights of the circus didn't chase many of the shadows away.

'So this is what you would do, after all the years that we have been through?' Papa's voice was distinct, filled with hurt and maybe a little anger.

'Papa, please.' The other man's voice was soft and embarrassed. 'I don't want things to end badly between us.'

'And how else were they supposed to end?' Papa demanded.

Hot on Syeira's heels, Andy rounded the corner by the converted bus and spotted Papa and Stanislas standing in front of the RV.

'This is what I had to do, Papa.' Stanislas was a short, compact man in his late fifties. His long black hair was shiny with dye and brushed the shoulders of his suit. He held his cane in both hands before him as though he might have to defend himself.

'Papa,' Syeira called.

Papa's head snapped around and his eyes were wide with emotion.

'What is going on here?' Syeira asked. Andy trailed close behind her, knowing that when tempers flared out of control between men to the degree he saw before him, violence sometimes happened before anyone knew it. They'd gone beyond the limit of the circus holo-projectors and Matt had winked out of existence twenty yards back.

'He deserts the circus, deserts us,' Papa accused, leveling a finger at the magician, 'like some thief in the night.'

'Even a rat will desert a sinking ship,' Stanislas replied sternly.

'Rats have never been counted on,' Papa said. 'If I had known you had such a taste for cheese, I would never have counted on you.'

'I am no rat.'

'Ha!' Papa exploded. 'And I say to you if it squeaks like a rat, then it must truly be a rodent. And this rat is leaving Cservanka Brothers to work for Cirque d'Argent.'

Syeira turned to the magician. 'Is this true?'

Stanislas gazed at her shame-faced, then lowered his eyes. 'Yes, Syeira, it's true.'

'Why?'

'Because we are nearing the end of our present contract,' Papa said, 'and Stanislas doesn't believe we will be given another one.'

'We will get another contract,' Syeira said. 'The sponsors will not turn us down.'

'You say this out of hope,' Stanislas replied, 'and out of loyalty to Papa.'

'Loyalty,' Papa interjected, 'is not a word I would think would find comfort in your mouth.'

'Papa,' the magician said softly, 'I am an old man now.'

'You speak as though we are not all getting older.' Papa shook his head, and Andy saw some of the softness return to his features.

'You never seem to age,' Stanislas said. 'No matter the hardship, no matter the trouble, always day in and day out you remain steadfast, Papa.'

'For me, there is no other way.'

'These people hold you here, Papa,' the magician said. 'Some of them believe in you, and others simply love you.' He smiled and wetness touched his eyes. 'I would say that most of them love you. I love you, even though we can't seem to agree on this.'

'Then why do things this way?' Papa demanded. 'Behind my back?'

'There was no other way to do it.' The magician spread his hands. 'Could I come to you and tell you that I'd lost faith, Papa? Lost faith in you and this circus, and myself?'

'Yes,' Papa declared.

'If I'd given you that chance,' Stanislas said, 'I was afraid you would have convinced me to stay. I couldn't allow that. Not this time.' He sighed heavily. 'I haven't many years left to me in this business.'

'That's not true,' Papa said.

'Ah, you were always generous, my friend. But you and I both know my hands are slowing. Were it not for those trained chimps and the elegant sense of timing I've always had, I would not be before an audience now.'

'And the Cirque d'Argent,' Papa demanded. 'What will they do for you?'

'They are going to pay me almost three times what I'm earning here. If I work a year for them – this year – it's the same as working three years for you. I need that money. You know my Lispeth is sick. She hasn't been well for a very long time.'

'I know,' Papa stated. 'I remember all those nights I stayed up with you as we watched over her.'

Tears trickled down Stanislas's face, silver in the moonlight. 'As do I, my old friend, as do I. Some of those days, I would not have made it without you.'

'But you can make it without me now.'

'I have to,' the magician whispered hoarsely. 'They offered me a three-year contract. That's nine years of pay for three.'

'You're still young,' Papa said. 'You could easily work another ten or twelve here.'

'And if I get to where I am unable to work?'

'I would see that you were cared for,' Papa replied. 'The same way I take care of all my people.'

'I wouldn't want to end up a pauper and be a drain on the circus,' Stanislas said. 'You know me. I have far too much pride for that.'

Andy felt embarrassed to witness the exchange. The war between the two men was over but the hurting was only now starting.

'You're going to leave Gertha, Marguerite and Faust behind?' Syeira asked.

'I have no choice in this,' Stanislas said. 'They belong to Papa, as does the very trailer I live in, and they have known no other home. I would not take them from that.'

Papa's shoulders slumped in defeat. 'Then there is nothing that I might offer you, my old friend?'

The old magician wiped his wet cheeks with the back of his hand. 'It would only shame both of us, Papa.'

Slowly, Papa nodded. 'Then I wish you Godspeed, Stanislas.' He offered his hand. The magician took the proffered hand, then Papa swept him into a big bear hug. 'May your voyage be a safe one, my friend, and may your heart never weary.'

Stanislas gripped the other man fiercely, tried to speak but couldn't, and stumbled away.

Syeira crossed to Papa, tears staining her cheeks. 'Stop him,' she whispered.

'I can't.' Papa dropped his arm across his shoulders. 'It is as Stanislas says, I would only demean us both. He sees that he has no choice.'

'But shows without Imanuela and the Great Stanislas,' Syeira said, 'fans are going to notice these things.'

'We will carry on,' Papa stated. 'We always have, my child. And as long as a Cservanka remains alive who loves the circus as I do, this show will continue to carry on.'

Andy watched the old magician disappear into the night, a shadow fading and absorbed by the dim white light of the secure parking area. His coat tails flapped in the light breeze.

Noise drew his attention to the RV. Three simian faces pressed against the glass, eyes bright as they watched Stanislas disappear. They were dressed in their costumes for the show. One of them waved goodbye.

Chapter Thirteen

'Andy, are you awake?'

Convinced he had to be having a bad dream, that no one could possibly be trying to wake him, Andy resisted the call at first. Then he realized the voice had been Syeira's, not his mother's.

'Yeah, I'm awake.' He sat up in bed, immediately slamming the top of his skull against a hard metal surface. He groaned in pain.

'Are you okay?' Syeira asked.

'Yeah. Just banged my head against the upper bunk to get alert quicker.' Papa had assigned him a berth on the clowns' bus. Ducking, he pushed himself into a sitting position on the bed's edge. His bare feet touched the chill tile of the bus floor.

Syeira stood in the open doorway at the back of the bus. Distant city lights glowed against the sky behind her.

'What's wrong?' Andy asked over the throbbing hum of the window air-conditioning unit that cooled the bus.

'Nothing's wrong,' Syeira said. 'It's time to go.'

The circus is leaving tonight. Andy yawned, trying to focus. 'What time is it?'

'Four.'

He'd been asleep for two hours. He couldn't believe it. Normally he stayed ready to go. In fact, he could probably do without sleep longer than any of the Net Force Explorers with the possible exception of Leif Anderson. But Leif's

143

payback once he crashed was an extended visit to the Land of Nod, not the catnapping Andy could get by with.

For the last three days, the length of the engagement Cservanka Brothers had in Alexandria, Virginia, Andy had cared for Imanuela, worked on the computer game design, and hung out at the circus. He'd also checked in with his mom at the clinic and at home a few times, but even in veeyar he didn't escape the exhaustion that seemed to haunt him.

'Andy.'

'Coming,' he replied, trying to keep the annoyance he felt from his voice. When Syeira closed the doors, he grabbed jeans and a pullover from the bag under his bed. Living in the converted bus wasn't exactly the lap of luxury. He pulled the clothes on, stepped into his cross-trainers, and raided his stash of beef jerky.

Outside, the circus had resurrected. Floodlights that created pools of illumination had replaced the colorful lights. The constant, hammering *ker-thump* of generators created a cacophony of sound. Strident voices rose above the thumping.

'What are we supposed to do?' Andy asked. Papa had been putting the finishing touches on a work schedule before the evening show. Most of the performers had set routines for the teardown. Some of the local men and teens had been hired to help with the disassembly of the circus.

'We're helping with the midway.' Syeira led the way through the tangle of power cords running from the generators across the ground. Elephants dragged and pushed equipment and concession stands onto flatbed trailers pulled by waiting eighteen-wheelers that had been rented for the occasion.

Everything seemed surreal to Andy. Maybe it had something to do with the lack of sleep, but he thought mostly it had to do with the way the tent city so quickly disappeared.

When he and his mom had seen the circus going up, he hadn't thought that much about it. Construction still went on regularly in various parts of Alexandria. But after spending so much time at the circus over the last few days, watching it go down affected him more deeply than he'd anticipated.

As he watched, the Big Top mushroomed out and slowly dropped.

'Are you okay?' Syeira asked.

'Yeah,' Andy answered. But his voice was surprisingly tight.

The group sped out of the shadows like a hunting pack.

Their furtive movements drew Andy's attention instantly. He stood inside a portable cotton candy concession stand where he'd been securing the equipment for the trip. The concession workers had already cleaned up after the blow-off, the time the main events in the Big Top had closed down and the audience had wandered through the midway for a final tour.

Carefully, Andy put aside the dishes he'd been packing and watched as the group filtered into the work going on around the circus. Metal gleamed at their feet and Andy could almost hear the whir of wheels on rollerblades.

Paved roads led into the parking areas around the circus grounds from four different directions. Andy assumed the intruders had come in that way.

He crossed to the door quickly, knowing the constant growling of the generators would mask any sounds he made just as it masked the noise the skaters made. He took his foilpack from his pocket and folded it into phone configuration. He pushed the earplug into place.

Mark Gridley answered on the second ring. 'Hello.'

'It's Andy.' He spoke softly so his voice wouldn't carry.

'I thought you'd run away with the circus.'

'We're leaving town this morning.' Andy passed through the concession stand doorway and moved in pursuit of the skaters. Moonlight kissed the dim gleam of a black skull with flaming eyes standing out against leather, then it was gone. 'I need you to stand by for a couple minutes. I think I just spotted a local skater gang called the Skulls invading the circus grounds.'

'Aren't those the guys you ran into at the mall?'

'Yeah. How much do you believe in coincidences?' Andy stayed low as he moved through the circus structures. Most of the performers and workers had gathered at the north end of the grounds, helping load some of the heavier equipment on the flatbed trailers.

'Coincidences happen,' Mark commented, 'but I'm not a big believer in them. I've got the Alexandria Police Department on rapid forward.'

'Good. I don't want to cry wolf.' Andy slid between two concession buildings. His Explorer training included night maneuvers and he knew sky-lining – spotting someone's form against a light source behind them – was a real danger with all the activity going on around him.

'The Skulls aren't here for a good reason,' Mark assured him. 'It might be better to call the police now.'

'Wait,' Andy cautioned. 'Those guys are also known to carry weapons. Maybe the mall confrontation wasn't just something that happened. But if the police are called in, I'm afraid things could get out of hand. It might be better to find out what they're doing here before we call in the cops.'

The Skulls headed straight for the area behind the midway where the offices were kept. Papa's wagon was there.

Andy trailed behind them, staying fifty yards back. He caught snatches of conversation over the drone of the generators but nothing he could really make out. The Skulls now carried their skates tied around their necks. They ran through the sideshow buildings that housed physical as well as virtual attractions. Those buildings were scheduled to be loaded last because they were among the lightest. Livestock and tents were loaded first.

Andy ducked behind Madame Elsa's fortune-teller's booth and watched as the Skulls gathered around the door to Otakar the Strongman's building. Closer now, Andy recognized Razor, the leader he'd fought in the mall. One of the skaters slipped a prybar from under his vest and handed it over.

Razor shoved the prybar into the doorjamb. The lock gave with a metallic snap that was buried in the other noise going on. In quick succession, the skaters filed into the building.

'Call the police now,' Andy said. 'They just broke and entered Otakar's trailer.'

'I'm on it.'

Still hunkered down, Andy crept closer. Mark kept the foilpack channel open, letting him hear the conversation with the police.

Quick as the Skulls had been about entering the strongman's set, they were even quicker coming back out.

Andy maintained the foilpack's phonelink but added the video connect, intending to take a vid of the crime. He moved slowly around the fortune-teller's booth and brought the foilpack up. Just as he viewed the scene through the aperture, ready to start rolling vid, a huge foot filled his vision, then turned everything black. He went flying backward.

Off-balance, Andy sprawled on his back on the ground. The foilpack spun out of his hand, dragging the little earplug he'd been using for audio feed away.

'Told you somebody was following us,' one of the skaters crowed triumphantly. He stood big and broad, his features clouded by the shadows and Andy's blurry vision. He stepped forward and grabbed Andy by the shirt, hoisting him to his feet almost effortlessly.

Andy tried to push free but couldn't find purchase. His arms felt weak and ringing filled his ears.

The skater grinned in anticipation. 'I'm going to bust you up.' He drew a fist back.

'No,' Razor ordered harshly. 'Leave him.'

The big skater grimaced. Then he shifted his weight and slammed Andy into the fortune-teller's booth.

The impact almost knocked Andy out, turning his knees to rubber. He went face forward onto the hard ground and couldn't seem to get his arms to take his weight. After a deep, shuddering breath, he finally had enough strength to push himself up.

The Skulls were already disappearing into the night again. But he was certain some of them were carrying packages.

Bright light bounced over the ground around Andy. 'What's going on?' a man demanded.

Andy turned, blinded by the light. He blinked and shook his head, feeling the headache take root. 'Get the light out of my face.'

The light moved away.

Spots danced in Andy's vision as he pushed back against Madame Elsa's booth and got to his feet on quivering legs. Still, he recognized Martin Radu.

'What happened to you?' Radu asked.

Andy pointed at the strongman's booth. 'Skaters broke in.'

Radu flicked the light over the gaping door. 'Is anyone in there now?'

Andy shook his head and instantly regretted it. The pain felt like an explosion inside his skull. 'They left. They took something out of there.'

Radu walked to the booth, starting to swear just after entering.

Still somewhat dazed, Andy managed to recover his foilpack on the ground, then walked into the booth after Radu. 'Mark?'

'I'm here, buddy,' Mark answered. 'How are you doing?'

'Feels like somebody walked a Space Marine battlesuit over me. The police?'

'On their way.'

Radu swept the flashlight around the booth's interior. Built-in cabinets held costumes and stage equipment. The strongman's barbells lay in the center of the floor. Each of the four bars contained large balls on either end labeled from 250 pounds to 1000. After all, Otakar was billed as the World's Strongest Man.

However, each of the barbell balls was hollow. They were

148

heavy, even though they didn't weigh as much as they were labeled. Most people, if they were allowed to try, couldn't lift them.

But the Skulls had known about the hollow barbells. Worse, they'd known something was hidden in them. Something was wrong about that.

'Is anything missing?' Patrol Sergeant Cranmer of the Alexandria Police Department asked. The grounds the circus had camped on were under the PD's jurisdiction.

Standing in front of the police officer, Papa shook his head. 'No.'

Andy hung back in the crowd, watching. Syeira stood at Papa's side while Radu paced only a short distance away.

Cranmer was tall and lean, clean-shaven features a little pink from sunburn. He considered the form he'd been filling out. 'Was there anything inside that particular booth they might have been after?'

Papa shook his head. 'No. Nothing. As you can see for yourself, it is only the strongman's booth. It's one of the small stage areas we carry for the sideshows along the midway. There are not even trinkets there for anyone to win.'

No way the Skulls broke into the sideshow for nothing, Andy thought. He touched his swollen, bruised lip, wincing at the electric pain that shot through it.

Approaching dawn turned the eastern skies gray.

'Well, Mr Cservanka,' Cranmer stated politely, 'I'm going to file this report about the break and enter, but don't expect a lot. With no lost property involved and you leaving town, this is going to be put on a back burner.'

'I appreciate your candor, sir,' Papa replied. 'However, there remains the matter of the attack on the young man. I don't want them to get away with that. Andy could have been seriously injured.'

Cranmer flicked his gaze to Andy. 'What about it, son? If we took you down to look at some mug shots do you think

149

you could identify the boys that were here?'

Andy hesitated a moment, covering it by touching his lip. Papa and Syeira looked at him. He knew it was the Skulls but he also knew that by the time he identified them, they'd have gotten rid of whatever it was they'd taken. And if he got involved to that degree, his mom would have to intercede for him since he was a minor – which could mean the chance to design the game and to go with the circus would be gone.

Plus, Andy was certain there was something more afoot than the Skulls embarking on a little vandalism. After the mall incident, he'd done his research. The Skulls trafficked in stolen goods and couriered contraband.

With a shrug, Andy said, 'All I know is that it was the Skulls. They were wearing the gang insignia.'

'Anybody can wear a skull jacket,' Sergeant Cranmer pointed out.

Resisting the impulse to argue, Andy said, 'Yeah, I guess so.' *But not just anybody would have known about those barbells. And I'm going to find out who told them.*

Andy sat in the passenger car of the Atlantic Corporation Transport train and yawned tiredly. The effort hurt his swollen lip. Judging from his grayed-out reflection in the window, though, the lip's puffiness had come down some.

Syeira's reflection stepped in behind him. 'You're awake,' she said.

He turned toward her, only smiling halfway because that hurt, too. 'Barely,' he told her. 'I feel like I'm about an inch away from dying.' It was late morning. He'd had three hours of sleep since the circus train had pulled out of Alexandria.

Other people, commuter travelers as well as circus performers, were in the seats around them. Most of them were asleep or scanning news headlines in papers or on personal digital assistants. The clacking of the train passing over the tracks sounded like a metronome.

'You should be sleeping,' Syeira said. She wore denim

shorts, a midriff tank, and a light tan jacket with the circus logo on it to pull it all together.

Andy tapped his watch. 'Time to go check on Imanuela.'

'I've already been out to her car. She's resting comfortably. Not a sign of trouble. Train travel is as familiar to her as your home is to you, you know.'

'Good.' Andy yawned again. 'I was afraid maybe she might get motion sickness. Still, I promised my mom. Gotta check her myself.'

'Want some company?'

'Sure.' Andy uncoiled from the seat and slid out into the aisle. He grabbed the medical bag from an overhead bin.

The flatbeds containing the animal cages were secured behind the passenger train. Imanuela's cage was up front, rigged with a portable holo-projector unit that fed off the train's power and telecommunications link.

Stepping carefully, Andy crossed the linkages connecting the railway cars as he worked to the front of the train, followed by Syeira, who moved like there really wasn't a railroad track passing beneath her feet at high speed. Andy let himself into Imanuela's enclosure, reminding himself that the thick transport cables holding it to the flatbed were engineered to hold it in place through a hurricane, even with an elephant inside it. The bindings only *looked* a little too flimsy for comfort. As he moved into the enclosure, Andy's stomach growled loudly enough to be heard over the sounds of the train.

'Want some breakfast?' Syeira asked as Andy took Imanuela's vitals.

'You can find that?' Andy asked in surprise. He'd missed the catered circus breakfast and had guessed that he wouldn't eat again until the train stopped in Columbia, South Carolina. He's slept through the stopover in Raleigh, North Carolina. Cservanka Brothers Circus had a week-long engagement booked in Mobile.

'Papa always travels with some food handy,' Syeira

volunteered. 'It might just be instant oatmeal and soup and crackers and stuff but he'll have something. And I made friends with one of the conductors. She'll let me use some hot water. It won't be fancy but it sounds to me like you could use the meal.'

'Anything would be great right now,' Andy replied. 'Imanuela's feed pellets are starting to look appetizing.'

Syeira left, hopping gracefully across the gap between the two moving railway cars like it was nothing.

Andy triggered the holo-projectors and called his mom over the foilpack. When she arrived, she noticed his lip immediately.

'Holo-Net mentioned there'd been some kind of trouble at the circus,' she said. 'What happened to you?'

Andy was an old hand at keeping his mom from worrying about things she couldn't do anything about. Single moms tended to worry more than most. 'It was dark last night and this was the first teardown I'd worked.'

'Teardown?' His mom touched his lip. Luckily, the holo-image didn't apply the pressure of a real touch.

'Taking the circus down,' Andy explained.

'Does this hurt?'

'No.' *If you were really here, trying this, I'd be jumping out of my skin about now.*

'So how did this happen?'

'I tripped and fell.'

Irritated satisfaction showed on his mom's face. She turned from him and looked Imanuela over again. 'I heard the circus had a break-in last night. Something about gang members?'

'The police figured it was a dare or vandalism,' Andy replied. 'Nothing was taken and no one was hurt.'

His mom nodded vaguely. They talked for a few more minutes and she agreed with him that Imanuela was doing fine. Straightening, his mom looked over his shoulder and said, 'Looks like it's time for me to go. Three's company.'

The little grin she gave Andy embarrassed him. He turned and spotted Syeira headed back toward him with a big paper sack in her hands. He said goodbye to his mom and she vanished.

'Everything okay with Imanuela?' Syeira asked.

Despite the straw and animal smells inside the elephant's cage, Andy detected the strong odor of hot chocolate coming from the bag Syeira held. 'Yeah. She's fine.'

'We could eat inside the passenger car,' Syeira said.

Keying on the prompt she'd given him, Andy said, 'Or?'

Syeira smiled. 'Or we could eat on top of it.'

'On top?' Andy looked at the passenger car's rooftop as it swayed gently back and forth. The prospect was way more attractive than it had any right to be.

'It's a lot safer than it looks,' Syeira said. 'Papa doesn't like me to do it but he doesn't yell at me much when he catches me.'

'I'm game.' Andy followed Syeira up the narrow ladder leading to the passenger car's roof and clambered over the edge.

Though burdened with the paper sack, Syeira managed the climb much more easily than he did. Her body seemed to adjust to the railcar's swaying like second nature. The wind was warm and didn't push against them as much as Andy had thought it would.

Halfway down the passenger car, Syeira sat down in crossed-leg fashion. She waved her hand and suddenly there was a red and white checked tablecloth hanging like a flag from her fingers.

Andy grinned in spite of the pain in his lip. 'Don't tell me. You've also worked with the Great Stanislas.'

'Yes. But only on special occasions.' She spread the tablecloth.

'What special occasions?' Andy sat across from her, surprised to be as warm as he was. It was early afternoon now and puffy white clouds moved across the blue sky.

Syeira mumbled as she passed out plastic containers.

Andy opened his cup and breathed in the hot chocolate

aroma. 'I didn't hear you. When did you say you worked with Stanislas?'

Syeira sighed. 'When one of the chimps was sick.'

'Oh.' Andy struggled to keep a straight face but couldn't. He burst out laughing, then moaned in pain.

'Serves you right,' Syeira stated. She lifted the paper sack. 'And there's nothing saying you have to be fed either.'

Andy's stomach growled again. 'Okay, that's not funny.'

Syeira passed out two ham and cheese sandwiches and kept one for herself, then added a plastic bag of whole dill pickles, and two single servings of fruit and yogurt.

'Wow,' Andy said in appreciation. They ate in silence and he tried not to wolf the sandwiches down, nibbling the pickles as a cunning subterfuge.

'Hungry?' Syeira asked, smiling.

'Good food,' Andy replied.

'Right.'

He gazed out at the forested countryside rolling past them. They were miles from any urban areas and the trees looked as though they could swallow up a small city.

'It's beautiful out here, isn't it?' Syeira finished with her meal and sat with her arms wrapped around her tanned legs.

'Yeah,' Andy answered, but he knew he'd feel more at home in a cityscape. 'It'd make a great battlefield for Space Marines.'

Syeira laughed.

Andy looked at her.

'I guess maybe we see different things,' she explained, watching the greenery roll by. 'I like coming up here and sitting because it clears my head. Lets me have a moment to myself.'

'Oh.' Andy felt a little humbled because he realized she'd chosen to share that moment with him and maybe he wasn't as appreciative as he should have been.

'I think Klaus and Marie are going to leave after Mobile.'

As tired as he was, it took Andy a moment to remember

Klaus and Marie were the trapeze artists. 'Did they make an announcement?'

'No. They won't do something like that. I just noticed that they're keeping to themselves.'

'Maybe they're just tired.'

'I've seen people come and go at the circus,' Syeira said. 'I've got a feeling.'

'Are they going with Stanislas? To the Cirque d'Argent?'

'I don't know. But I do know that if they leave, I'd better be ready to fly by the time we reach St Louis.'

'Are you ready?'

Syeira hesitated, her gaze lost somewhere out in the forest. 'I'm not sure. Uncle Traian thinks so.'

But Uncle Traian isn't going to have to fall again, is he? Andy only felt a little guilty for thinking that. The realization that Syeira might be on the trapeze for a real performance, possibly without a net if Traian had his way, was scary.

Syeira wrapped her arms around herself more tightly and grinned sheepishly. 'Maybe it's a little colder out here than I thought.'

Andy glanced at his cup, but the hot chocolate was gone. So were the sandwiches, pickles, and yogurt.

'You're finished. We can head down,' she said.

Feeling a little embarrassed and nervous all at the same time, Andy said, 'Or we could sit a little closer. Use the tablecloth as a wrap. Share the warmth.'

A long beat stretched between them, then Syeira said, 'Okay.' She slid across the top of the train until she sat beside him. She handed him the checkered cloth square.

Andy was immediately conscious of her warm body against him. She shivered. Before he knew what he was doing – *no, stop!* – his arm was around her shoulders. He pulled the tablecloth around both of them.

Her shivering stopped. 'That's better,' she said. 'Thanks.'

Andy shrugged, which he discovered was kind of uncomfortable while he was hanging onto someone else. He looked at the train. 'I've never ridden on a train. Not outside of veeyar. And not this way ever, even in veeyar.'

'We could truck the circus around but taking the train is a lot less complicated.'

'I still can't believe it all fits on here.'

'Actually, Ringling Brothers and Barnum and Bailey Circus was the first to really use the rails to move their show around in the 1930s and 1940s. They were experts on transporting just about anything by rail. When World War II came along, the American military went to them to discover how to better move men and hardware for the war effort.'

'Really?' Andy was amazed.

'Papa told me about it. Ringling Brothers and Barnum and Bailey had built specialized train cars to handle the big tents and animals, as well as all the booths and the midway rides. Before they did that, they'd had to operate with skeletal set-ups or spend a lot of time putting the show together.'

She continued, telling Andy more circus history. Ringling Brothers and Barnum and Bailey, she told him, had begun as separate circuses, huge competitors, but had been affected by the arrival of the movies and other entertainment that had downsized the live entertainment sector of the market. As she spoke, Andy felt her growing heavier and heavier inside his arm. After a while, she went silent. Soon he heard her snoring, rocking to the sway of the train.

He smiled, enjoying the feeling of just holding her sleeping in his arms. It was the first time in his life that he could remember really enjoying just sitting still.

The train slowed just a bit as it rounded a curve and started up a steep grade. The cars clanked and jostled a little more. Andy tightened his grip on Syeira, surprised at the way she continued to sleep. The linkages clanked and the cars jerked as the pulling engine controlled their inertia.

Movement six cars back drew Andy's eye.

Martin Radu stood between the cars, holding a foilpack to his face. He had his other arm hooked around the ladder near him but his hand gestured angrily. Evidently he felt Andy's gaze on him because he glanced up, spotted Andy, then retreated between the rail cars where he couldn't be seen.

Andy's curiosity became even more aroused. Before turning in that morning, he'd called David Gray, a fellow Net Force Explorer and the friend who'd convinced him to join the program. David's dad was a police detective, and David had access to some databases that weren't available, or even known, to the general public. Andy had asked David to look into the Skulls to see what kind of information he could find on the skater gang.

Despite Radu's insistence that nothing had gone missing from Otakar the Strongman's booth, Andy knew that something had been taken. He'd seen the Skulls leave with it. He just didn't know what had been hidden inside Otakar's hollow barbells.

But he was pretty sure by now that Martin Radu *did* know. And was somehow involved in the theft.

Chapter Fourteen

'A clown's face,' Petar Jancso said as he diligently applied the heavy white foundation to his own features, 'is the most important thing he'll ever create. Clowns are born with big hearts filled with love, and all that love comes out on their face touched by humor or sadness.'

Andy sat on a stool next to the dwarf and watched as Petar continued with his transformation. The makeup room was at one end of the RV, everything neatly in its place in little built-in drawers.

Petar started drawing in his eyes, then paused and glanced at Andy in the lighted mirror. 'You can work up any act, take it anywhere you want to go, and put any number of stories behind it, but as long as you live, the face you invent will be your face.'

Despite a serious bout of preoccupation over what was going on, Andy couldn't help but be interested in Petar's words. They'd arrived in Mobile, Alabama the night before last, slept in, then started putting the circus together yesterday morning. Miraculously, they'd gotten it together in time to open tonight. Andy felt bone-tired, crushed flat as an empty gelpack.

'Do you know how a clown claims his face?' Petar asked.

'No,' Andy answered, wishing he knew how to bring up what he really wanted to talk about. The good thing was that he felt he really could trust the little man.

Petar's hand moved automatically. Years disappeared from his face along with lines. Blue and green circled his eyes. The red rubber nose plopped into place. 'You have to take a photo in makeup and send it in to the Clown and Character Registry. Know what they do with it there?'

'I don't have a clue.'

Petar grinned, partially at Andy and partially to try out the makeup. 'They paint your face on a goose egg and keep it in the registry.'

'A goose egg?'

'Sure,' Petar replied. 'It's tradition. Painting a clown's face on a goose egg goes back to the fifteen hundreds. Only then it was for the clown, to help him remember what face he wore. Later that habit became part of the registry.' The dwarf took down his wig from beside the lighted mirror. 'But that isn't what you came here to talk about, is it?'

'No.'

Petar adjusted the wig. 'Then what?'

'Remember that night that the skater gang broke into Otakar's booth?' Andy said evenly.

The little clown nodded.

'Well, they took something.'

'What?'

'I don't know. But I saw them holding packages when they came out of the strongman's trailer.'

'What kind of packages?'

Andy shook his head. 'I wasn't close enough to tell.'

Petar touched his rubber nose. 'Have you told Papa?'

'I tried to but he insists that nothing was taken.'

Understanding dawned in the little clown's eyes. 'But you're thinking maybe it was something Papa didn't know was there?'

'Maybe.' Andy shrugged. 'I just find it too convenient that the skater gang was trailing Syeira in the mall that day, then they turn up a couple days later to raid the circus.'

'Maybe they were mad about you fighting them in the mall,' Petar suggested.

'I don't think so. I've got a friend whose dad is a detective on the Washington, D.C. Police Department. David checked out the Skulls in department files. They've graduated from misdemeanors these days. They've been ferrying felonious cargo for the last three years. They make a ton of money, all of it untaxed. They're businessmen now, not kid punks out for trouble.'

A frown turned Petar's smile upside down. 'So they're not exactly the type to come out to the circus on a lark.'

'No.'

'So what are you going to do?'

'Keep my eyes open,' Andy answered. 'The same as I'm asking you to do.'

'You know,' Petar said slowly, 'you could have been wrong about confiding in me.'

'If I had been,' Andy said with a grin, 'I'd know better where to start looking now, wouldn't I?'

'Get a move on, Andy,' Emile the stilt clown urged as he strode between the sideshow booths on his impossibly long legs toward the Big Top. 'Word is that we're going to be playing to a straw house tonight.'

'I know.' A straw house meant they'd nearly sold out every seat for the circus show that evening. Mobile, Alabama was turning out to be circus-friendly. Andy felt good about that. 'Where's Syeira?'

'Last I saw her,' Emile called out just before he disappeared around a tent, his tall hat just barely visible above it, 'she was with Papa. At his trailer.'

Andy made the turns automatically, wending his way through the backyard – that's what the performers called the area where they prepared for their acts. They'd set up the circus the same way as they had in Alexandria, going for the general configuration they normally used. That was the practice all circuses followed when they could. The circus felt familiar, homelike, that way. There was an old circus story of an animal trainer in a one-ring circus who gave his dog a bone every night. And every night the dog buried it under the same wagon of the circus. In the morning the circus pulled up stakes and moved on to the next town. And the dog never figured out why the bone he'd buried was never where he left it.

But right now, with the tension of knowing that something was going on, Andy didn't feel much at home, no matter how familiar the layout had become.

Martin Radu hadn't been around the circus much lately, although that wasn't suspicious to anyone in the circus. As the twenty-four-hour man, Radu had to finish prepping all the advertising and advance work, making sure everything was in place and ready.

But Radu's long absences, Andy knew, also gave the man plenty of time and privacy, two things all the rest of the performers conspicuously lacked, to pursue other activities.

David Gray had, at Andy's request, checked Radu's background through Interpol and FBI files. As an international clearing house for criminal files with up-to-date cybernetic resources, Interpol could generally be counted on to find things. Unfortunately, Radu didn't have a criminal record either in the United States or abroad.

At least, not one that's traceable. Radu had come from the carnage still raging in the Balkans. The history he'd given before joining the circus checked out, but David had pointed out that most of the Eastern European satellite countries still had a lot that went on that no one knew about. And tons of records had been destroyed in the conflict, including more than a few that were intentionally lost.

The only thing that Andy really had against Radu was a feeling that something was wrong, and over the last few years he'd learned to trust those feelings. Maybe Maj could have pulled something more concrete out of the air if she'd been around, but he wasn't sure enough of his facts to bother her at this point.

One of the things he'd repeatedly heard Papa say was that

circus business was circus business. No jurisdiction really wanted to deal with any problems that came up in a circus. Out of Romania as they were, international law was also a factor.

In retaliation to any violence or disagreement in a circus that spilled over into a community, the local law enforcement agencies usually came down hard on the circus. Inspectors wrote citations out regarding health and safety issues, closed midway rides and confiscated livestock and equipment. And usually the Immigration and Naturalization Services were called in to verify green cards, taking days of productive show time away.

Going outside the circus for help wasn't a good idea. At least, not yet.

Andy stepped to one side of the aisle between tents and personal trailers as the bareback riders came through with their ponies. The girls and their mounts all wore pale lavender plumed headdresses. Syeira wasn't among them.

'Hey, Kalifa,' Andy called.

Kalifa was a petite Somalian girl with big eyes and coal-black skin. Her smile was wide and generous. 'Andy,' she said, pulling her pony to a stop beside her. She and her family had fled her country to escape its civil wars when she was just a girl.

'I thought Syeira was going to be with you,' Andy said.

'No. The plans have changed since Klaus and Marie are quitting.'

'They're quitting?' Andy couldn't believe it. He'd seen both Klaus and Marie that morning.

Kalifa looked sad. 'They are packing now. A representative from Winskus Circus has made them an offer. They are flying out tonight to join them in Paris before the end of the week.'

A sick feeling twisted through Andy's stomach. 'Where's Syeira?'

'With Traian,' Kalifa answered. 'Getting ready for tonight.'

'She's going to fly?' Andy's words were barely audible even to his own ears.

'The audience loves women trapeze fliers,' Kalifa replied. 'The danger is the same for a man. But a pretty young woman like Syeira, she can capture their hearts, make them beat for her while she dances with death.'

'Yeah.' Andy's own heart was hammering. Syeira had practiced with Klaus and Marie that morning, and she'd fallen into the net three times while Traian had berated her.

'I've got to go,' Kalifa said, pointing at the other riders disappearing around the tent ahead of her. 'But I will be cheering Syeira's debut tonight.'

Andy nodded, not trusting himself to speak. He waved, then trotted toward Papa's trailer. *Maybe I can talk her out of it.* But even as he thought that, he knew Syeira wasn't someone easily talked out of a course of action.

When he reached Papa's trailer, he rapped on the door but got no answer.

'Papa's not there.'

Andy turned and spotted Madam Elsa wrapped all in her black fortune-teller costume. 'Where is he?'

'He's inside,' the old woman said, 'but he's on the Net. At the Wallachia circus.'

'Is Syeira with him?'

'Yes.'

Andy crossed over to Elsa. 'You know about Klaus and Marie?'

The old fortune teller nodded. 'Yes.'

'Is Syeira going to fly tonight?'

'She plans to. Papa is against it but she won't listen.'

Andy thought desperately. 'Maybe Traian could—'

'Traian listens to no one these days,' Elsa stated quietly. 'The doctors may have saved his life by prolonging it with their machines, and given him a new existence on the Net, but they lost the best part of him. We no longer have his heart.'

'I'm sorry,' Andy said.

Elsa covered his forearm with her hand. 'I'm done with my

grieving, young man. I still love what remains of Traian, but I have buried the man that I knew. Syeira will not listen to Papa but perhaps she will listen to you. You are in her heart as she is in yours. Go to her. Talk some sense into her.'

Andy ran back to the midway. He passed through the light crowd milling around the games and the concession booths. Most of the audience had already gathered inside the Big Top.

The midway also featured several computer-link chairs that could be rented by those wishing to access the Wallachian circus. He dropped into the chair and leaned his head back. When the laserbeam receptor made his implants tingle, he felt the jolt that launched him onto the Net.

Andy stepped into eighteenth-century Wallachia with his next breath. Pedestrian traffic flowed around him, going both ways. Judging from the trendy street clothes on some of the people around him, the Mobile audience was really enjoying the virtual circus as well as the real one. And, too, there were all the other Net visitors who might be dropping in from all over the world. Virtual Wallachia wasn't limited in any way to the visitors linking in from the midway.

A barker with a thunderous voice stood by the Wallachian front gate. 'Come see those lovely equestrians,' the barker shouted, waving his colorful hat and pointing toward the Big Top with his cane. 'Daring darlings, every one.'

Part of the crowd peeled off and entered the tent.

Andy summoned an icon that appeared in the air before him, said Syeira's name, and pressed it.

A shimmering rectangle opened in front of him, establishing a head and shoulders shot of Syeira. 'What are you doing here, Andy?'

'I came to talk to you.'

'Look,' Syeira said sharply, 'I really don't need any more pressure right now.'

'No pressure,' Andy promised. 'I promise. Just good common sense.'

A finger hooked the edge of the shimmering rectangle and pulled it wider, revealing Papa sitting beside Syeira. 'Come on,' Papa said.

Andy grabbed the edge of the rectangle and pulled himself through.

When Andy looked again, he stood on a hill overlooking Wallachia. A breeze whipped through the tall grass and the nearby trees. The brown canvas tents of the Cservanka Brothers Circus looked like toadstools in the heart of the city in the valley below.

'Over here,' Papa called.

Andy turned, realizing that Papa and Syeira must have joined up with one of the gypsy bands that roved the area around the virtual city. He and Syeira had seen them on other excursions but had never visited with them.

Some of the gypsies were programmed as near-AI characters designed to interact with visitors, but others were real gypsy hackers who'd gotten online and whom Papa had permitted to stay. Making allowances for the gypsies in the Net Force security programs Andy had installed had been tricky.

More than a dozen vardoes, the colorful wagons gypsy bands lived in and worked out of even in the current year of 2025, sat in a circle around a bonfire. Andy recognized a Bow-topped wagon, a Cottage-shaped wagon, a Brush wagon, a Straight-sided wagon and a Reading wagon.

The Reading vardo had proven the most popular, possessing characteristic large wheels and a wide body which sloped outward as it went toward the eaves. The rear wheels were larger than the front ones, and spindles worked in a cunning design around the vardo. The horses which pulled it when the gypsy caravan was moving stamped restlessly under a nearby copse of trees.

Kettles and pots hung over smaller fires by the bonfire, filling the air with the smells of cooking spices and meats. Gypsy families sat around the large circle, watching the dancing women swirling around the bonfire in their colorful skirts. Most of the dancers were near-AIs.

Papa and Syeira sat in the front of Papa's wagon. Papa worked at a piece of wood with a small knife. Long curls of pine fell at his feet while he shaped a wooden elephant with its trunk curled up from the wooden block. One of the superstitions in the circus claimed that it was bad luck to take a picture of an elephant with its trunk down.

'Andy,' Papa greeted with a nod.

Syeira didn't say anything.

'I just heard about Klaus and Marie.' Andy walked over beside the vardo. The living quarters in the vehicle were visible through the front door behind Papa.

'It is a sad thing,' Papa commented. 'I worked with Klaus's father, God rest his soul, and helped raise that boy.'

'He's a man full-grown, Papa,' Syeira said.

'And with a man's pride.' Papa nodded. 'I understand these things.'

'Klaus and Marie had to leave now?' Andy asked.

'They were given no choice,' Papa said.

'This act was meant to hurt Cservanka Brothers,' Syeira said. 'Winskus Circus is also funded by the same international sponsors we have. They have three more years on their contract after this one. There has been some talk that our international sponsors will fund only one circus in the future. By taking Klaus and Marie, they think they will become the clearer choice for receiving the funding.'

'And there's nothing you can do about this?' Andy asked. The wild gypsy music and the twirling dancers remained on the periphery of his awareness.

Papa shook his head.

'You could have put them under contract and prevented their leaving,' an accusing voice snarled.

Andy glanced over his shoulder and saw Traian had joined them.

'A contract, brother?' Papa asked in disbelief. 'We've never had a contract with anyone in the circus.'

'You sign contracts all the time,' Traian argued.

'Not,' Papa said, 'with performers. While they are here, they are to be treated as family. They are our family. They will not be indentured.'

'And so,' Traian said, folding his arms, 'they feel free to leave you any time the grass appears greener.'

Papa sighed. 'These are hard times. Not just for the circus but for our people too.'

'*Our* people,' Traian said, 'would never leave Cservanka Brothers.'

Papa said nothing, and Andy felt bad for him. It was one thing to have to face bad news but it was another to have Traian rub it in.

'There will be more desertions,' Traian said. 'You know this, don't you?'

'Yes.'

'Since Stanislas and Klaus and Marie have left,' Traian stated, 'a dam has been opened. If you do not stop it, all the others will leave you, too. Cservanka Brothers will be no more.'

Papa rolled the rough elephant shape in his callused palms, his knife blade winking brightly as it caught the light from the bonfire. 'Perhaps it will be time, then,' he said quietly.

'Time for what?'

'Time for us to think about taking the circus away from international touring.' Papa glanced at the town at the bottom of the valley. Torchlight and lanterns lit up the streets and the midway around the Big Top was alive with activity. 'We still have Wallachia.'

'A make-believe circus!' Traian threw his hands into the air as he stalked back and forth. 'No one wants a make-believe circus!'

'Those people down there appear happy with it.'

'Faugh!' Traian shook his head violently. 'What they want is the real circus. They want to sit in the bleachers, watch as sudden death spins in the trapeze above them, waiting half-expectantly and half-afraid for blood to be spilled.'

'That is your version,' Papa said. 'I believe the audience wants entertainment, laughter and surprise.'

'You dishonor Mavra's memory, brother,' Traian accused.

Andy saw the wet sheen in Papa's eyes and knew that Traian's words had stung.

'Stop it, Uncle.' Syeira stood on the wagon, towering over Traian.

'Ah, but you have your grandmother's fire,' Traian said, white teeth flashing.

'You will not hurt Papa.'

Traian waved the order away. 'He hurts only himself. You're too young to see this.' He glared at Papa again. 'Mavra loved the flying trapeze, Anghel, or have you forgotten? She was never more alive than when she was in front of an audience, suspended high above the ground, in a dance with death.'

'But, then, she's not alive now, is she?' Papa whispered.

Surprisingly, tears sprang from Traian's eyes. Lithely, he vaulted to the wheel and wrapped an arm behind Papa's head, pulling his brother's face into his shoulder.

Traian's proxy looked fifty years younger than Papa did but Andy knew from articles he'd read that Papa was only three years older than the trapeze artist.

'No, brother, she's not with us anymore,' Traian said fiercely, 'but she will never go unremembered. Not for a moment.' He took Papa's tear-streaked face in both hands. 'But she would not want you to give in so easily. She would want the circus to go on.'

'No,' Papa said, '*you* want the circus to go on, Traian. You refuse to see that it has nowhere to go.'

Traian dropped to the ground. 'How can you say that?'

'My son left the circus as soon as he was able,' Papa said, 'and I am no longer young. Who will guide Cservanka Brothers should I grow unable?'

'We have Syeira,' Traian cried, gesturing toward her. 'You have kept the circus all these years that you might leave it to her.'

'No, I've kept the circus all these years because I loved it. And what else was I supposed to do? I am no farmer, no data processor. I am a clown.'

'You are a circus owner.'

'Do I own it or does it own me, Traian? I ask you this because I no longer know the answer. Everything I do is to feed this circus, to keep it going one more day. Sometimes I think I was wrong to do that.'

'Syeira loves the circus,' Traian objected. 'Ask her.'

'I do, Papa. I could not imagine a finer life than the one I have had so far.' Tears tracked Syeira's face as well. 'With you and with the circus.'

'See?' Traian exclaimed.

'I do see,' Papa agreed. 'I have seen how you have pushed her into attempting the trapeze, how you would sacrifice her life tonight if you thought it would buy you one more chance to keep your aerialist act alive.'

'There will be no sacrifice,' Traian responded.

'And should she fall tonight? Will you be using a safety net?'

'She will not fall.'

'Just as you would not fall? Or my wife?' Papa whispered.

With the Net proxy in place, Traian's face remained cold, as implacable as marble. He switched his gaze to Syeira. 'Come. We don't have much time to prepare you for your act tonight.' He held out his hand.

Syeira hesitated, glanced at Papa, then took her uncle's hand.

'Syeira,' Andy said.

'I've got to go,' she told him.

Confusion and anger and fear all thrummed inside Andy, sparking like a Space Marine thunderflash going off. He watched as Traian and Syeira both vanished. He turned to

Papa. 'What are we going to do?'

Papa turned his hands up, letting the knife and the unfinished carving dissolve into golden pixels that quickly disappeared like dying embers from the bonfire. The jaunty gypsy music suddenly seemed incredibly out of place.

'We watch,' Papa said in a thick voice. 'We have no other choice. We watch – and we pray.'

Chapter Fifteen

Ka-boooooom!

The thunderclap of detonation echoed around the Big Top. Dark charcoal-colored smoke boiled from the cannon's mouth before the person inside came shooting out.

Seated in the bleachers watching the show, Andy smiled despite his nervousness as the clowning-ball arced from one side of the left ring to the other. The gunpowder was all flash, noise and smoke, and not a propellant at all. The cannon itself was spring-loaded.

The flying clown bicycled his legs and waved his arms, then crashed into the pirate ship that had been created from huge foam blocks. A Jolly Roger flew proudly from the ship's prow.

Despite the fact that the human projectile hadn't really touched them, the clowns dressed in loose-fitting pirate costumes waving rubber cutlasses went down like tenpins. Then the boarding party of hero clowns that had fired the cannon rushed among them with fully operational cream pies and vanquished their foes.

After the final obligatory humorous lines had been played out, the spotlights dimmed on the ring. Another spotlight opened on the ringmaster in the center ring.

Andy's stomach spasmed as he realized the man was standing where the safety net had been that morning. *The same safety net that had caught Syeira each time she fell this morning.*

'Ladies and gentlemen,' the ringmaster announced in his rolling basso voice, 'tonight Cservanka Brothers is proud to announce the dawning of a new star under the Big Top.'

Even though he didn't want to, Andy glanced up. There, in the upper reaches of the Big Top, shadows clustered on both sides of the flying trapeze.

Matt sat calmly beside him in holo-form, his hands resting naturally between his knees. 'It's going to be okay.'

Andy fidgeted constantly, feeling like he was coming apart at the seams. 'You didn't see her falling during practice.'

'We're not here to watch her fall.'

'Tonight,' the ringmaster went on, 'join me in welcoming the talented Miss Syeira!' He waved and the spotlight sped from him, picking up Syeira as she ran to the center ring from the tent flaps.

Syeira faced the crowd and bowed in three directions. Her costume was brief, barely covering her, figure-hugging black and soft aqua. The aqua cape over her shoulders reached the sand.

The crowd roared its approval and thundered applause.

A clown rushed up from the shadows with an armload of red roses wrapped in paper. The clown doffed his hat and presented the roses to Syeira. She took the flowers, kissed the clown on the cheek, and stepped into the rope loop that had dropped behind her. She held onto the rope with her free hand as the other aerialists pulled her up. The spotlight tracked her.

Andy watched her go up and up and up. His mind, ever active, splintered, tracking down every conceivable action that could go wrong. He felt like he lived a thousand lifetimes in those few seconds.

Syeira stepped out of the rope even with the platform on the left. Another girl, one who would never leave the safety of the bars, took the roses from Syeira and placed them securely out of the way.

Quiet fell over the crowd.

High in the Big Top now, Syeira looked tiny. She presented herself to the crowd again, curling one arm above her head and smiling. Behind her, arms folded across his chest, Traian stood like he had as much to risk as the aerialists waiting to perform.

'There's Papa.'

Andy followed Matt's pointing finger and spotted Papa in the shadows near the right ring. Papa wore his clown suit and makeup but he wasn't making balloon animals for the kids in the audience the way he normally did. His eyes were totally locked on the flying trapeze.

Even though she'd never performed on the trapeze bars before an audience, Syeira teased them like a pro. She shrugged out of the aqua cape, letting it flutter to the sand below, emphasizing how great the distance was. Then she took the trapeze bar hooked to the pole beside her. She flipped it out experimentally, letting it glide back and forth on its own.

On the other side, Jorund – an aerialist who'd come from Norway – grabbed the other bar and swung out across the distance. He performed a few easy maneuvers, arcing his body high, releasing for a moment to reverse his hands, then flipped upside down to make his hands ready for Syeira.

Syeira swung out on her bar then, going through her own exercises. She moved effortlessly, totally graceful.

'She's good,' Matt commented.

'It only takes one mistake,' Andy whispered.

Like a seasoned pro, Syeira warmed up, getting her arc to match Jorund's, getting her speed and height up, getting ready to let go. She pulled herself into a sitting position on the trapeze bar, and fell backward in a sudden tumble that left her hanging from her folded knees.

She reached for Jorund but he only got one hand.

'No,' Andy breathed, almost coming up from the bleachers.

Syeira released her hold, then concentrated on swinging the bar again. This time Jorund caught both her hands and she unfolded her legs, dangling from the man's grip, each of them holding the other by the wrists. She dismounted on the platform opposite where she'd begun.

She bowed when she was safe, and the crowd responded a little. Simply being ferried from one platform to another wasn't what they'd come to see.

The swings came faster. Jorund took Syeira by the hands again and she folded up, holding onto his forearms while he grabbed her by the ankles. When she was in place, swinging upside down from her partner's hands, the other bar was put into motion again. She grabbed the bar as it came toward her and Jorund released her.

Andy tensed, knowing the routine only got harder from this point on.

Syeira progressed from simply grabbing hold of her partner to letting go her trapeze and grabbing his hands. Each time she seemed to freeze in mid-air, chilling Andy to the bone. On the return back to her own trapeze bar, the swing adjusted and timed by one of the aerialists waiting on the other platform, Jorund released her and she flipped once, catching the bar.

'Oh, man,' Andy groaned. And even though he whispered, the words carried over the people around him. Only silence filled the Big Top.

On the way back to Jorund, Syeira released the bar and twirled in a skater's twist two complete revolutions. Jorund's catch was a near miss that caused an eruption of applause from the audience when everyone saw that she was safe.

Still in motion, Syeira swung back, going into the double somersault that was the high point of her routine. That morning, Andy had only seen her complete three of the five attempts.

Finishing the second somersault, her hands gripping her legs held tightly together and straight out before her, rolling up into a ball, she snapped open like a spring. Her hands reached for the bar, trying to rake it in as it started away from her.

Andy just knew she'd missed. His heart seemed to stop as he stood.

'No,' someone in the crowd pleaded.

'She missed,' someone else whispered hoarsely.

Syeira reached desperately, managing to get one hand on the bar but the other missed.

Then the lights went out and total dark filled the Big Top.

For a moment Andy thought he'd been knocked offline. He'd chosen to use one of the computer-link chairs the circus provided and attend the circus performance in holo rather than being physically there. As a holo, he didn't have to get lost in the crowd.

With strobing, eye-burning intensity, the emergency lights flared to life around the inside of the Big Top. The spotlights had thrown out light bright as day in center ring, but the emergency lights only created a vague, hazy twilight.

Standing now, Andy stared up at the flying trapeze.

Syeira dangled by one hand from the bar.

Andy moved, stepping up over the crowd, walking on air, stair-stepping up quickly. In normal holo-projections, someone in holo had to obey everyday physical laws like gravity and not being able to walk through walls. On the Net, things were different because anything went.

He was able to run up the air because of a program Mark Gridley had designed that circumnavigated the physical laws. When Andy had used the circus computer-link chair, he'd accessed Mark's program from his own archived files.

Around him, people panicked and surged toward the lighted exits. Shouting voices and piercing cries of scared kids filled the air. Most of the out-of-city holo-visitors had disappeared along with the power. Matt was still there because Andy had patched him through the computer-link chair he was using.

Andy ran, gaining height, streaking for the lone figure dangling from the trapeze bar.

'Syeira!' he called.

She swung, frozen, looking down at the ground so far away. She made no response.

'Syeira!' Andy closed on her rapidly, scanning the single hand she had wrapped around the trapeze bar. *Are her fingers slipping?* 'Syeira! Snap out of it!'

Dully, her head came up and she struggled to focus on him. The trapeze swing's arcs lessened, barely moving ten feet now.

'Andy,' Syeira whispered. She reached for him with her free hand.

'No!' Andy shouted.

Shocked, she drew her hand back, suddenly twisting and off-balance as she hung by the one arm.

'Grab the bar,' Andy commanded. 'Grab the bar so you don't fall.'

Syeira flailed, shifting her weight, and grabbed the bar with her other hand. She pulled herself up into a seated position but Andy could see she was trembling.

Andy glanced around, expecting that the power would have been renewed and shocked that it wasn't. 'Can you swing back to the platform?'

'Yes,' she croaked.

'Then do it,' Andy ordered, 'before things get worse.' He looked for Traian, surprised to find that her uncle had vanished as well. *Probably came through an outside Net hook-up and got cut off.*

He stayed with Syeira as she pumped her legs. When she got close enough, the male aerialist grabbed the trapeze bar rope and pulled her in. He helped her to the platform, then offered her a rope to slide down. Andy floated down after her, moving as effortlessly as if he were in zero-gee. They touched ground at the same time.

'What's going on?' Syeira asked in a voice that cracked.

Andy shook his head. 'Don't know.' He spotted Papa by one of the main exits, calling out to people and directing them with an orange glowing hazard light cone. 'Some kind of power failure.'

'We have our own generators,' Syeira reminded him. 'And then there are back-up generators.'

'I know,' Andy said. 'Wait here.'

'Where are you going?'

'To try to find out what's going on.'

The fleeing audience blocked the exit, filling the doorway. Rather than risk any program integrity field interference, Andy ran for the wall beside the door. A brief chill touched him as he passed through it. Then he was outside.

Emile the stilt-clown towered above the fleeing crowd. 'Calm down, folks,' he cried. 'Slow down before one of the kids gets hurt.'

Unfortunately, the crowd was too panicked and confused to listen very well. They scattered around Emile and someone hit him hard enough to nearly knock him from his long legs.

'Where are the generators?' Matt asked. He stood at Andy's side.

'Behind the backyard.' Andy took off through the crowd, weaving through them as he ran. He briefly considered logging off but decided he had a better chance to see what was going on if he remained in holo-form.

'Where's the backyard?' Matt asked.

'Behind the Big Top.' Andy dashed through the midway, glancing at the darkened hulks of the concession stands and sideshow events. Whatever the power shortage was, it was complete except for the internal systems like the virtual circus in Wallachia and the computer-link chairs and holo-projectors.

A crowd coming out of the Hall of Terror maze blocked the way ahead.

Without hesitation, Andy stepped into the air and leaped over them. He hit the ground running on the other side.

The generators were mounted on five three-quarter-ton trucks that were parked closely together. The systems were tied into a main electronic board housed in a small trailer. The generator cables wound like fat, black pythons across the ground and plugged into the hook-ups on the trailer's side.

The trailer sat dark and silent. Sparks flared inside it and thick smoke poured from the open door and windows. Petar Jancso stood in the doorway peering inside, a handkerchief pressed against his lower face.

'What happened?' Andy asked.

'Looks like a circuit board went out,' the little clown replied, pointing at the red fire extinguisher at his feet. 'I put out all the flames I saw but there could be more.'

The odor of burning plastic warred with the strong scent of ozone in the air.

Andy stepped up the short flight of steps leading into the trailer and peered inside. The smoke made it impossible to discern anything. White frost from the fire extinguisher still dappled some surfaces. 'Did you see anyone when you got here?'

Petar coughed and shook his head. 'I was the first one here.'

Other circus performers arrived, all wanting to know what was going on.

'Where's Radu?' Andy asked.

'I saw him around the animal pens only a little while ago. I've been trying to keep an eye on him.' Petar only spoke loud enough that Andy could hear.

Andy left Petar there answering questions from the other performers who were just arriving.

'The smoke may have upset the animals,' Matt pointed out as they sprinted for the animal corrals. 'Their sense of smell is keener than ours.'

Imanuela! A shiver of dread ran through Andy, surprising him that he could have any terror left to feel after the last few moments.

The animal handlers were already hard at work calming things when Andy and Matt arrived. The elephants moved restlessly in their enclosures, and the horses trotted skittishly.

The trained dogs barked incessantly, adding to the confusion.

Andy raced around them, heading for Imanuela's corral. Pale gray smoke from the electrical fire in the trailer wisped through the area.

His hopes were in vain. Imanuela had lowered her head and was pulling against her ankle chain, rattling it. Her eyes rolled wildly in fear. She flapped her ears and trumpeted. She surged forward again. Usually docile, Imanuela had never tested her fastenings before, but the combination of the smoke and panic in the air, her difficult pregnancy, and the meds she was on to control it, all contributed to the elephant's loss of control.

Two handlers, dressed as clowns, abandoned their efforts to try to control her. She trumpeted again and pulled hard. The pillar she was tethered to shivered.

Andy stopped short of Imanuela's corral and started calling out to her, hoping to get her to listen to his voice. With all the other noise and confusion going on, he didn't know if that was possible.

Some of the panicked circus visitors ran through the animal area. A tiger growled at a group that got too close to its cage. Two women in the group screamed and dodged away, falling to the ground and taking a half-dozen other people with them.

The straw house, filled to capacity, was working against the circus now.

'Imanuela!' Syeira came at a dead run.

Andy stepped in front of her, instinctively thinking to hold her back from the cage. Syeira didn't even see him until it was too late, then she ran through him like he wasn't there – which he wasn't since he was only a holo. He felt a cold chill as the programming tried to resolve the conflicting data.

'Don't!' Andy yelled at her back. 'She doesn't know what she's doing! She could hurt you!'

Syeira vaulted to the top of the corral, talking as soothingly to the elephant as she could in a loud voice. Then Imanuela pulled again. The chain holding her leg snapped. Trumpeting, she ran out into the open, scattering people in all directions. Whether by design or panic, Imanuela ran back toward the dark circus tents, cresting the tide of fleeing circus visitors.

Andy hesitated, looking back to where Syeira had fallen. She pushed herself up. 'Are you okay?' he asked.

'I'm fine,' she said. 'We have to stop Imanuela before she hurts herself.'

Or someone else, Andy thought.

'We've got trouble,' Matt said. 'The local police have arrived.'

In disbelief, Andy watched the spinning red and blue lights of the police car swing into view near the Big Top. The driver raced through the midway section, spotlights playing over the dark tents and booths. Then the driver saw Imanuela heading straight for the car.

The police car's nose dipped as the driver floored the brakes. A huge dust cloud boiled up behind the vehicle. The police officers kicked their doors open and took positions behind them. Even at the distance Andy could tell one of them held a semi-automatic pistol and the other had a shotgun. Both leveled their weapons at the rampaging elephant.

Imanuela never broke stride.

Chapter Sixteen

Andy ran, losing the holo-enforced gravity and real-time restraints by accessing Mark's program and overriding the holo-projectors. Even moving fast as he was, he was afraid the police officers would shoot Imanuela before he could intercept her.

Although the average African elephant stood ten to thirteen feet tall at the shoulder, in his enhanced holo-form Andy had no problem vaulting up onto Imanuela's back with two hands like a cowboy trick rider. He ran across the elephant's back, waving his hands to attract the attention of the police officers.

'Hold up!' the police officer with the shotgun shouted. 'There's a kid up there!'

In holo-form, Andy knew Imanuela couldn't feel his weight but could nevertheless see and hear him. Still weightless thanks to Mark's utility program, he slid down Imanuela's head, appearing in front of her.

The elephant stopped suddenly, throwing her weight back and stopping only a few feet short of the police car.

'Easy, Imanuela,' Andy said. 'Just take it easy. Everything's going to be all right.'

Imanuela rocked from side to side, shifting her feet, obviously ready to start running again. She coiled her trunk, trying to wrap it around him, but her sinuous snout only passed through Andy. She trumpeted in frustration.

Then Syeira was there, pulling on one of Imanuela's ears to get her attention. The elephant coiled her trunk around

Syeira and lifted her up. Syeira clambered adroitly to the top of Imanuela's head and sat on her neck. Talking gently, but loud enough to be heard above the confusion rampaging through the circus grounds, Syeira guided the elephant away from the police car and back toward the animal cages.

When Andy glanced at the police officers, he saw that Matt was already running interference, announcing that they were both Net Force Explorers. Andy was glad to let him do it.

Confusion and panic still reigned the circus grounds. More police arrived, their flashing lights strobing the darkness that had descended over the Big Top, the other tents and the booths along the midway. It was hard to believe that the area had been full of laughter and amusement only minutes ago.

Andy sat up from the computer-link chair in the gaming area of the midway. The main lighting in the booth was gone, victim to whatever had knocked out the other systems, but the emergency lights revealed that he was the only one left in the room.

He pushed himself out of the chair and ran outside. Glancing to the left, he spotted Imanuela and Syeira retreating in the harsh glare of the police car's headlights. To the right, Papa was talking to a group of clowns and circus performers.

Not certain what he was supposed to do, Andy turned and headed toward the animal cages. He wanted to make sure Imanuela was all right.

Just before he reached the back of the police car blocking the way, he saw someone stumble and fall out of the corner of his eye. He turned, staring down the narrow alley between concession stands, thinking it was a circus-goer, thinking maybe it was someone having a heart attack.

As he sprinted between the concession stands, he slipped his foilpack from his pocket and reconfigured it into a phone.

The shadowy figure pushed up weakly from the ground. A shaft of red light, followed by blue, whipped across the man's features and Andy recognized him as Martin Radu. The twenty-four-hour man clutched his side in apparent agony.

Just before Andy got to the end of the alley between the concession booths, a man stepped into his view and backhanded Radu across the face. Obviously weakened, Radu dropped to his knees.

Confused and a little afraid, Andy skidded to a stop only a few feet away. He remained hidden in the shadows of a corndog booth.

The man yelled at Radu in a language Andy couldn't understand. He moved closer, then filled his fists with Radu's shirt and jerked the man to his feet.

Radu protested weakly in the same language, covering his face and head by wrapping his arms around them.

Andy breathed quietly, scanning the area. Behind the man who held Radu were two other men and a woman. All three men were dark complexioned, with dark hair and eyes. Andy would have hated to try to pick them out of a line-up.

But the woman was different. Where the men seemed to project angry menace, the woman held a cruel elegance. She stood almost six feet tall, an impressive figure, broad-shouldered and slim-hipped like a professional athlete. Andy guessed she was in her thirties from the way she acted, though based on her appearance she would have passed for ten years younger. Her chestnut-brown hair was pulled back in a French braid. She had high cheekbones and a wide, generous mouth. She wore a dark bronze Armani suit. She also wore wraparound sunglasses that had a particular glint to them that reminded Andy of some of the nightvision shades Net Force agents used in urban areas for night maneuvers.

With all the noise and confusion going on around the circus, no one else even noticed these people.

The woman talked quietly in the same language the men and Radu used. All of them, Andy noticed, listened to her speak; there was no interruptions and no questions.

And when she finished, Radu nodded, making no move to

brush away the trickle of blood that ran from his split lip to his chin.

The woman's voice turned glacial. 'Mazerak,' she barked.

Instantly, the big man standing in front of Radu reached inside his jacket and brought out a 10mm pistol. He pushed the muzzle into Radu's face.

Terror spread across Radu's features as he tried to bend backward away from the weapon.

The woman said something else.

Radu's reply this time was much longer. And the name Cantara was repeated three times.

Without another word, the woman turned and walked away. The man with the pistol held Radu there on the ground until the woman and the other men were well away.

Andy had to restrain himself from rushing the man with the gun. The only thing stopping him was the fact that the guy seemed like a total professional. If he surprised them, Andy felt certain the man would kill Radu, then turn the pistol on him. And if Radu was convinced that he was about to die, Andy was certain the man wouldn't just sit there.

Finally, the man with the pistol smiled coldly. He pulled the weapon away and touched his forehead with it in a brief salute. Then the pistol disappeared and so did the man.

Andy released a tense breath he hadn't even been aware that he was holding.

Gasping, his mouth rounded with effort, Radu fell forward and barely caught himself on his hands. His body shivered uncontrollably for a few seconds, then he pushed himself up on shaking arms and legs. A dark stain covered the side of his shirt and Andy knew that it was blood.

Briefly, Andy considered calling one of the police officers over but he got the feeling that Radu wouldn't press charges – or even admit what had just happened. And without Radu's compliance, Andy and the police would never find out what had just happened here.

Andy also had the feeling that the woman wouldn't allow

herself to be easily arrested. Since so far nobody but Radu had been hurt, Andy didn't want that to change.

Radu placed his arm back over his side and started walking, weaving from side to side. As soon as he reached a more populated area, he was spotted. He waved off other circus performers who offered help and assaulted him with questions and demands, and ignored the customers who were getting over their initial panic and were now getting irate.

Quietly, staying within the shadows, Andy trailed along behind Radu. Following the woman didn't seem like a good idea.

A few minutes later, Radu made it to his personal trailer. When he fumbled with the doorknob and key, he left blood smears on the trailer's white finish. Before he entered, he wiped the door clean with his shirttail.

Andy's mind worked on overtime, trying to figure out how Radu and the woman and her followers fitted in. Obviously they were mad at Radu and it probably wasn't anything to do with the circus or they'd have talked to Papa as well.

So what was it?

He remembered the way Radu had entered the strongman's booth back in Alexandria, and he remembered how Radu had been upset although he'd said nothing had been taken. And then there were the open barbells, revealing all the empty space inside.

For the moment, Andy shelved the speculation. He didn't know enough to make any concrete guesses. He slipped through the shadows and got close to Radu's trailer.

Unexpectedly, the lights came back on around the circus, stripping away most of the shadows. Luckily the one Andy was standing in remained. He sidled down the trailer to the bathroom area. Most of the small, personal trailers were set up with a dining area/office in the front half, with a bed and small bath in the back. The sound of running water came from the bath.

The window was just out of Andy's reach.

Balancing himself carefully, Andy put a foot on the tire and pushed himself up, pressing his palms against the side of the trailer to maintain his balance. He leaned sideways and peered into the small window.

Radu stood in front of the washbasin and took off his bloody shirt. His face held none of the terror Andy had seen earlier. Radu was totally dispassionate, even when he saw the small, bloody hole in his side.

Andy knew then it was a bullet hole.

Twisting around, Radu gazed at his back in the mirror. The bullet had gone completely through the flesh, leaving a slightly larger exit wound than the entry one. Both wounds still bled. The man knelt and removed a small first-aid kit from under the sink. He selected the bandages and medicines expertly.

Judging from the scars on his torso, Andy figured that Radu had gotten plenty of experience with knife and bullet wounds. There were even clusters of burn scarring. Martin Radu hadn't lived a quiet or peaceful life.

Still, Andy wondered if the woman represented old business that Radu couldn't outrun anymore, or if she was new business, the force behind something that was going on now.

Radu took a needle from the first-aid kit and threaded it with surgical nylon as though he had done it all his life. After making sure that the wounds were both clean, he pushed the curved needle through his flesh, then tied off the first stitch.

Andy's knee buckled without warning, giving way to the uncomfortable position he was in atop the tire. His leg thumped the side of the trailer.

Radu's head whipped around and he stared at the window. A small pistol appeared in his hand like magic. 'Who is there?' he demanded.

Andy pushed away from the trailer, dropping to the ground and sprinting back toward the circus. He glanced over his shoulder and saw Radu's face shoved up against the window screen. Andy was certain he hadn't been seen because the light in the trailer would have worked against Radu.

But he still had no clue what Radu's encounter meant.

'Come on, Andy. It's time to get up.'

Andy struggled through layers of sleep, not really waking up, just kind of reaching a lucid grogginess that he assumed would pass for social function. He looked around and saw that several of the clowns in the trailer were already gone, but at least today they hadn't all beaten him to rising.

Still dressed in last night's clothes, he swung his legs over the side of the bed, discovering that he still had one shoe on. It took a semi-serious search to find the other shoe.

He looked through the open doorway at Syeira. 'Has something happened?' His mind flip-flopped back and forth between Imanuela and Martin Radu. He hadn't told anyone what he'd seen last night, not even Matt. Before he did anything he wanted to figure out what it was he was supposed to do.

'Everything,' Syeira replied.

Andy grabbed his toiletry kit and a fresh pair of jeans and a shirt. He joined Syeira outside. The circus performers all headed for the cookhouse. They ate lunch at different times during the day, but Papa insisted that they all eat breakfast together.

'Everything?' Andy asked. 'Want to give me a Cliff's Notes version?'

'It's the Holo-Net,' Syeira said disgustedly. 'It must have been a slow news night because what happened last night received a lot more coverage than we would have expected.'

'They say bad press beats no press.'

'Only an idiot would say that.' Syeira took long strides, making Andy hurry to keep up.

The smell of baking breads, frying meats and tangy spices filled the air inside the cookhouse. During a show, the cookhouse doubled as a dining area for the customers grazing from the concession stands in the midway. Long tables with built-on folding benches on either side filled the cookhouse's central area.

No one at the tables had started eating yet. The cooks watched over the grill area and the ovens but they weren't serving out.

Papa sat at his customary small table at the end of the service line where he met with performers over breakfast. He had a regular routine with some of them to discuss various aspects of the circus, as well as concerns about acts and equipment needs. Sometimes those breakfasts even managed to just be social visits, but not very often.

Today, his face held none of the usual ebullience. He sat quietly, nodding to a few of the performers.

Andy took his cue from Syeira and remained quiet. The silence in the cookhouse was almost intolerable. Usually even when everyone had only gotten a few hours of sleep, the place was a madhouse. Conversations in a dozen different languages were held from one end of the cookhouse to the other. There were also practical jokes and pranks, and the clowns weren't the worst of the lot.

Martin Radu was one of the last dozen or so to arrive.

Papa stood up from his small table and somehow the quiet got even quieter. 'My friends,' he said, 'my family, all of you are aware of the problems we had last night. Some of you know about the reports on Holo-Net.'

Emile blew a raspberry. 'If there'd been any real news yesterday, they wouldn't even have covered what happened here.'

'Is the city council asking us to leave?' Radu asked quietly.

Papa shook his head. 'No. I called them this morning and left a message saying we would be leaving by tonight.'

'Why, Papa?' Claire, one of the bareback riders, asked.

Papa faced the assembled performers. 'This circus has lost two acts over the last few days. We need to take stock and make sure we are ready for our next engagement. If we leave now, we have eight days to get ready for our debut in St Louis, Missouri.'

'But, Papa, how we gonna make our nut by cutting back on work like that?' Josef was a skinny old man who habitually wore overalls and an engineer's hat. He was a mechanic and usually worked on the kiddy rides as well.

The nut he referred to, Andy had learned, was a term for the cost of doing business. In the old days, when a circus rolled into town, policemen acting on behalf of the towns that had agreed to host them, had actually taken wheel nuts off the wagons, not returning them to the circus until the agreed-upon price for allowing the performance was paid to the town.

'It's just a few shows.'

'And I know about them shows, Papa,' Josef went on. 'They bring in lots of money, money we ain't gonna have now.'

Instantly, many of the performers began talking in hushed tones. Various levels of concern, worry and fear tightened their voices.

Money, Andy had discovered over the last few days, was always a concern at the circus. Especially with the endowment contract so close to being at an end.

'You will get your pay,' Papa promised. 'Have I ever stiffed any of you?'

'I'm not worried about you, Papa,' Josef said, looking a little guilty. 'I'm just worried about them banks. Sometimes they say you got the money, sometimes they say you don't got it. I don't know about them banks.'

Papa shrugged. 'Then I can pay you in advance, Josef.'

The old mechanic scratched the back of his neck and didn't meet Papa's gaze. 'I'm just a little nervous, I guess. I always know a chicken in the pot is worth two in the bush, you know?'

'I know,' Papa replied gently.

'If you can pay a check like that,' Josef said, 'then I guess maybe we're okay.'

'How can you do this?' In a twinkle of light, Traian appeared in the cookhouse only a few feet from Papa. He was dressed in a flamboyant trapeze costume with a high collar. 'Are you going to run this circus, Anghel? Or are you going to let them do it?'

Papa shook his head. 'This is none of your concern, Traian.'

'Of course it's my concern,' Traian stated angrily. 'This is the Cservanka *Brothers* Circus, remember? This isn't Anghel's Circus.'

'Traian, please, this isn't the time—'

'Wrong. This is exactly the time.' Traian whirled on the performers seated at the tables. 'Do you know why Papa is shutting down the show?'

No one dared answer. Andy knew it was because any voice would become a target for Traian's wrath.

'The power supply last night,' Traian said, 'was deliberately destroyed.'

Chapter Seventeen

Conversation started in the cookhouse then and there was no holding it back. Andy glanced at Syeira, who nodded.

'We've got traitors in our midst,' Traian declared over the dull roar of voices. 'I look at you and wonder how many of you are really true to this circus.'

Some of the performers turned away.

Traian continued to pace angrily, his eyes raking the circus performers. 'How dare you question Papa's loyalty when treachery is everywhere around us! And now, he offers to pay you eight days wages for lazing about, and you want that in advance! You should be working among yourselves to drive out the weak ones, the ones who don't believe in this circus!'

No one could meet Traian's fierce gaze.

'You don't know what a real circus is,' Traian declared. 'You're supposed to be a family. Yet here you are, worried about your own problems.'

'They are real problems,' Josef retorted.

'Yeah,' Traian said, 'and every time you've had a problem, this circus has been here to take care of you. Or have you forgotten that?'

Without warning, Traian winked out of existence.

Andy knew the holo-projector power had to have been switched off.

Papa stepped from behind the counter. 'Well,' he stated quietly into the silence. 'I guess enough has been said about that. We'll be leaving for St Louis as soon as I can make the travel arrangements.' He turned and walked out of the cookhouse.

The silence in the building was complete for a short time. A few of the performers glanced at Syeira, who tried in vain to ignore them.

'I think I'm going to skip breakfast,' she told Andy. 'I don't think I have much of an appetite now.'

'Would you mind company?' Andy asked.

Andy held out a fistful of feed to Imanuela, who snuffled it up quickly with her trunk and shot it into her mouth. *It's good to see that not everyone has lost his or her appetite.*

'You didn't have to come out here with me.' Syeira sat on the corral fence. Since they'd left the cookhouse nearly half an hour ago, she'd been totally silent. 'You could have gone back to bed or had breakfast.'

'Sure,' Andy agreed, 'or I could have tagged along with you and been a friend. I'm kind of happy that I chose the friend thing.'

'Me, too,' Syeira admitted. 'I'm sorry to be such a grouch.'

'You're worried. It's allowed.'

'Shutting the circus down for the next few days is going to hurt Papa financially more than he's letting on.'

'He's been in this business a long time, Syeira. Probably he knows what he's doing.'

'I'm scared, Andy. More scared than I can ever remember being.'

'Even more scared than last night when you almost missed the bar?'

Syeira shivered. 'You know, it's weird, but at the time I wasn't even thinking of the fall.'

Andy couldn't believe it. 'That would have been the first thing that crossed my mind.'

Syeira shook her head. 'It's different up there somehow. It's not about falling, it's about flying.'

'I couldn't do that.'

'Uncle Traian says most people can't. He said that even the flyers that perform over a net can't forget about falling. That's why they keep the net there.'

'Personally, I think the net is a good idea.'

'There are more people who die in a car accident than a fall from a trapeze bar. Flying isn't the problem.'

'Do you really think you're ready for it?'

'I don't know,' she admitted. 'Yet. The circus is the biggest problem. Losing these days here in Mobile is going to wither Papa's financial cushion into nothing to finish the year out. Unless we have some stupendous shows.'

'There's no reason to think that won't happen.'

'There are plenty of reasons to think that might not happen. Klaus and Marie are world-renowned flyers, Andy. They drew audiences wherever we went. Stanislas has his own following. Several people have seen his act on the talk shows and special features on Holo-Net. Papa is afraid other performers are going to leave, too.'

'What about what Traian said? About the power manager unit being sabotaged? Was that true?'

'Yes.'

'Why would someone do that?' Andy asked.

'Uncle Traian thinks it was done by one of the other circuses coming up for reconsideration at the same time we are.'

'What does Papa think?'

'Papa,' Syeira said, 'doesn't know what to think. I've never seen him like this. That's what has me worried most of all.'

Andy moved cautiously through the mirrored maze he had designed, wary of all the splintered images that moved when he did. The images were of a clown thirty feet tall, the painted face and red bulbous nose looking amusing and menacing at the same time.

Without warning another clown slid into view, joining his image reflected in the mirrors. The painted smile looked predatory and chilling.

Seated in the control cockpit of the clown battlesuit, hands and feet encased in cybernetic feedback gloves and boots, Andy swiveled around and brought his right arm straight out. The enemy clown loomed before him, its arm also raising. Andy dropped into a squat as his opponent's hand morphed, becoming a cannon mouth.

A cream pie blasted from the cannon mouth, ripping through the air. Thanks to the programming he'd written, the spinning pie remained vertical, ignoring air friction and gravity, sailing like a missile. The cream pie slammed against the mirrored wall only a few feet above Andy's head. The gooey pie dissolved into the mirrored surface almost at once.

Now you're mine! Andy fired back in retaliation, catching his opponent full in the chest with three cream pies.

Sparks and black smoke coiled around the clown as it stutter-stepped and jumped. The clown battlesuit rattled back and forth between the mirrored walls, then fell backward, going stiff as a board. By the time his opponent fell on his back, his hands joined over his chest and a cluster of white lilies appeared in them.

GAME OVER spelled out in huge green letters in the air.

'Want to play again?' Andy asked. Despite the fatigue that filled him from the last six days of hard labor on the game, he was excited. The circus had moved to St Louis during that time, set up the tents, and was ready to open the doors.

'No,' Martin Radu said. 'You've beaten me six times in a row. I'm convinced that you're much better than me.'

At least no one is holding a loaded cream pie at your head. Andy and Petar had watched Radu over those six days, but the man had never done anything suspicious. Actually, Petar had watched Radu the most because nearly every waking hour Andy had was spent on the game.

'What about the game playability?' Andy asked. He'd created four major game environments, borrowing every game design engine released to the public that he could get his hands on. Besides the Hall of Mirrors battleground, he'd also created a Wallachia scenario involving a vardo race while firing at enemy forces (cream pies and lightning bolts that shot from hand buzzers), a hunt through the circus grounds, and a deep space mission that had been the most taxing of all. Even with Mark Gridley's help, Andy had been surprised at how well the deep-space clown vehicles maneuvered.

'I like it,' Radu said. 'Take me through the deep space mission again. I want to see it once more.'

The targeting program for the deep space mission had been a work of art, Andy knew. He and Mark had worked on it for three days solid. They'd borrowed some of the research and programming Maj Green had developed for her Striper fighter-sim and extrapolated on it. Where Maj's fighter jet could fire air-to-air missiles and air-to-ground missiles from short ranges, the circus game could launch wire-guided cream pies for hundreds of miles. There was, Andy knew, nothing like it out in the gaming field.

Most shooter games preferred their action up close and personal, down and dirty to the max. Radu had specifically asked for the long-range scenario, explaining that it would require more skill for advanced players, and that it would be more of a challenge.

Andy had agreed but the targeting capabilities on the long-range game were definitely cutting-edge. Even a beginning player wouldn't have too much difficulty getting up to speed to fight a long-range mission sim.

'Opposing clowncraft?' Andy asked.

'No. I'll ride with you.'

Andy summoned up the game scenario icon, entered the two-player co-join mode, and tripped the activation code. The clown battlesuit shimmered and winked out of existence.

In the next heartbeat they were skimming earth's outer atmosphere, tracking enemy targets. The clown theme remained but the ship this time followed the basic configurations of a space shuttle that ferries goods and passengers to and from space stations.

Radu sat beside Andy in the co-pilot's seat. If the bullet wound in the man's side gave him any discomfort, he never showed it.

Andy gazed out at the star-filled black space.

'Warning,' a soft, feminine voice stated. 'Unidentified craft are quickly approaching.'

Andy brought up the weapons screen and flew toward the targets. The skirmish with the two opposing clownshuttles was brief, leaving both craft disabled from cream-pie attacks. Andy watched the clownshuttles fall back into earth's gravity well, sprouting lilies just before they burned up in the atmosphere.

'They can't handle me,' Andy said, too tired to restrain his pride in the game. 'I taught them everything they know.'

'You did good, Andy,' Radu said.

Yeah, well, what about you? Are you behind the circus sabotage? Who were those people – that woman and the freaks with the pistols? What were you fighting about? The questions hammered inside Andy's mind but he didn't ask them. Whatever was going on, he *knew* Radu was behind it. And after seeing that gun in Radu's hand when he'd spied on his trailer, Andy had decided to keep his eyes open and his profile low. He was going to call in the cops when he had enough evidence to put Radu away without endangering Papa's circus. All the trouble was centered on or against this circus, and nobody other than Radu had been hurt so far, so Andy had felt justified in sitting on what little evidence he had until he had the whole picture in hand and could safely bring in the law to stop the attacks on this world he'd come to love. 'Thanks.'

'How confident do you feel about the design and your skills?' Radu asked. 'I've got an opponent for you if you think you're ready.'

Andy looked at the man, his suspicions flaring. 'Sure.'

Radu brought up a phonelink icon and pressed it. A viewscreen didn't open up, but the woman's voice sounded in the clownshuttle cabin clearly. 'Are you ready to play?'

'Yes,' the woman answered.

'He is quite good. I hope you don't find yourself embarrassed.'

'I assure you,' the woman replied. 'I am quite good myself. Don't worry about me.'

Andy felt chilled. Even though she was speaking English now instead of whatever language she'd spoken a few nights back, he recognized her as the woman who'd threatened Radu.

'Let her into the game,' Radu told Andy.

Andy opened the game up to the incoming signal, but held off lowering the pass/don't pass architecture that allowed access into the game. Virtual and real guests of the circus were allowed into the games when they purchased their tickets.

'How familiar are you with gaming?' Andy asked.

'Very,' the woman replied.

'Check your onboard mapping and skills archives,' Andy advised. 'The files there will download pilot's skills as well as debris involving the terrain you're going to be exposed to.'

'I've already done that,' the woman said. 'Space is space, after all.' She sounded like she'd already been there, whether in real life or on the Net.

Andy wondered which. 'I'm Captain Andy,' he introduced himself, hoping he would get a name.

'You may call me Harpy,' the woman replied. 'Major Harpy.'

Okay, Andy thought, *now she's pulling rank on me*. He grinned despite the weirdness of the situation. With all the threats the woman had made to Radu, why would he want her to take a tour of the circus game? And why would she be interested?

A blip fired on his sensor screen.

'I have you on my screen,' the woman said.

'But not in your sights,' Andy quipped. He took evasive action, skimming into low earth orbit, staying just out of the gravity well's clutches. The planet spun slowly beneath him, blue seas and brown landmasses covered over in places by white clouds.

'No,' the woman admitted. 'Not yet.' Her confidence was undeniable.

'Have you flown suborbital fighter craft before?' Andy asked. His sensors indicated the woman had cut in her thrusters. In the present mode, fuel and armament were endless and didn't have to be parceled out.

'Many times.'

For real or just in a gaming environment? Andy couldn't shake the merciless image of the woman staring down at Radu.

'How did you design your sensor array?' she asked.

Andy watched the kilometers separating them disappearing in heartbeats. She definitely wasn't holding anything back. 'it's based on GPS programs available to meteorologists through weather satellites. I also piggybacked some public news feeds.'

'So you can pinpoint places that actually exist in different countries?'

'Sure.' Andy shrugged. He dropped out of the suborbital path and plunged earthward. The woman continued to close the distance, almost within firing range now. 'Mr Radu felt that it was important game-players be able to fly over their own cities. Kind of a fun thing to do. If you'll hold off for a moment, I'll show you something.'

'Proceed. I will spare you for the moment.'

Andy cut the clownshuttle comm and glanced at Radu. 'Nothing wrong with her confidence.'

Radu didn't look at him, continuing to watch the earth sweeping up at them from below. 'No. She's very sure of herself.'

'I tend to be full of surprises.' Andy sideshifted through the game environment by accessing his edit tools. In the next eyeblink, they were above the circus in St Louis. The

Gateway to the West gleamed above the dirty brown Mississippi River. The business skyline of the downtown sector rose in towering skyscrapers. Paddleboats, real and virtual, plied the slow-moving river.

'You can access the outside world?' the woman asked.

'In a sense,' Andy said. 'We can see them, but they can't see us. I don't have access to holo-form projectors, just live-link satellite feeds. We can't interact with the real or online environments the city controls like you can in holo-form.' He brought his weps up and fired a spray of cream pies at the Gateway arch. 'See?'

The cream pies hammered the arch but disappeared almost instantly, leaving no trace behind.

'It's just as well we can't play in holo-form. I wouldn't want people turning in reports about UFOs to the local law enforcement agencies or to Net Force,' Andy said.

'And you can do this all over the world?' the woman asked.

'Not yet,' Andy said. 'But I've added in all the cities that the circus is going to visit over the next few months.'

'But adding others worldwide is no problem?'

Andy couldn't help wondering why she was so interested, but then again, maybe she was a lubefoot, an expert on Net programming. In addition to possibly being a cold-blooded killer or circus saboteur.

'It won't be a problem at all,' Andy said.

'Very impressive.'

'Want to take a look at Antarctica?' Andy asked.

The woman sounded amused. 'Why do you have Antarctica programmed?'

'It's glacial,' Andy responded. 'There's a lot of interesting terrain. I've programmed in avalanches and atmospheric phenomenon.'

'And you think you have your best chance there?'

'Yeah. You're still wanting to play?'

'Of course. I live for the thrill of the hunt.'

Andy believed her. He accessed the edit tools again, adding

a splashy rainbow-colored science-fiction movie special effect that was decades old and really cheesy by current standards.

When the special effect faded, they were racing across the frozen tundra. Winter white spread in all directions, making it hard to see some of the sudden upthrust shelves of ice that rose as much as fifty and sixty feet high.

Andy flew nap-of-the-earth, depending on his instruments and his familiarity with the terrain to make the difference. Plus, there were some things about this particular Antarctica that the woman couldn't know.

Andy adjusted the yoke, shedding more altitude. He ran scarcely twenty feet above the ground. A polar bear leaped away from a hole broken through the ice, a galloping hulk in white fur. Andy heeled the clownshuttle over to the left, standing it on one wedge-shaped wing. Normally the clownshuttle didn't handle like a fighter jet in normal atmosphere, but the specialty programming allowed it to. Despite being heeled over, the G-forces kept him and Radu pressed back in their seats.

'How good is she?' Andy asked. He checked his sensors, seeing that the woman had located him on her sensors and was again closing the distance.

'I've never seen anything she couldn't handle.'

So why are you along? Andy wondered. *Is it because she wants you here, or do you want to see if she's as good as she thinks she is?*

'I've found you, Captain Andy,' the woman said.

'Yeah, well, you still have to catch me.' Andy dipped down into a huge canyon nearly two hundred feet deep, shaped like someone had hit the ice with a gigantic ax. Jagged white walls filled the view on both sides. He descended within the canyon, having no more than ten to twenty feet on either side of the clown shuttle to use. It couldn't have flown in the canyon horizontally.

The other craft closed the distance like a homing missile.

Chapter Eighteen

As Andy flew through the Antarctic terrain, the canyon became rockier, and the straight split suddenly widened and fragmented into a choice of three different canyons. He selected the one on the right, watching the three-dee mapping instrumentation.

The woman flew into the middle or left canyon because the clownshuttle's sideward-looking sonar suddenly lost the ping. The overhead GPS satellite connection still showed him both craft however.

Working quickly, Andy dropped speed, knowing that he'd only get one chance for the maneuver he had in mind. He popped up from the canyon and put full flaps down, creating intense air drag that tried to pull him and Radu from their seats. The three canyons continued to run mostly parallel. He watched the screen as the woman's clownshuttle passed him by.

Rolling to the left, Andy watched the GPS images and aligned his clownshuttle behind hers. She didn't immediately pop into the sky, telling him that she was definitely a pro in gaming if not in actual aerial combat. He kicked in full thrusters as he settled into the canyon. This one was wider, allowing him to fly level. He rested his hand lightly on the stick, thumb near the firing buttons.

The woman broke in over the comm. 'Very clever.'

'Pull,' Andy said.

'Pull? Oh, I see. As in skeet shooting.'

'Yeah.' That was precisely the idea Andy had in mind.

'Perhaps I'm more capable than you believe.'

'We're going to find out.' Andy sped through the canyon. 'You see, I know that this particular canyon ends soon.'

The woman remained on course.

Andy felt pretty good. He'd taken Matt Hunter and Mark Gridley in these canyons, getting on their tails and waiting till they popped up to cream-pie them from the sky.

Without warning, the woman's clownshuttle rose up above the canyon walls.

Andy went after her, expecting her to break to the left or right, or kick in full afterburners and hope to outrun him. Then the dropping distance between the two craft turned into a blue as the numbers spun. Andy was closing too fast and he knew it. Why had she cut her speed? It didn't make sense.

Then he got visual ping, knowing he could see her with his naked eye. He glanced up from the instrumentation and spotted the silvery gleam in front of him. 'Time to get splotzed.'

The woman didn't say anything. Maybe she didn't have any last words.

Andy dropped his thumb, vetting both heat-seeking Boston Cremes less than a mile out. Impact and detonation was only seconds away.

The woman held steady just long enough that he believed she'd accepted the inevitability of defeat. Then she jettisoned the on-board flares, creating a multitude of sparks across the sky that were intended to confuse the heat-seekers. As soon as the emergency maneuver was carried out, she pulled back hard, executing a barrel roll that was an absolute marvel to behold.

Andy juked hard to the right, avoiding the crystalline ridge of mountains to his left. He only had the one move open to him, and he knew that she had to be aware of it.

'Now,' the woman said, 'pull.'

'She has you,' Radu commented glumly.

Andy didn't say anything. He watched as the woman barrel-rolled into position behind him.

She attacked, opening up with the twin machine guns that fired miniature cream pies. They slammed into the clownshuttle's sides, rattling the whole craft.

'You can't get away,' Radu said.

'Since escape is out of the question,' Andy stated calmly, 'I guess destroying her is the only way out.'

Radu looked at him.

Andy only smiled, jettisoning his own flares when the woman fired her two Boston Creams. The flares took out both homing missiles. He rolled the clownshuttle over, climbing as he spiraled over and over, getting his GPS position and streaking straight out to sea.

'You can run,' the woman taunted, 'but you can't hide.'

'I'm not hiding,' Andy growled. He kept the afterburners open as he flew, running thirty and forty feet above the terrain. The Atlantic Ocean gleamed ahead of him, only a few miles – a few heartbeats – away. If he reached the beach before she gunned him down, he had a chance.

She opened up with her machine guns, hammering him at every opportunity.

'You should concede now,' the woman advised.

Andy shook his head. 'I don't quit. Ever.'

'This is a game.'

'Game or not,' Andy said, 'I don't quit.' He rolled, staying low, actually dragging a wingtip through deep snow on a craggy ridge. Cream pies pelted the terrain around Andy.

'You're young yet,' the woman told him.

'No,' Andy replied grimly. 'I know a secret.'

'What?'

Andy scanned the damage indicators scrolling in over the instruments. He was a wreck waiting to happen, a corpse on the move. 'Never play against the guy who built the game.'

The sparkling green ocean – flat as a tabletop – spread

outward from the rocky beach. Black and white bodies lined the shore.

Andy didn't know how many penguins lined the water's edge but he was close enough that he could have seen them if he wasn't flying so fast. He accessed his files, bringing up one of the new traceback utilities Mark had designed for use against Net Force software he often got the opportunity to test out.

'And if you defeat the game's designer?' the woman asked.

'Then he didn't do everything to you he could have,' Andy said.

The cream-pie assault hammered the clownshuttle again. 'I think you're too self-aggrandizing.'

'Not me,' Andy said, looking back and grinning. He watched as the woman flew over the penguin rookeries. 'You see, I know the penguins are my friends.' He tampered with the game-time, slowing events down so that he – and his opponent – could see the penguins below.

The penguins moved incredibly fast, reaching inside their tuxes and pulling out huge blasters that never could have fit under a coat. All the penguins pointed their weapons at the woman's clownshuttle less than forty feet above them. When they opened fire, violet rays lanced from the blasters and perforated the opposing clownshuttle.

The woman's plane went to pieces, turning into a rolling orange and black comet that arced toward the ocean.

Andy hit full flaps and watched the burning debris rocket past. Somewhere in there, he knew, the woman was being forcibly logged off the Net. He lifted his right hand, accessing the traceback utility, and fired a beam of green light that was masked from everyone but him.

The green light touched the wreckage just before it disappeared into the ocean. Hopefully, it touched the woman as well.

'You beat her,' Radu gasped.

'Yeah,' Andy said. 'Pretty cool, huh?'

Radu didn't say anything.

'Who would guess that penguins in Antarctica all have Double-Oh classifications?' Andy asked. He took a casual sweep back over the shoreline.

All the penguins stood and saluted him smartly.

Andy heeled the clownshuttle over and saluted them back.

'Hooray for Captain Andy,' the penguins shouted. 'Hooray for Captain Andy. He's our hero.'

Andy hooked a thumb over his shoulder at the rookeries. 'Flattering but kind of a little over the top, you know?'

Radu didn't look happy at all.

Andy guessed that there was no telling how much trouble the man was going to be in for being part of the embarrassing episode. 'Do you like the game?'

'Yes,' Radu answered. 'Very much. When can you have it up and running?'

'Tomorrow night,' Andy answered. 'By the time we open for the first show.'

'Good.'

Andy felt the warning tingle as the traceback utility let him know it had made contact with its target. 'I've got to go. My mom's calling.' The traceback had a definite short shelf life – and that was if it didn't get discovered somewhere along the way.

Radu nodded. 'We'll talk later.' Then he logged off the Net and disappeared.

Andy shoved his hands upward, pulling free of the seat harness and phasing through the clownshuttle's roof just as it started to nosedive toward the ocean. He held his right hand up. Immediately, a shiny green line shot down from the sky and coiled around his wrist.

So far, so good.

The green line yanked and Andy went with it, spinning free of Antarctica. He passed from the game environment onto the Net in an eyeblink.

He left the St Louis Netscape behind, watching as the Net

shifted and revealed itself as a Mercator map. With the traceback utility, he was disguised as logoff feedback, part of the SAVE/DON'T SAVE question programming. Usually Mark's traceback archived itself in the time/date stamp or a visual component icon since both of those were generally attached to any ongoing application.

The traceback bounced him around through a hundred Net nodes in heartbeats. From six different translation points within the United States he flashed through over forty connections in Europe, through a sophisticated array of satellite translations designed to slow down nearly all traceback utilities, then back into the black-market sector operating in Russia that spread out to the rest of the world.

By the time he reached Russia, Andy had armored up with one of Mark's crashsuit utilities. This version was stripped down, no frills and basically no joy in Andy's eyes, but it was hard to detect.

In one of the Russian nodes, he almost triggered an alarm that would have ended the transmission and peeled off the traceback. The node was a security construct with a design like a hammock spider's web, three-dimensional and layered.

He bounced between the lines, wary of crossing strands that would have reached out and trapped him like he was a passing fly, then triggered the Net's auto-logoff features. He jumped and ran along the strands, slid down some like a fireman and climbed others.

At the very end, nearly free of the security construct, a last-minute strainer in the form of a mechanical spider five times as large as he was appeared. The sharp-edged claws snapped closed all around him, searching for him. Andy raced close enough to reach out and touch the spider. The crashsuit morphed, taking on the metallic chitinous spider armor, covered with wicked, curved hooks just as the arachnid before him was.

Then he was gone, passing for a brief stay in the Middle East where he went through four more security nodes. Then he returned to the United States, to St Louis, landing in a cyber café in the tourist area along the Mississippi River. As his holo-form translated into the cyber café, he overlaid it with a proxy of a friend from Bradford Academy that wouldn't draw any attention. The woman wouldn't recognize him.

Inside the cyber café, the green line faded, turned so translucent that even Andy had trouble seeing it. The cyber café sported fifty computer-link chairs and most of them were filled.

But Andy recognized the woman as she got up from the chair she'd been occupying. She was dressed street casual today, in a blouse and slacks that made her look positively touristy.

As she got up, she glanced around warily, the half-smile on her lips never touching her eyes.

In holo-form, dressed in jeans and a pullover, Andy acted like he'd only come in for the Net link. He lay back in the nearest chair. Since he was in holo-form, the chair didn't recognize his existence, but no one watching him would know that.

The woman left the cyber café, stepping out onto the street and hailing an autocab.

Andy stood and went to the window. He couldn't follow her in holo-form. Trying to trace her through the Netscape of the city without a signature would be impossible.

The woman got into the autocab and closed the door. The autocab pulled into the line of traffic in the next instant.

But not before Andy managed to access an image utility and upload some candid shots. He had no clue who she was, but he figured it was a real possibility she was known to people in the security business.

He logged off.

'Is that a rattlesnake roasting on that spit?'

Andy glanced up from the campfire and spotted Mark

walking over to join them. Andy glanced back at the spit over the dancing flames. A sharpened stick threaded through the snake's body, bunching it up into bends that made it look like a pretzel.

'Yeah, it's a rattlesnake.'

'Gross.' Mark looked hypnotized as he sat on the rocks near Andy. 'What's that thing in its mouth?'

'A jalapeño pepper,' Andy replied.

'And that's supposed to add flavor or something?'

'Nah, it just looks cool.'

'Right.' Mark shook his head. 'You know, I'm beginning to think you're spending too much time in this veeyar.'

'Rattlesnake is one of Cactus's best things.'

Cactus sat quietly near the roasting spit, occasionally turning the cooking meat and basting it with a thick red sauce.

The campfire reflected in Mark's eyes. 'Roasted rattlesnake as a culinary dish?'

'Roasted snake tastes just like chicken.'

'Must make the chickens happy.' Mark looked warily around at Cactus and the other four Pony Express riders gathered at the campfire. 'You guys aren't going to break out into song any time soon, are you?'

'No. That's a different kind of cowboy.'

Mark pointed at a covered pot hanging from another pole over the fire. 'That smells like beans.'

'Yeah. They go good with roast rattlesnake.'

Mark shook his head. 'This is not going to be pretty.'

'You didn't come here to talk bar-be-cue,' Andy said. 'You found out something about the woman.'

'Her name is Cantara bin Kadar bin Yazid Al-Fulani,' Mark said. 'She's an international terrorist.'

Andy digested that but still didn't understand how that would tie the woman to the Cservanka Brothers Circus. 'She was in Net Force files?'

'In a lot of them,' Mark agreed. 'My dad even chased after

her a few years back. But he never caught her.'

Andy gazed into the campfire, watching the hot, bright embers lunge up at the sky only to go black a few feet up. 'What does she do?'

'Mainly, she sabotages computer programs and cyber systems.'

'That might explain what happened to the lion-tamer's program.'

'That's not really an important target,' Mark pointed out.

'Depends,' Andy said, 'on what the real target was. So who is Al-Fulani working for?'

'She's independent these days,' Mark answered. 'At least, that's what the files I looked at say about her. She started out as a hacker in Jerusalem, just learning the Net and how to get around in it without paying for all the services.'

'Did she get arrested?'

Mark nodded. 'Seven times before the age of eighteen, all of them offenses that required stays in juvenile detention areas.'

'Where were her parents?'

'She left them when she turned fifteen, lived out on the streets, and did strictly cash-and-carry break-and-enters from cyber cafés. Just before she turned eighteen, a splinter group of Middle Eastern terrorists asked her to join them.'

'I take it she did.'

'Oh, yeah, and she's done monster business since. A few years ago she appeared to drop out of the terrorist business and into the black-market sector. Net Force doesn't have a lot of information on her from that time.'

Andy turned that over in his mind, trying to find the common denominator that put the woman with the circus. 'What about Martin Radu?'

'I couldn't find out anything about him. After being born, Radu seems to have lived a very quiet life for the next thirty-three years. He only really showed up in reports six years ago when he started working for the Cservanka Brothers Circus.'

'Is the ID legit?'

Mark nodded. 'Birth certificate and fingerprints check out.'

'Then why aren't there any more records?'

'Eastern Europe isn't exactly forthcoming with their information even these days. Radu only showed up because he started moving around internationally. Passport and visa stuff. Databases in those instances crosscheck each other, collating information. Whatever Radu did in Romania remains in Romania unless you talk to someone from there.'

'I told you about all the scars he has?'

Mark nodded. 'Romania still isn't a peaceful country in some respects. There are pocket groups of terrorists and militia throughout those countries. I'd say having had a rough life wouldn't be too unusual.'

'There are a lot of guys at the circus who don't have scars like that. I don't think Radu has walked the straight and narrow.'

'Probably not.'

'And what is Al-Fulani doing here in the United States?'

'According to the Net Force information sheet I got my hands on, she's been heavily involved in the black-market sector, moving materials and software into the Middle East.'

'What kinds of software?' Andy asked.

Cactus leaned forward and pinched a hunk of meat from the roasting rattlesnake, put it into his mouth and chewed deliberately. Then he put more sauce on and turned the spit again. The meat sizzled and snapped.

Mark looked a little green in the campfire light. 'I think I'm going to be sick.'

'That,' Andy informed him, 'would totally put off the other appetites around here. What software is Al-Fulani moving?'

'Anything military spec that she can get her hands on. The Middle East, except for Israel, is far behind the rest of the world. Don't you remember the history lessons Dr Dobbs gave regarding the Gulf War?'

'Desert Storm, Desert Shield?'

'Yeah. Iraq had Scud missiles and no real delivery systems, remember?'

Andy nodded.

'The same situation still pretty much exists in the Middle East,' Mark went on. 'The various terrorist groups active there have upgraded their weaponry since the Russian break-up, but they still don't have the delivery systems in place.'

A cold chill ran through Andy as he suddenly put the places together. 'They're pretty much limited to line-of-sight engagements.'

'Yeah,' Mark said. 'And since most terrorist groups are smaller than standing armies, they can't get involved in a head-to-head confrontation without getting wiped out.'

Andy knew that. Terrorists operated on the theory that if they could work from within a group, show cause for change and strike with anonymity, they could create that change – or at the very least strike fear into the hearts of the governing bodies they wanted changed.

'Why don't they have better delivery systems?' Andy asked. 'A GPS targeting program wouldn't be that hard to build if you had access to the right programs and information.' He knew, because he'd done it himself – in the last couple of weeks.

'Let's say they had the right programs and information,' Mark said. 'They still have to have Net access. Unless they have access through some other means.'

Andy nodded, remembering. Net access was blocked to unidentified entry points. Hackers moved through the systems disguised as some bit of data, and then they downloaded whatever they went there to steal and got offline. Directing a missile to a distant target – an aggressive action on the Net that would be instantly recognized by defensive utilities in place – took far longer than a hacker's sudden slash or riposte.

'What if,' Andy asked, 'a targeting system was in place, only it was disguised as something else?'

'Wouldn't happen,' Mark said confidently. 'What programmer skillful enough to do that would be stupid enough to do that?'

'That's the scary part,' Andy admitted, 'because I think it was you and me.'

Chapter Nineteen

'We can't bring Martin Radu in. If you were going to report this, that night in Mobile would have been the time. The police officers on the scene there would have some leeway to act, because of the emergency situation.'

Andy stared in disbelief at Captain James Winters. He sat in holo-form the next morning across from the Net Force Explorers liaison in Winters' personal office. 'You've got to be kidding.'

Winters leaned back in his chair. He was tall and lean, browned by years of exposure to harsh elements and sun, hair cropped short, every inch the military man that he'd trained all his adult life to be. He was dressed in a dark suit and tie, on his way to a funding meeting in Washington, D.C.

'Based on what you've told me, Radu hadn't done anything that would allow me to issue a search warrant, much less a warrant for his arrest,' Winters said.

'I saw him with Cantara Al-Fulani.' Andy pushed himself out of the chair and paced in front of the folder-laden desk. 'I saw her order one of her men to put a pistol to Radu's head. I thought they were going to kill him.'

'If they had,' Winters said softly, 'maybe we could have gotten involved.'

'You could get involved now. Al-Fulani is a known terrorist and wanted fugitive.'

Winters sighed.

Andy knew he had that affect on the man. Winters sighed

when Andy's short attention span kept him from seemingly tracking everything that was said – although Andy figured he always heard the important parts. And Winters sighed when Andy paced. Of all the Net Force Explorers, Andy knew he was probably the one who tried Winters' patience most of all. Andy lived a lot of the time on the edge of stepping over the line but he always knew where the line was – which to Winters was probably the most irritating thing about him.

'I only have your word that Al-Fulani was there,' Winters pointed out.

'And my word's not good enough?' Andy put as much indignation in his voice as he could, drawing upon years of experience of listening to indignation in the voices of others.

'It is for me,' Winters said. 'In fact, I'm going to put undercover men there at the circus on the offchance that she will show up again. But you have to remember, Al-Fulani might not have even been there in person. You might have been looking at a holo-form.'

Andy shook his head stubbornly. 'All the outside lines to the holo-projectors were blown in Mobile.'

'Maybe she had a back door into the system.'

Andy rolled his eyes.

'I'm just playing devil's advocate here,' Winters pointed out.

'She's in St Louis,' Andy said. 'I tracked her there.'

'I heard you say that,' Winters replied, 'and I'll notify the appropriate authorities so they can look for her.'

'According to the files I've seen, Al-Fulani skips across international lines like it was nothing. They're not going to catch her. You have to trap her.'

'How?'

Oops. A plan – he needed a plan . . . Andy froze, thinking furiously. 'I haven't got that part worked out yet.'

'If it's any consolation,' Winters said, 'neither have a lot of other people who've been doing this a lot longer than you have.'

'That's no consolation. What about the game I designed for the circus?'

Winters spread his hands. 'It's a game, Andy. You did a good job on it. It's a legitimate application of available software. We can't arrest Radu for commissioning it or anyone else for using it, until they actually do try to use it to target a missile. We can arrest them for that. It comes under the heading of international terrorism – and there's plenty we can do once that happens. Mark has confirmed that what you developed could be stripped down and used for targeting missiles but we now know that Net Force can safeguard against it. Mark's already turned over everything he's got to us. He's designing lock-out codes, and so are some of the personnel here at Net Force. We hope that will end any threat from that corner.'

'Maybe. But Al-Fulani is still free out there.'

'She'll fall.'

'Maybe if you brought Radu in . . .'

'For what?'

'On a conspiracy charge, for starters.'

'Do you have proof that Radu was working with Al-Fulani?'

'I saw them together.'

'Doesn't mean anything,' Winters said gruffly. 'Without his testimony against her we don't have a case. Sure, we could bring him in and question him if he comes voluntarily, but I'll bet he won't come voluntarily. If you're right, he has too much to hide. If you're wrong, well, circus people don't much like law enforcement people. There's a lot of history there. Either way, he's not going to admit to working with her. Think about it. Even if the Justice Department cuts him a deal, Al-Fulani's people would find him and kill him.'

'Maybe he'd talk *because* he's afraid. What about that bullet hole I saw?' Andy asked. 'Her people shot him. He has a wound in his side.'

'If he'd gone to a doctor, it would have to have been

reported. He didn't and it wasn't.'

'You could examine him, make him tell you about it. At the very least he's guilty of covering up a crime. And maybe he'll understand that his best hope of getting through this alive is to put her away.'

'Andy, no one can look at him without his consent or a court order,' Winters replied. 'Getting a court order from a judge would prove difficult, I think maybe even impossible. If the bullet could be recovered, and since it went through Radu the chances of that are slim, the weapon it matched up to has probably already been disposed of. There's no trail back to Al-Fulani.'

'Radu could testify against her.'

'Sure, but do you think she's told him where she is? We stand a better chance of catching her if we leave him in place and watch him.'

Andy paced some more. After he and Mark had talked last night, he'd slept fitfully. The clowns in the trailer he was staying in had talked about the circus potentially breaking up. None of them were for it but they all agreed that unless something was done, that was exactly what was going to happen.

He'd wanted to see Syeira, to talk to her and get his head clear, but he knew he couldn't talk to her about Radu and Al-Fulani. He felt guilty about keeping something so serious from her for so long. But she hadn't been available anyway. She was getting ready for the high-wire act that would open tonight.

He felt like too many things were crashing down on him. Imanuela wasn't looking as good as he would have hoped, and his mom was even thinking of flying down to check on her this weekend. And if she felt she needed to be here in person, that only meant bad news for the elephant and her baby. On top of that, the circus that he'd come to love seemed to be falling apart. And the girl that he cared about in ways he'd never even imagined was going up on a trapeze without a net tonight, risking her life to thrill an audience who would never even get to know how special she was.

Then, Radu and Al-Fulani, who'd fooled him into creating a program that could, at least temporarily, give terrorist groups a shot at big-time missile launches, seemed to be on the verge of getting away.

Andy stopped pacing, turned and looked at Winters. 'I think that Al-Fulani deliberately sabotaged the power supplies in Mobile so she could get in and find Radu.'

'Maybe.'

'If she or her people did,' Andy said, 'they nearly killed Syeira on the high wire.'

'Don't make this too personal,' Winters said softly.

'Too personal?' Andy shook his head. 'Al-Fulani almost killed a friend of mine that night, Captain Winters. It doesn't get any more personal than that. I'm not going to allow it to happen again.'

Winters sighed again. 'Look, I understand how you feel but we have protocol to go through. Radu's record is darned near spotless. A case has to be built against him; we can't just grab him without cause. And, right now, what law has he broken? You brought the game to us before it was used by any of the terrorists. No crime has been committed there. The game is legal, and Radu commissioned it for the circus. No laws broken there. You saw him get shot and beaten up by a terrorist. That's not a crime either. Thanks to you, we've got reason to suspect him. We just don't have enough to bring him in.'

'Al-Fulani's already wanted.'

'You're right. That's one thing in our favor – she's got outstanding warrants for all kinds of crimes. The minute we find her, we can pick her up and put her away. But she remains to be caught.'

'Then catch her.'

'How?'

Andy looked up at the ceiling. 'I don't know.'

'Neither do I. But I promise you, Andy, we're going to try.'

'Sure.'

Winters looked at him. 'I'd like you to think about leaving the circus. You may be in danger.'

Andy shook his head. 'They don't know I'm on to them. And if I left suddenly don't you think that would be suspicious?'

'They don't know you've discovered anything yet.'

'What if they run a test on the system in the next couple days? If the lock-out programs work and I'm gone, they're going to know I gave them up. Like you said, then they'd find me, no matter where I hide. If I'm here, I can fuzz things up, crash some equipment that could cause the problem or something. Besides, I can't leave anyway,' Andy said. 'Imanuela needs me.'

'I'm sure another veterinarian could be brought in.'

'I took this job on. I mean to see it through.'

Winters' face hardened, and Andy could tell he was dangerously close to the no-tolerance limit. 'You don't have a history of seeing that many things through, Andy.'

Andy shrugged. 'With all due respect, sir, when it comes to my friends, that statement's about as wrong as it gets.'

'Point taken.' Winters leaned forward again. 'I assume you're not planning on leaving the circus, then?'

Andy grinned with more enthusiasm than he felt. 'What, and give up showbiz?'

'You look worried.'

Andy glanced up, seeing Papa suddenly standing in front of him in white-face. 'No.'

Papa adjusted his red rubber nose. 'A clown knows these things, Andy. They wear smiles to cover broken hearts.'

Andy glanced to the west, watching as the sun sank over the horizon, splintering one final time from the big silver arch near the Mississippi River. He sat on the corral and watched Imanuela eating hay.

'Okay, so maybe I'm a little worried,' Andy admitted. He'd

fumed all day since the meeting with Winters that morning, and he'd racked his brain trying to figure out what he was supposed to do. Maybe there was nothing he could do.

Papa leaned against the corral, his fringe of bright orange hair fluttering under the small cap he wore with an elastic band under his chin. 'What do you worry about?'

'Her.' Andy nodded at Imanuela.

'I, too, but I know that she has you here, and your mother not so very far away. I take heart in that.'

'Yeah.'

'And you worry about my granddaughter,' Papa said softly.

'A lot,' Andy admitted.

Papa smiled gently. 'You like her.'

'Yeah.' Andy broke the eye contact, feeling slightly embarrassed. He gazed toward the Big Top, seeing the Cservanka Brothers Circus flag fluttering bravely at the top. The show was due to open in less than an hour.

'Have you ever been in love,' Papa asked, 'before?'

Andy started to say something flip, something about not being in love now but only in heavy like, but he looked into Papa's knowing eyes. 'No,' he whispered.

'And this scares you, too?'

'Like you wouldn't believe.'

Papa nodded and smiled. 'Good.'

'Good?'

'Love's supposed to be like that.'

'If it was up to me, I'd change the operating parameters,' Andy said honestly, 'because this really bites.'

Papa laughed then, loud guffaws that broke Imanuela's singleminded pursuit of food. The elephant trumpeted briefly and flapped her ears with leathery cracks.

'Mavra had that effect on me,' Papa said wistfully. 'No matter how uncomfortable it gets, you should cherish that feeling.' He paused. 'I know Syeira feels the same about you.'

'You do?'

Papa nodded. 'I can see it in her. And, usually, when she

creeps out on top of the trains when we travel from one city or country to the next, she likes to be alone. She takes her books and a sack lunch. You're the only person she's ever invited.'

'You knew about that?'

'Sure.'

'I'm surprised you let her do that. My mom sure wouldn't have.'

'Yet you went.'

Andy only felt a little guilt.

'Parents, even grandparents, can't always choose what their children do.'

Andy was silent for a moment, feeling a little guilty. 'Just so you know,' he said, 'I asked her not to go up on the trapeze tonight. Or at least to use a net.' For the last few days, the local HoloNet had been running commercials for Cservanka Brothers Circus, and one of the chief attractions was Syeira leaping from trapeze bar to trapeze bar, flying through the air with the greatest of ease. Only the commercials didn't show that she'd been working over a net, and they didn't show the times she'd fallen during the shoot.

'As did I,' Papa said, 'but I fear she's not going to listen to either of us. She's very strong-willed, like her grandmother and great-uncle.'

Andy watched Imanuela, worrying about her, too. From what his mom had said, it wouldn't be long before the baby came in spite of everything they had tried. 'I don't think Syeira got all her strong will from her grandmother and Traian, Papa. I think a lot of it comes from you.'

'I'm just an old, broken-down clown, boy.'

'You're the man,' Andy said, 'who's managed to keep this circus together for decades, despite everything. Traian doesn't see that.'

'Traian has his own misfortunes to carry.'

'And most of these performers don't see what you do, either.'

'They are children in many respects,' Papa said. 'Professionals, yes, each and every one, but still they live the dream, and they feel the hunger of wanting to be more, to do more, to go faster and farther than they've ever gone before. It is a natural thing.'

Andy waited a long time, then he asked, 'Do you think the circus is going to stay together?'

Papa adjusted his red rubber nose again. 'I don't know. I hope so. Sometimes, my young friend, you just have to take each day as it comes.'

The last waning daylight shot deep red forks into the bank of purple and amber clouds to the west, and darkness seemed to roll over the corral, letting in a chill off the Mississippi River that hadn't been there in the light of day.

Abruptly, the lights of the circus flashed on. Bright neon colors traced the rides and lit up the Big Top. The concession booths along the midway lit up as well, forming little islands of illumination. Jaunty calliope music filled the night.

'It's showtime,' Andy said, but instead of the usual exhilaration that had been filling him with each coming performance, he felt fear squirming inside him. He dropped from the corral fence.

A true grin twisted Papa's bright red lips and his eyes twinkled. 'Truly, there is no greater life.' He put his arm around Andy's shoulders and hugged him. 'Come on, Andy, let's go to the circus and forget all our worries for a while. After all, that's what circuses are for.'

Maybe, Andy thought, *but you don't know about Radu and Al-Fulani.*

The performances lacked the crispness that usually marked them. They were sluggish and the timing was off, like they were exercises instead of joyful pursuits.

Andy watched the clowns do their bit in the right ring and listened to the audience laugh at the staged antics. Maybe the audience couldn't tell the difference, but he could. The electricity that usually marked the evening's entertainment was missing.

He gazed around the crowd surreptitiously, looking for the Net Force agents Captain Winters had promised to send. He didn't see any likely candidates, but then, if they were good agents, he wouldn't.

At the end of the bleachers, next to the main entrance into the Big Top, Martin Radu watched the performances with a blank expression, his arms crossed over his chest.

The clowns finished, disappearing in a cloud of confetti. Crupariu, who gave the most wooden performance Andy had ever seen the man give, followed them. However, Napoleon's growl scared several of the nearby audience members. Petar came next, and had the audience howling with laughter at his antics.

Then complete darkness descended, and Andy's heart started pounding fiercely.

'Ladies and gentlemen!' The amplified voice rolled throughout the Big Top. A spotlight opened up on the center ring, revealing the ringmaster. He doffed his hat, holding it in one hand as he bowed deeply. 'Cservanka Brothers Circus is honored to present a new aerialist who will thrill you and amaze you with her skill and expertise, with her daring and bravado. Soon you will see her flying, defying death, with amazing beauty and grace.' He pushed his hat in the direction of the flying trapeze.

Another spotlight, this one bigger, dawned on the flying trapeze. Five performers, two on one platform and three on the other, bowed, then waved to the crowd.

Andy listened to the quiet that had fallen over the crowd. It was an expectant hush, and in that moment he hated them for it.

One of the male flyers tossed a rope down. It was threaded with glitter so that it sparkled as it spun on the way down. The hoop tied at its end looked to Andy entirely too much like a hangman's noose.

'Ladies and gentlemen,' the ringmaster cried, 'join me in welcoming – in her maiden flight taking place right here tonight in St Louis – the lovely, the bold, Miss Syeira!'

Syeira sprinted toward the center ring, her arms driving and close into her sides. When she reached the ring's edge, she pushed off on one foot, throwing herself high into the air. She flipped and landed lightly on her feet, throwing her arms high and arching her back like an Olympic hopeful.

Despite the fear that he felt, Andy felt a smile twist his lips. He felt certain he'd never met another girl like her, and probably wouldn't ever again. Then, in the same instant, he grew angry with her all over again for risking her life like this.

Gracefully, she stepped into the waiting rope loop. Jorund hauled her up as she twirled, holding onto the rope with one hand while she waved to the audience with the other.

'Mommy, that girl's going up into the air,' a little red-haired girl sitting close to Andy cried out, pointing.

'I know, dear. Be quiet and let's watch.'

The little girl's voice lowered into a whisper. 'Mommy, she not careful, she could fall a long ways.'

Even the kids understand, Andy realized. And they were all mesmerized.

Up in the flying trapeze, Syeira stepped out onto the platform. She took the bar offered to her, bent her knees a couple times, then focused and swung out.

The circus band played a drum roll that escalated in intensity. After swinging out a few times, Syeira went into her exercise routine. She swung back and forth, getting higher and higher. She moved from there into a handstand on the bar, holding her body in line until gravity overtook her, then flipping through the bar. Reaching the apex of another swing, Syeira let go the bar on the upswing, then flipped one hundred and eighty degrees, reversing direction effortlessly.

Andy forced himself to breathe, thinking for a moment that he'd forgotten how.

One of the aerialists on the other side of the trapeze tossed

Syeira the other bar. Swinging toward the other bar, holding onto the first bar with one hand, she caught the second bar and switched over, arcing quickly back toward the other side of the trapeze.

She stopped on the other platform opposite Jorund and waited. Quickly, Jorund reversed his position, hanging upside down.

The crowd fell totally silent and the band's last chorus died away as Syeira launched herself from the platform. Her arc was mismatched with Jorund's arc at first. Even though Andy knew the mismatch was on purpose, he felt his stomach tighten in nervous anticipation.

Then the arcs matched. Syeira swung her legs up and Jorund grabbed them. He carried her to the other end of the trapeze, then back again so that she could reach out and grab the approaching bar easily. They swung apart again, getting faster and higher.

Just when Andy thought he couldn't stand the suspense anymore, Syeira sailed from the bar, drawing her legs in close, whipping around in a double somersault. Then she straightened out, reaching for Jorund.

People gasped near Andy, nearly driving him nuts with anxiety.

In the next moment, Jorund snapped his hands around Syeira's wrists. The stunts came more quickly, executed flawlessly.

Andy barely breathed. Then, after seemingly forever, Syeira performed a triple somersault with a twist, like she had all the time in the world, like she'd suddenly gone weightless, like she would never fall.

Then gravity claimed her, bringing her down from the high apex, her costume flashing as the spotlights bathed her. Jorund swung back toward her, hands wide, arms reaching, looking inches too short.

Andy started up from the bleachers, halfway to his feet, his heart in his throat.

Jorund seemed to pluck Syeira from the air, grabbing her wrists. They swung back to the platform and the other aerialists grabbed Syeira and helped her to the platform. The spotlights narrowed their focus, clinging to Syeira, who struck a pose and smiled broadly.

In that instant, Andy knew she'd never walk away from the flying trapeze. She'd found something up there that she couldn't find anywhere else. Part of him was sad but the rest of him was happy. Not many people got to do the things they really cared about.

The spotlight shifted again, picking up the other aerialists that were already in motion. The band struck up a lively tune, buoying the crowd's mood.

In that moment, Andy saw Martin Radu turn and walk out of the Big Top.

Chapter Twenty

Andy pushed himself up and stepped quickly down the bleachers, excusing himself as he bumped into audience members. By the time he reached the ground in front of the bleachers, he'd stepped up the pursuit of Martin Radu to a near run.

He slowed after he went through the tent flaps. For a panicked moment he thought he'd lost Radu, then he spotted the man walking through the midway, obviously heading for the personal trailers and RVs.

His heart thumping steadily, Andy threaded through the crowds spilling over from the Big Top. After talking with Winters, knowing Al-Fulani wasn't the type to make mistakes, and knowing that Net Force would be reluctant to engage a terrorist group in the midst of the circus, Andy had cobbled together a desperate plan. Andy knew Winters wouldn't have approved it in a hundred years, no matter how desperate he'd gotten.

But after the way the terrorist leader had nearly cost Syeira her life, there was no way Andy was going to just let the woman walk away. Not if he had a good chance to take her down.

Radu remained wary as he walked through the midway. He glanced behind himself often but Andy drifted along easily, shadowing the man without being spotted. Martin Radu wasn't the first person Andy had followed. All right, so maybe he *was* one of the few that hadn't been in a game scenario online, but still, Andy figured he had his share of experience.

The circus midway in all its glory moved around Andy, throwing bright lights into the night's darkness, chasing shadows away in one heartbeat, then retreating before them in the next. Purple and green lights from the Octopus danced through the air as the amusement ride swirled and dipped. Laughter from the riders cascaded across the area, then taunts rang out to the people still waiting to ride. A half-dozen teenage girls ran in a pack, waving wildly at other girls who screamed excitedly to see them.

The magic of the circus was upon them. Anything could happen amid the tents and rides.

Andy knew the visitors weren't aware how true that was. He swallowed hard, his throat drier and tighter than he'd expected. But he didn't turn from the chase. Clusters of people swept by him and he avoided them as if he was wire-guided, touching nothing.

Radu left the midway and stepped into the shadows, moving through the parked RVs and buses till he reached his own. The shadow that moved across one of the curtains told Andy that Radu wasn't arriving to an empty house.

Andy took out his foilpack and configured it to phone function. He called out a number. 'Petar?'

'Yes,' Petar answered, sounding very nervous.

'It's time to empty the funhouse.'

Petar hesitated. 'Andy, are you sure about this?'

'Yes,' Andy replied, halting in the shadow of an RV as Radu let himself into his trailer. 'How many people are in there?'

'Maybe fifteen or twenty. Jorge says it's been slow so far. The funhouse is holo-equipped, so the holo audience can attend as well, but it's just not a big draw. Too "Plain Jane." '

Yeah, yeah, yeah, save me the sales pitch. Andy's stomach flip-flopped. 'Make sure you get them all,' he said.

'I will. I'll check the control booth myself.'

'Good. Have you checked the computer-link chain in the booth?'

'Yes. It's still operational.' Petar hesitated. 'I'd feel better if you told me what this was about.'

'No, you wouldn't,' Andy promised him. He pushed his breath out, trying hard not to hyperventilate.

Shadows played across the closed blinds inside Radu's trailers. Whoever Radu's guests were, they weren't making pleasant movements, but at least none of the shadows seemed to be holding pistols.

Andy didn't know for sure what Radu had done that had drawn Al-Fulani down on him; he figured maybe he'd never know. That was fine with him. Radu might not have done anything. Maybe it was simply that this deal was big enough – especially with all the money some of the Middle Eastern terrorists would invest in something like the targeting system – that the woman wanted to handle the deal up close and personal. Andy really didn't care what had brought her here. He just wanted to make sure she never came back again.

'Okay,' Petar called back a moment later, 'everyone's out and we just closed the funhouse to the general public.'

'Get out of there,' Andy said.

'Why?'

'It's better if Radu doesn't see you. He might suspect something's wrong.' Andy ran all the programming through his mind again. He'd spent hours putting all the special software into the system that he needed for tonight.

He'd also pass-coded his clown game with a software trap that let him know if it had been downloaded from the circus operating system. The software protection programming had kept the game from being downloaded over the Net. The game had been downloaded once that morning. Radu had no way of knowing that Andy had layered in a bogus copy. Without all ten passcodes, the game programming downloaded the bad program, which was designed to fail completely the first time someone tried to boot it up on their computer, and to take the computer out, too, just for good measure.

A hand dropping on Andy's shoulder nearly stopped his heart. He turned, not knowing whom to expect.

The man was clean-cut and smooth-shaven, of average height. He wore jeans and a loose pullover. And, Andy figured, a concealed weapon under that pullover.

'Hey, kid,' the man greeted in a neutral whisper. His eyes never left the trailer. 'What are you doing here?'

'Same thing you are,' Andy responded. 'Trying to capture a known terrorist.'

'Oh, no, let me guess,' the man said. 'Andy Moore?'

'Don't I match my file photo?'

'Got a little more sun on you than the picture showed. And maybe a little less common sense. Winters warned me about you.'

'You know Al-Fulani's in there?' Andy asked.

'A person we believe to be Al-Fulani is in there,' the agent admitted.

'You want to tell me how you plan on getting her out of there without turning this circus into a bloodbath?' Andy demanded.

The agent's face remained neutral. 'No.'

'Let me clue you in,' Andy offered, feeling more at home cracking wise than playing this straight, no matter how dangerous it was. 'A can opener isn't going to do the trick. If you brace Al-Fulani, she's going to go down shooting, along with any people she brought along. And a lot of innocent people are going to get hurt tonight.'

The agent shrugged. 'So we take her down when she leaves the circus.'

'And if she leaves during the rush after the circus is over?'

'Leave this to the professionals, kid.'

'Do you plan on picking me up and taking me out of here kicking and screaming? Your suspect might notice that.'

'You wouldn't do that.'

'No,' Andy said. 'You're right. But I'm not going to walk away from this, either.'

'Kid,' the agent said, 'don't make this hard.'

'Without me,' Andy said, 'you guys don't stand a chance. You have to take her right here and right now.'

Evidently sensing that Andy was about to make his move, the agent reached for him.

But Andy wasn't there. The agent's short, quick grab missed, and anything longer would have drawn attention. Andy kept moving, walking backward and talking to the agent.

'Wish me luck.' He was smiling. *So, okay, I meant to make contact with Net Force, just maybe not so soon.*

He turned and continued walking toward Radu's trailer, feeling the Net Force agent's eyes boring into his back. Captain Winters was going to be madder than Andy had ever seen him if he pulled this off. If he didn't pull it off – well, it just wasn't going to matter how mad Winters was.

Feeling a little sick and excited all at the same time, Andy approached the door to Radu's trailer. He took a couple quick breaths, pumping his system with oxygen, getting ready for the effort he was about to make.

Angry voices sounded inside the trailer. Mostly it was the woman, and though she spoke in the language that Andy didn't understand, he figured he knew what they were talking about.

He rapped his knuckles against the door.

The angry voices quieted.

Andy rapped again.

'Go away,' Radu commanded. 'I'll talk with you another time.'

Andy was aware of the faces pressing against the windows on either side of the door. 'Mr Radu, it's Andy Moore. I'm guessing that you're probably wanting to talk to me now. Especially if you found out you couldn't burn a copy of the game.'

The door lock worked.

Radu swung the door open, his mind obviously busy trying to figure out what he was supposed to say, how he was supposed to act.

Heart thumping fiercely, praying his presence was not working against the Net Force agents in place around the circus, Andy looked at Radu. 'Or maybe I'm wrong.'

Radu struggled, trying to find something to say.

'Get him inside,' Al-Fulani ordered.

A big man pushed Radu aside, glanced around suspiciously, then fisted Andy's shirt.

'Hey.' Andy slammed a forearm into the man's wrist hard enough to break his grip, and took a couple steps back. 'Play rough and I'll take my toys and go home.'

'Step back and give him room,' Al-Fulani ordered. She stood at the back of the trailer, her arms crossed over her breasts. Her eyes narrowed as she studied Andy's face.

Radu and the man stepped back.

Andy straightened his shirt, swallowed hard and hoped his knees wouldn't buckle. *Syeira went up on that trapeze tonight without a safety net*, he told himself. *I can do this.* Still, his knees quivered.

Al-Fulani waved the three men back in the room, giving Andy more space. But it was only a token concession. Andy knew the woman felt certain they could overpower him easily.

'What are you doing here?' Al-Fulani asked.

'Trying to keep from getting ripped off,' Andy answered.

'Who sent you here?' Radu asked.

'No one.'

'Liar.' Radu was so mad and scared he was shaking.

Andy didn't blame the man. Either way this played out, Radu knew he wasn't in control of his world anymore. Al-Fulani had him by the short hairs and now Andy knew he wasn't what he proposed to be. 'Talk bad to me and I'll go somewhere else. Not unless you've got someone really good at computers. Better than me. Since I designed something your people haven't, I figure I'm better than anyone you've got.'

'You're cocky.' Al-Fulani took a half-step forward.

Andy shrugged.

'I like that.'

'He's a Net Force Explorer,' Radu warned.

'So? You worry too much,' Al-Fulani said. 'Net Force is not in the habit of sending children to do their dirty work. If they were involved, this boy would be miles away, even if they had to lock him up to keep him out of it.'

Andy knew the woman was only buttering him up, buying time. He remained by the closed door, letting them think he felt confident about getting outside the door before they could get to him.

'What do you want?' Al-Fulani asked.

'Money,' Andy said. 'A lot of it.'

'Why would either Mr Radu or myself pay you money?' the woman asked. 'The game is not all that good.'

'That's true,' Andy said. 'It is kind of generic. But Mr Radu asked me to include GPS programming. At first, I didn't understand why he wanted that. It seemed kind of dull. He said it was to allow all the people in the different places the circus visited to include their own cities and countries in the game. A lot of games have realistic terrain in them, but none that I know of combine real-time GPS programming.'

'So?' Al-Fulani asked.

'So I got to thinking that a game like that, enhanced like it was, would make a good missile targeting system for some country or group that doesn't have a good delivery system.'

Al-Fulani didn't say anything.

Andy smiled. 'It's funny. I never thought anything about it until yesterday. When you and I went head to head in the game?'

'I recall. You cheated.' A small smile twisted the woman's lips.

'I don't like to lose.'

'In that, we share something.'

'The way I see it,' Andy said, 'you're going to make money off the program I wrote. I want some of it.'

'You could have talked to Mr Radu about that.'

'Yeah, well, after seeing how you and your men handled him in Mobile, I figured he wasn't exactly the top guy.'

Radu's face darkened with fury.

'How much?' Al-Fulani asked.

Radu turned toward her. 'You can't be serious. You're not going to pay—'

'Shut up,' the woman ordered. She kept her gaze on Andy. 'How much?'

'Ten million dollars,' Andy said.

'You're a minor,' Al-Fulani pointed out. 'Even if I had that much money, how could I possibly get it to you?'

'Cash,' Andy replied, knowing that much cash would cause too many problems crossing the different international borders to make it viable. Not to mention the problems he'd have hiding it under his bed.

Suddenly, a loud thump sounded against the trailer door. Andy glanced at it, like he was surprised that one of the terrorist's people had blocked the door from outside.

Al-Fulani smiled. 'Oh my, it seems you find yourself constantly outmaneuvered. And this time there are no penguins to save you.' She waved to the three men, urging them forward.

Without hesitation, grateful for the movement now, Andy spun and hurled himself toward the bay window at the front of the small trailer. He crossed his hands in front of his face. Glass shattered and he went spilling through, landing on his stomach on the ground. The noise, he knew, wouldn't even be heard over the normal sounds of the circus.

He groaned as he pushed himself to his feet and took off in the direction of the funhouse like death itself was coming after him. *It would have looked more impressive if I'd landed on my feet.* But falling, having to struggle to get to his feet, he knew that was more believable, that they'd believe he was actually fleeing for his life. And he knew that was true to a greater extent than he liked to think about.

But he had to be the bait to set the trap.

'Get him!' Al-Fulani called out behind him.

Andy heard running feet slap against the hard ground at his back. The chilling sound of a silenced bullet whistled by his ear. He grabbed the corner of a trailer and yanked himself around it, pulling out his foilpack, configuring it for phone, and punching a call through to Captain James Winters' private number. The Explorers liaison might be monitoring the op at the circus, but he wouldn't let his personal phone go unanswered.

Winters answered on the first ring. 'Andy? What are you—'

'Sorry,' Andy said, already drawing deep lungfuls of air, 'don't have the time or wind for long explanations.' He dodged again, ducking behind another RV. Glass shattered as a bullet cored through a window behind him. 'I need you to keep your men back for a couple minutes.' He gasped, grabbing more air, driving his feet hard against the ground as he ran a broken pattern. He stayed inside the maze of the trailers and buses, both to make it harder to shoot him and to mask the fact that he was talking over the foilpack.

'Are you out of your *mind?*'

'No, sir.'

'Do you really have a handle on this, son?'

'Yes, sir,' Andy replied. 'Al-Fulani and her men believe I have what they need. They're coming after me. I'll draw her into a position where you can take her down in the open without anyone else around. I promise.'

Winters hesitated only a moment. 'Don't let them catch you.'

'No, sir,' Andy said. 'That's the whole idea.' Tersely, he explained what he needed of the Net Force agents. Surprisingly, Winters didn't ask questions. Andy realized then that when the chips were down and an op had gone into motion, Winters was a player. Just like him.

But Andy also knew Winters was going to have a long talk with him when the current situation was over and done with. And then there'd be the whole issue with his mom. Not a pleasant prospect. If he lived long enough to experience it. He figured if the terrorists got him, at least he would be spared a couple of nasty lectures.

'There! There he is! Take him down but don't kill him! We need him alive!'

Andy heard the man yelling behind him and knew they'd closed some of the distance while he'd been talking on the phone and trying to stay out of their line of sight. He folded the foilpack and shoved it into his pocket.

Risking a glance over his shoulder, Andy saw that Al-Fulani was racing after him, too. *Good. She's got the whole crew coming after me.* Now all he had to do was stay loose and alive for a few more minutes.

Evidently, Al-Fulani's men were equipped with personal comm-links because they all vectored in on Andy when he broke from the line of trailers and hotfooted it out onto the midway.

Terror was still breathing down his neck when one of them exploded from right behind him, rushing from the sheltering bulk of a bus. The man kept his weapon close to his body and reached to grab Andy with his free hand.

Andy dodged to the left, then caught sight of a man breaking from that direction as well. He set his sights on the corndog stand directly in front of him and ran for his life. Surely he could outrun a bunch of terrorists!

A line stood at the service window, and many of the people were watching Andy approaching at a dead run. Both men closed from the sides ahead of him and he knew if he tried to turn back or pause, the men behind him would take him.

Trying to get into the crowd would only slow him down, too, he knew. And then there was the chance of some would-be hero in the crowd wanting to impress his girl by jumping Andy and holding him for his pursuers.

Andy raced for the corndog stand, highlighted by the wash of blue lights hanging under the awning. A small Dumpster sat on the side. Without hesitation, Andy leapt up onto the Dumpster, immediately hurling himself up to the top of the corndog stand, praying that the roof would hold and not let him fall through.

Three long, hollow booming strides and he was across. He threw himself off to the ground, landing hard but staying on his feet, pushing himself to run like he'd never run before. The distance-eating effort paid off.

The funhouse lay directly ahead of him. A hooded skeleton with a scythe stood over the entrance, illuminated by neon green lights. The scythe swung repeatedly, flashing green fire in its wake. VAULT OF HORRORS scrolled over the entrance in an arch.

An OUT OF ORDER sign hung on the door.

For one terrified moment, Andy wondered if Petar had accidentally forgotten and locked the door when he'd left. If he had, Andy had nowhere else to run. Al-Fulani and her people would have him, and Winters' op would be seriously hamstrung by the crowds of circus-goers.

'Hey!' a young man shouted to Andy's left.

Stay out of it, Andy thought. *Just back off and go away.*

The guy hesitated for just a moment, then Al-Fulani yelled, 'Stop him!' The guy dropped into a crouch, like maybe he'd played football at some point. He was medium built but broad, like he worked out a lot.

If the guy got hold of him, Andy knew even if he got away, he'd probably be too slowed down to reach the funhouse before Al-Fulani and her people caught up with him. Less than ten feet in front of the would-be hero, Andy threw himself into a body-sacrificing baseball slide on his stomach, head forward. He slid roughly under the guy's outstretched arms, feeling hide go under his chin and from his stomach because his shirt was too thin to provide enough protection.

Even before he completely stopped sliding, Andy pushed up with his arms, getting his feet under him, ignoring the fire in his lungs and the pain in his stomach and chin. *Not going to quit*, he told himself fiercely. Despite the exertion and the tension, Andy's legs felt good. And his lungs were still not knifing him – he kept himself in shape.

He sprinted all the way to the funhouse door, humped up and pumping with everything he had left. *Don't look back, don't look back. Concentrate on the door.* He skidded at the end of the run, turning sideways to slam into the door. He hit the release bar, glancing back to see Al-Fulani's men closing on him.

The door opened inward and he pushed his way inside.

The interior of the funhouse was dark but outside light gleamed on the stainless-steel surfaces polished mirror-bright that made up the maze. Andy trailed a hand along the right wall, running fast, despite the soft mattress in the floor that made footing suddenly seem treacherous. Dozens of his reflections chased after him.

He counted the mirrored panels, working through the twists and turns of the maze that he had memorized. Even though he was expecting it, the hologram of the skeleton – moldy green like it had been fresh-dug from a grave – rising from the floor in front of him pumped his adrenaline up another level and nearly froze him in place for just an instant.

The skeleton screamed in mortal agony and swiped a bony hand at Andy.

I hate that thing, Andy thought.

Men's voices, talking in the language that Andy didn't understand, sounded in the maze passageway. The conversation galvanized Andy into action again.

More holos shimmered and popped into existence. Spiders and ghosts mixed with holo creatures from the Black Lagoon and Frankenstein. Andy rounded the next corner and saw a vampire raise its ugly head from the tender throat of its latest victim. The vampire turned into a bat and flew at Andy, fangs gnashing.

When he'd first come to the funhouse after joining the troupe, Andy had had a blast in it. The funhouse *was* fun, with just enough imagined terror to really put an edge on things. Coming here with Syeira at another time had made him feel like it was kind of cheesy. The funhouse just wasn't Syeira's kind of place at all. Being with her made the funhouse feel juvenile and she just didn't get the same excitement out of it that he had. At the time, Andy wished she had experienced the same feelings.

Now, though, with Al-Fulani and her goon squad breathing down his neck, the darkness inside the funhouse took on a whole new level of terror.

'Andy Moore,' the woman called out.

The back of Andy's neck prickled, but he kept quiet and didn't quit moving. He counted the mirrored panels, hoping he had the count right.

'You can run, but you can't hide,' Al-Fulani taunted.

'You told me that before,' Andy said. His words didn't sound very brave with the quaver in his voice.

Al-Fulani laughed and the sound rolled over the funhouse, occasionally punctuated by the screams of various holos that leaped out to scare attendees. 'You cheated in the game,' she said.

'Never play against the guy who built the game,' Andy replied. He came to another junction, with just enough light in the area to see the three passageways ahead. He was right where he wanted to be. He headed into the left one, tripping another holo.

A leather-masked madman with a chainsaw suddenly stepped out from around a nonexistent corner. The chainsaw spat sparks and the sound thundered in Andy's ears, temporarily deafening him.

With effort, Andy didn't flinch, striding through the flesh-chewing swath the masked man cut in the air. The hologram kept moving, and so did Andy. He felt the blood from his torn chin drop on his chest, warm in the funhouse's chill. He trotted into the left passageway, still counting the stainless-steel panels on the right. The passageway curved around to the left.

A gunshot sounded behind Andy, followed immediately by a barrage of foreign words that couldn't be anything other than obscenities. Al-Fulani shouted commands.

Andy stopped his count and pressed against the panel he'd stopped in front of. Nothing happened. *Don't panic*, he told himself, letting out a breath. *You couldn't have missed it by more than one.* He pressed the panel ahead of the one he'd chosen. It didn't move either. *Or two. Surely you couldn't have missed it by more than two.*

'You could give yourself up, Andy,' Al-Fulani offered.

Andy could still hear the gunshot ringing in his ears. *Right.* Forcing himself to remain calm, he went back to the original panel he'd chosen, trying not to wonder how close the woman and her henchmen were getting. He counted one back of it – and pressed.

'Things would go easier for you if you give up,' Al-Fulani said. 'All I want is that game.'

Yeah, right. Like you're going to let me live, trusting me not to tell anyone about your scheme. 'I don't give up,' Andy replied. 'Never have, never will.' The panel clicked back six inches and he shoved it to the side, stepping into the funhouse's control center.

'You should make it easy on yourself,' the woman said. 'My anger is not a good thing.'

'Probably not,' Andy agreed, feeling more confident as he slipped the hidden door back into place. He turned and crossed the small room to the computer-link chair, flopping into it and lying back. 'But I know a secret.'

'Never play against the game designer,' Al-Fulani said. 'I know. But we're not playing a game now.'

The implants in Andy's head pulsed as he logged onto

the Net. His body stayed in the chair. His holo-form appeared beside it. All the fatigue and pain he'd been feeling evaporated as he adjusted his implants to block it, leaving only the dull echoes of that pain behind in his real body. In holo-form, he moved lightly on his feet, dressed in the same clothes he'd been wearing.

'No, we're not playing a game now,' Andy agreed. 'Back in Mobile when you caused the power outage, you nearly killed someone I care a lot about.'

'You took back the game out of revenge?' Al-Fulani sounded like she couldn't believe it. 'There's no percentage in vengeance.'

'Like terrorists don't harbor grudges.' In holo-form, Andy stepped through the maze wall back into the passageway. Back on the Net, he opened a virtual connection, giving it Captain Winters' number.

'Andy,' Winters answered.

'Are the agents in place?' Andy's real self whispered as his holo-form waited, listening to the footsteps echoing through the funhouse.

'Almost. Are you safe?'

Andy grinned in spite of the fear that still thrilled inside him. 'Sure. I've got them right where you want them. The funhouse is isolated, confined, empty except for me and them, and they aren't expecting your people.'

'This could still go badly.'

'Yes, sir, but it's better than the trailer she was in, where she had too many people around, lots of cover, and a nice field of view to shoot your people. Anyway, it's too late to keep it from going now.' Andy waited. 'Let me know when the agents are in place.'

'And if Al-Fulani's people find you?'

'They won't,' Andy insisted. He stood in the maze, his holo-form legs trembling with repressed energy. Back in the control booth, his real self accessed the funhouse monitors, seeing that Al-Fulani had spread her people out to cover more ground. That kind of worked in his favor because they'd wait to shoot, wanting to make sure they weren't shooting each other. Besides, they didn't want to kill him until they had the key to the game upload in hand. That would buy him some time.

Andy plotted the courses through the maze that would bring them all back together, then put up holos of the metal panels over passageway selections to fool them into going the way he wanted them to.

'Hold it!'

Andy spotted Martin Radu just ahead of his holo-form. The circus twenty-four-hour man had a pistol in his hand. With only a thought, accessing the funhouse's online menus, Andy brought up a ghost holo, triggering its release from the stainless-steel panel beside Radu. The ghost-holo reached for the man with hooked, bony fingers, unloosing a blood-curdling howl that made Andy's teeth ache.

Startled, Radu turned and fired. The bullet flared from the stainless-steel panel and ricocheted through the funhouse, igniting brief sparks in its passage. By the time Radu was able to notice him again, Andy had turned and fled up the passageway.

Al-Fulani barked out orders.

'She's telling them to be careful with their weapons,' a calm voice said in Andy's ear, 'that she needs you alive, at least for now.'

'Thanks, Captain Winters, that's nice to know,' Andy said drily. He drew up a map overlay of the funhouse maze, lit up the terrorists' positions, and watched them converging, moving toward the area he wanted them in.

'Andy Moore, you're in the hands of Captain John Carter,' Winters said. 'Net Force special ops.'

'When you care enough to send the very best . . .' Andy cracked. 'Are your men in place, Captain?'

'Yes. We could take it from here.'

'No,' Andy replied. 'This is my game. We do it my way and

maybe nobody gets hurt.' He rounded the next turn in the passageway. It opened on a large room where blue-tinted ghouls were hauling a fresh corpse from an open grave.

Andy blanked the ghouls out of the funhouse maze, took a deep breath, and stared at the cemetery landscape that covered the whole back wall. It gave the illusion of no way out, and that was exactly what it was going to be.

He turned, tracking Al-Fulani, Martin Radu and the other terrorists on the map overlay. He crossed his arms over his chest and waited, standing in front of the cemetery wall, no way out but the grave.

Two of the male terrorists came out the passageway first, dropping into shooter stances with their pistols shoved out before them, pointing right at him.

Andy smiled at them. 'Welcome to the party.'

Al-Fulani, Radu and the other men arrived hot on their heels. It was the woman who first sensed that something was badly wrong. She held her weapon uncertainly and backed away.

'Never,' Andy said, 'never play with the guy who built the game.' Then he accessed the funhouse virtual edit tools and removed the wall showing the cemetery landscape.

When guests normally finished the maze, they had to walk through the graveyard to get out. Once they were through the holo, the back door out of the funhouse was revealed.

Now, when the cemetery landscape holo melted away, it revealed twenty heavily armed Net Force agents in body armor standing behind portable bulletproof shields. They held M16A4 rifles pointed at the terrorists.

Al-Fulani jumped toward Andy, reached a hand out to grab him, pointing her pistol at his head. 'Don't,' she ordered, 'or I'll shoot the—'

Andy watched the surprised look fill her face when her hand passed right through him. She took a stunned step back.

'It's my game this time,' Andy said. 'And I play to win. You see, I know a secret. Net Force is my friend.'

Captain John Carter identified himself, then ordered the terrorists to put their weapons down very slowly. He also told them that the building was surrounded. Voices outside the walls confirmed this. The bad guys complied. Before Carter could start reading them their rights, Andy had something he wanted to say.

'Game over,' Andy announced. 'You lose.'

Epilogue

Andy stood in front of the Vault of Horrors and watched as Net Force loaded Al-Fulani, the other terrorists, and Martin Radu into a specially equipped full-size Dodge van. All of them were handcuffed, and Captain Carter saw to it they were bolted to steel rings welded to the floor. The position didn't look comfortable at all.

The sideshow just out of reach of the midway had drawn a lot of spectators. Flashing lights from the Net Force light-bar-equipped vehicles mixed with the lights from the whirling rides.

Captain Winters stood beside Andy. Even in holo-form, Winters gave off massive amounts of recrimination. Andy blew it off for the moment, though, because he was feeling pretty good about everything.

'You took a lot of risks out here tonight,' Winters said without looking at him.

'They paid off,' Andy said, not feeling like backing down.

'We're going to talk about that at a future date,' Winters promised. 'A very *near* future date.'

'Yes sir.' Andy didn't mind. He'd get chewed out for a while, maybe a long while, and there'd probably be a little grounding, but in the end everyone would have to agree that he did a good thing even if he didn't do it in the approved manner. After all, he figured people generally put lines around life for a guy like him to cross. As long as he crossed them for the right reasons.

'Andy, Andy!'

Sudden fear surged through Andy when he recognized Syeira's voice. He turned toward her and saw her running toward him from the midway.

'This is the young lady?' Winters asked.

'Yeah,' Andy replied, feeling a goofy grin fix itself to his face. It pulled at his scraped chin but he didn't mind at all.

'Andy,' Syeira gasped, grabbing him by the hand. 'Papa needs you. It's Imanuela. The baby's coming.'

'No,' Andy responded, drawing back. He'd felt kind of good about being given the hero's hug for saving the circus from the terrorists, though he didn't know how Syeira had found out so quickly. But now he felt the coldest fear he'd felt in a long time.

Syeira looked at the Net Force agents as they closed the van doors. 'What's going on here?'

'I'll tell you later.' Andy held onto her hand as she pulled him toward the corrals. He ran beside Syeira, matching her step. His stomach and chin hurt and he thought he was going to be sick just thinking about birthing a baby. He wasn't ready for something like that.

'Hey Rube!' The hue and cry of the circus performers echoed up and down the midway. 'It's Imanuela. She's having the baby. The baby's coming! C'mon! We gotta go see, make sure she's all right!'

By the time Andy and Syeira arrived at the corral, they had a crowd of circus performers and attendees in tow. Papa was in the corral with Imanuela, standing beside her and stroking her trunk, talking to her softly.

Andy froze outside the railing as the crowd continued to gather. The rides along the midway shut down but the lights remained on.

Syeira glanced at Andy. 'What's wrong with you?'

Andy stared at Syeira with wide eyes, his heart palpitating. His palms were all sweaty. 'I can't do this,' he croaked.

'Andy,' Syeira said softly, 'Imanuela can't do this by

herself. She needs help. She's in pain.'

'Doc Andy, Doc Andy.'

Andy turned and watched Emile, the stilt clown, striding high above the gathering crowd.

'I've got your bag, Doc Andy.' Emile held the bag up. His painted face showed worry.

Automatically, Andy reached up and took the bag from the stilt clown. The bag felt like it weighed a thousand pounds.

'Andy,' Papa called. 'Please come and help her. She's a brave old lady but I know she's scared. I can feel it in her.'

Imanuela trumpeted anxiously, coiling her trunk around Papa's arm affectionately.

Reluctantly, feeling more out of control than he had even when being chased by Al-Fulani, Andy climbed over the corral. *Oh jeez, oh jeez, oh jeez, I am so not ready for this.*

The area beside Imanuela suddenly rippled, and in the next instant Sandra Moore stood next to the elephant.

'Mom,' Andy croaked.

She looked at her son. 'I'm here.'

'I don't think this is a good idea,' Andy said.

His mom looked Imanuela over. 'And I don't think we have a choice.' She glanced at her son. 'You can do this. I will help you.'

'Sure,' Andy said, taking a deep breath. 'I can do this.' He glanced around the corral. *I can do this with all these people watching.* Then he remembered that the circus was being broadcast on the Net, including the animal corrals. *I can do this even with the whole world watching. But this is not what I want to do.*

An hour and a lot of hard work later, the baby elephant was born. It was two hundred pounds of soft, rubbery, wrinkly gray flesh, bigger even than Andy was.

Once he was sure the baby was doing okay on its own and Imanuela was taken care of, Andy sank tiredly to the ground,

Andy sat frozen, totally blown away. 'Wow.'

'Wow?' Syeira repeated.

'Yeah, wow,' Andy admitted. 'I'm kind of new to the vocabulary when we get to the area of wowness.'

'Me, too,' Syeira said, and she took his hand in hers.

If you enjoyed this book here is a selection of other bestselling titles from Headline

TOM CLANCY'S NET FORCE	£5.99 ☐
Created by Tom Clancy and Steve Pieczenik	
TOM CLANCY'S NET FORCE: HIDDEN AGENDAS	£5.99 ☐
Created by Tom Clancy and Steve Pieczenik	
TOM CLANCY'S NET FORCE EXPLORERS:	£3.99 ☐
THE DEADLIEST GAME Created by Tom Clancy and Steve Pieczenik	
TOM CLANCY'S NET FORCE EXPLORERS:	£3.99 ☐
VIRTUAL VANDALS Created by Tom Clancy and Steve Pieczenik	
TOM CLANCY'S NET FORCE EXPLORERS:	£3.99 ☐
ONE IS THE LONELIEST NUMBER	
Created by Tom Clancy and Steve Pieczenik	
TOM CLANCY'S NET FORCE EXPLORERS:	£3.99 ☐
THE ULTIMATE ESCAPE	
Created by Tom Clancy and Steve Pieczenik	
TOM CLANCY'S NET FORCE EXPLORERS: END GAME	£3.99 ☐
Created by Tom Clancy and Steve Pieczenik	
TOM CLANCY'S NET FORCE EXPLORERS: CYBERSPY	£3.99 ☐
Created by Tom Clancy and Steve Pieczenik	

Headline books are available at your local bookshop or newsagent. Alternatively, books can be ordered direct from the publisher. Just tick the titles you want and fill in the form below. Prices and availability subject to change without notice.

Buy four books from the selection above and get free postage and packaging and delivery within 48 hours. Just send a cheque or postal order made payable to Bookpoint Ltd to the value of the total cover price of the four books. Alternatively, if you wish to buy fewer than four books the following postage and packaging applies:

UK and BFPO £4.30 for one book; £6.30 for two books; £8.30 for three books. Overseas and Eire: £4.80 for one book; £7.10 for 2 or 3 books (surface mail).

Please enclose a cheque or postal order made payable to *Bookpoint Limited*, and send to: Headline Publishing Ltd, 39 Milton Park, Abingdon, OXON OX14 4TD, UK. Email Address: orders@bookpoint.co.uk

If you would prefer to pay by credit card, our call team would be delighted to take your order by telephone. Our direct line is 01235 400 414 (lines open 9.00 am–6.00 pm Monday to Saturday 24 hour message answering service). Alternatively you can send a fax on 01235 400 454.

Name ....

Address ....

....

....

If you would prefer to pay by credit card, please complete:
Please debit my Visa/Access/Diner's Card/American Express (delete as applicable) card number:

Signature .... Expiry Date..............

'To Papa,' Traian called from the front row, 'the man who holds all of this, all of us, together.'

A brief round of applause was quickly broken up by another trumpet from Imanuela.

Syeira came over and sat by Andy, their shoulders touching. Andy noticed with some relief that she was no cleaner than he was. But he still thought she was pretty.

'Boy,' she said, smiling, 'you're a complete wreck.'

'Look who's talking,' Andy retorted.

She laughed at him, seeming to glory in her part in birthing the baby elephant.

Andy wiped uselessly at his grimy forearms. 'Man, this just simply can't get any worse.'

'A name,' Papa told the crowd. 'We have our new baby and he must be named.' He pointed a white-gloved hand in Andy's direction. 'I propose that we name him Baby Andy, in honor of the young man who brought him into this world.'

The circus performers and the audience clapped enthusiastically, drawing more disfavor from Imanuela. 'Baby Andy, Baby Andy,' the crowd chanted. Even Captain Winters was smiling, and Andy's mom had to turn away from him to keep from bursting out loud with laughter. 'Baby Andy, Baby Andy.'

'Okay,' Andy said quietly, 'so maybe I was wrong about things not getting any worse.'

Syeira smiled at him and shook her head. There was a gleam in her eyes that he hadn't seen before. 'You did pretty terrific tonight.'

'So did you,' Andy said. 'When I saw you up there on the trapeze, my heart was in my throat. But you were so graceful, so—' he hesitated. 'It was like nothing I'd ever seen. I don't think I've ever been so amazed and scared and thrilled all at the same time.'

Without warning, Syeira leaned in and kissed him on the mouth. 'You haven't,' she told him, 'seen anything yet.'

every muscle aching and his senses on overload. He looked down at his shirt and pants, realizing for the first time what a mess he was.

'You did good, Andy,' his mom told him. 'I'll fly out in the morning and take a look at both of them.'

'Sure,' Andy replied. He drew his knees up and rested his forearms on them. He glanced at the crowd surrounding the corral, amazed at how quiet all that many people could be in one place. Traian had joined the watchers. Even Captain Winters had stayed. All of them oohed and ahhed over the baby elephant.

Papa, still in white-face though sweat had washed it away in places, approached Andy and patted him on the shoulder. 'You did good, Andy.' He bent down, came closer to Andy's ear. 'And you asked me earlier if I thought this circus would stay together?'

Andy nodded.

Papa's eyes twinkled and there were tears in them. 'I tell you this now, so we both know. This circus gonna be together always. People go from families, they always do, but it's the little ones and the new ones that keep making everything new again. Tonight I watched my granddaughter fly, and I loved her for doing it. And tonight I watched a new member of our family be born, brought into this world by your own hands.' He shook his head. 'Now could I ever believe something like this would end?'

'I don't know,' Andy said honestly. He was deeply aware that there wasn't a clean spot on him.

Papa clapped him on the shoulder, then turned to the waiting crowd. He lifted his voice, made it strong. 'We have a new baby tonight!'

The crowd cheered, drawing a warning trumpet from Imanuela, who curled her trunk around her baby protectively.

Papa put his finger to his lips in exaggerated clown pose and the crowd quieted immediately.